MALAFORMED REALITIES

VOLUME EIGHT

THOMAS M. MALAFARINA

**HELLBENDER
BOOKS**

an imprint of Sunbury Press, Inc.
Mechanicsburg, PA USA

HELLBENDER BOOKS

an imprint of Sunbury Press, Inc.
Mechanicsburg, PA USA

For information about special discounts for bulk purchases, please contact Sunbury Press Orders Dept. at (855) 338-8359 or orders@sunburypress.com.

To request one of our authors for speaking engagements or book signings, please contact Sunbury Press Publicity Dept. at publicity@sunburypress.com.

FIRST HELLBENDER BOOKS EDITION: June 2024

Set in Adobe Garamond Pro | Interior design by Crystal Devine | Cover design by Lawrence Knorr | Edited by Lawrence Knorr.

Publisher's Cataloging-in-Publication Data
Names: Malafarina, Thomas M., author.
Title: Malformed realities / Thomas M. Malafarina.
Description: First trade paperback edition. | Mechanicsburg, PA : Hellbender Books, 2024.
Summary: Thomas Malafarina strikes again with 12 spine-tingling tales of horror.
Identifiers: ISBN 979-8-88819-198-9 (softcover).
Subjects: FICTION / Horror | FICTION / Short Stories (single author).

Designed in the USA
0 1 1 2 3 5 8 13 21 34 55

For the Love of Books!

For my incredible and beautiful wife, JoAnne.
I know you dislike me dedicating all my books
to you and fawning over you like a lovesick schoolboy.
But even after more than three decades of marriage,
you still manage to bring that schoolboy out in me.

CONTENTS

INTRODUCTION

Welcome to the eighth edition of my short story collection series, Malaformed Realities. It's hard to imagine that we are in our eighth volume already. If any of you have been reading the series from the beginning, you are aware that back in Volume 7, I surpassed 200 short stories written. This is not me bragging about the number but just me being amazed at how the ideas keep coming.

I never sit down intending to write a short story, novella, or novel. I just go about my business of living, and eventually, the crux of an idea will pop into my head, and I'll make a note of it. I assume these ideas are thrust upon me by my unseen army of muses who seem to enjoy relentlessly tormenting me. Once the idea is firmly implanted, I have no choice but to start writing and see where the story leads me. I never know where it will go at the onset, making it even more fun.

Apparently, my muses have not yet tired of sending me inspiration upon inspiration, as the stories keep coming. Heaven knows I have not grown tired of receiving these ideas and acting as their loyal scribe. *Malaformed Realities Volume 8*, like the others, is a mixed bag of assorted stories, including a few with a humorous lilt. You might like some, you might like all. Who knows, you might not like any. There's not a lot I can do about that, as I don't sit down to write with any particular reader in mind.

Some authors write for fame, and some for fortune. Since early in my writing career, I accepted that my writing would bring me neither;

I write what I want, how I want, when I want. I think that amount of creative freedom is about all any writer could ask for.

So, sit back, relax, put your feet up, and hopefully enjoy the latest edition of Malaformed Realities.

THOMAS M. MALAFARINA
June 2024

NIGHT VISION

As Chuck sat in his car, waiting for it to warm up on that chilly Autumn morning, he found himself thinking about technology. He concluded it might be time to install one of those remote car starter thingies. If he had one of those gizmos, he could stay inside his warm house until his car was toasty and comfortable. The chilly car and ice-cold vinyl seats would become a not-so-fond memory. There would be no more sitting and shivering with his teeth chattering like a set of novelty wind-up choppers as he waited for the car to achieve an acceptable level of warmth.

Chuck wasn't intimidated by modern technology; he embraced it. One good example was his car's backup camera. Chuck loved having the camera and considered it a lifesaver. He would be the first to admit he was one of the worst drivers in the world when it came to traveling backward. However, with his backup camera, he considered himself a champ.

Not only did the camera allow him to see any obstacles in his path, but through the use of its superimposed green, yellow and red safety lines, it told him how close he was getting to whatever was behind him. As if that was not incredible enough, the camera displayed its image in color during the day and had a night vision feature for after sunset.

It had taken a bit longer than Chuck had hoped for him to become accustomed to using the camera. However, once he tried it a few times, he was hooked. He especially liked the night vision feature with its eerie, almost black-and-white picture that cut through the darkness like a Samurai sword. Chuck felt the camera gave him a sight previously reserved only for nocturnal animals. It was a feeling of power he found hard to put into words.

Every morning as he left for work, he backed down his driveway using his backup camera to guide him, keep his car on the asphalt pavement, and not veering off onto his lawn, which had previously done more than he cared to mention. Since he left for work before sunrise, the night vision feature was essential.

The morning he first saw the thing in the camera was like any other workday. Chuck cautiously backed down his driveway, watching carefully with his night vision camera. As he got a few feet from the end of his driveway, something shot past his rear camera. Chuck slammed on his brakes, certain he must have hit whatever had run behind him.

But he hadn't felt any impact, and the thing had been moving so quickly that Chuck could not identify it. As he looked at the display of his backup camera, all that was visible were the recently filled-in cracks on the roadway's asphalt. Chuck had noticed that the thing that ran across his camera was large, and he believed it ran on all fours but wasn't sure. He didn't think it was a deer; it didn't seem big enough to be a deer. But he was confident it wasn't a cat or a small dog either. It impossibly appeared to be the size of a large man. Yet no man Chuck had ever known could run on four legs.

He grabbed a flashlight from his glove box, got out of his car to verify he had not struck anything, and checked for possible damage if he was wrong about not hitting it. Chuck could see his car was undamaged in the dim flashlight's minimal glow. He breathed a sigh of relief and turned to go back into his vehicle. That was when he noticed a strange scent in the air. It was very faint and almost undetectable. It had a smell that was very woodsy, animal-like, and feral. Then he saw something on the ground below his rear bumper. He reached down and picked it up from the ground.

Chuck carried it into his car, where he hoped to examine it using his overhead light. He was sure it was the fur of some animal. As he sat in the car, he felt the coarseness of the piece of hair, realizing it was not from a rabbit or any similar creature. This fur clump was much longer than Chuck initially realized and was more like something he would imagine coming from a goat or similar animal. He sniffed the piece of fur and determined it carried the same scent he had detected earlier but much more potent at such proximity.

As far as Chuck knew, no goats lived within several miles of his subdivision. Perhaps someone had a pet goat that got away. Then he recalled the size of the thing he thought he had seen and realized it couldn't have possibly been someone's pet. When he thought of pet goats, he figured someone might have one of those tiny pigmy goats that were no bigger than an average-sized dog. What he had seen was far more massive than any such animal.

Realizing he had better get moving or risk being late for work, Chuck tossed the piece of fur out the window and continued backing down the driveway. Within a few seconds, he was on his way to his job. Chuck had entirely forgotten the early morning event when he arrived at his office.

The following day, Chuck headed for his car again and dropped behind the steering wheel, still half-asleep. He started his engine and put the car in reverse. He recalled the previous day's encounter and decided to pay closer attention to his backup camera. The night vision was active and showed the way was clear for him to back out onto the street.

Suddenly, something moved across his camera's field of vision, momentarily blocking his view. Chuck quickly turned in his seat, but he saw nothing behind him when he did. Nor did he see anyone or anything running away. Unlike the previous day, the creature appeared to have been walking upright on two legs. He had gotten a better look at whatever the thing was, and now He was sure it was a goat-like creature. But how could that be?

To the best of his knowledge, goats didn't walk upright on two legs. They didn't vanish into thin air either. Also, judging by what he had so briefly seen, Chuck would have put the thing at close to eight feet tall, another impossibility. What in the world was happening?

This time, Chuck didn't get out of his car. He didn't know if he had imagined things or if there was something wrong with his backup camera. Perhaps light had reflected somehow from a distant car and caused a shadow to pass over his camera. Maybe that could cause the night vision camera to display something that wasn't there. Yes, that made much more sense than considering the possibility of a goat-like monster, which made no sense whatsoever.

So, once again, Chuck headed off to work. However, this time, the events of the morning stayed at the forefront of his mind. He thought about it all during his commute. Then he recalled something he had forgotten about as he sat at his desk. He felt like an idiot for not remembering it earlier. He had a sophisticated motion doorbell camera also equipped with night vision capability. It was tied to an app on his smartphone to either watch a previously recorded segment or watch events happening in real-time. He could do it all on his smartphone.

Chuck opened the app as he sat alone in his cubicle. He had arrived early, so he didn't have to worry about anyone seeing what he was doing. He selected the option for viewing previously recorded events and saw a listing labeled "5:15 am". The next listing said, "5:20 am". His car was not visible by the doorbell camera, so 5:15 was when he walked out the front door. Chuck remembered looking at his dashboard display as he backed out of the driveway, and the clock read 5:26.

That meant the doorbell cam must have picked up some movement seconds after seeing the image in his backup camera. Chuck heaved a deep, apprehensive sigh as his finger hovered over the play button. He was curious to know what the doorbell camera might have picked up, yet part of him was unsure if he wanted to know. He pressed the button.

At first, he couldn't see anything in the eerie night vision display. Chuck watched the scroll bar advance. There were only 45 seconds of recorded play permitted with his service. It was activated by motion, and the recording started. Once completed, the recording stopped, and the image was transferred to storage on the cloud.

Chuck watched it to the end, then replayed it several more times. He thought he saw a blip on the video near the start. But what that might be, he couldn't tell. It came and went faster than his eye could follow. Chuck decided to try and drag the scroll bar slowly from left to right, allowing the video to advance practically a frame at a time.

It took several attempts, but when Chuck was about to give up, the picture stopped on a still image, and Chuck's blood turned to ice water.

"What . . . what, in the name of all that's holy is that?" He said aloud in shock. Chuck realized he had shouted in his surprise and quickly looked around to see if anyone else had arrived. He was pleased to see they had not, and he was still alone. He returned his gaze to the image frozen on his screen. It was an image from some nightmare world where sane people had no business venturing.

The image was a goat, or perhaps a better description would be a goat-like creature. It stood upright like a man, but it appeared to be over eight feet tall. It was muscular with massive ram horns that curled back from its skull. But the worst part of the frozen picture was the expression on the beast's face.

The creature stared directly into the lens of the doorbell camera as if it knew the camera was recording it. That icy stare held so much blatant hatred that it caused Chuck to shudder involuntarily. He wondered what the horrid beast was and what it was doing on his street. He took a screenshot of the monster.

Chuck realized how close he had come to bumping into the monster with his car. What would he have done then? If the beast were only slightly injured, it would have been angry and likely attacked him. Chuck was staring at the image on the screen when he heard a noise in the cubicle next to his. It was Bob Heckler, his coworker, and his friend.

"Morning, Bob," Chuck called.

"Morning, Chuck," he replied.

"Hey, Bob. Could you stop over here for a minute? There's something I want to show you."

"Ok. But it better not be work-related. I haven't had my second cup of coffee yet, and my brain ain't quite with the program," Bob said as he shuffled out of his cubicle and entered Chuck's.

"Look at this for me, Bob, and tell me what you see."

Bob looked at the screen for a moment, then said, "Well, it looks like a picture from one of those security cameras with night vision."

"It is. It's from my doorbell cam."

"Cool. I didn't know you had one of those," Bob said.

Chuck was becoming impatient, "That doesn't matter, for now, Bob. I was hoping you could tell me what you think that image is that the doorbell cam caught. Look closely and tell me what you see."

Bob stared at the screen for a few more seconds and said, "Well, I don't see much. I see your front yard, and I can see the sidewalk and street beyond that. That's about all I see."

Chuck was perplexed, "That's it? That's all you see?"

Bob said, "I can only see whatever I can see. Is there supposed to be something else I should be looking for, maybe something in the background or off to the side? Because I don't see anything."

"Let me look at that," Chuck retorted. When he looked at the video shot, nothing out of the ordinary appeared on the screen. It seemed as Bob had described it: the front lawn, the sidewalk, and the streets, nothing else.

"What's the matter, Chuck? You look surprised like you expected to see something else. Is everything ok?"

"Yeah . . . I mean no, not really . . . I thought I saw something on the video, but I must have been mistaken."

"What did you think you saw?"

"Um . . . nothing really, Bob. Forget it. We'd better get to work before Mavis The Monster gets in and sees us screwing around."

"Amen to that, brother. You know old-man Moneybags Martin has that old hag watching everything we do. Do you know why I heard her desk is positioned outside the bathroom? Moneybags put her there to count how many times each of us goes to the can and how long we're in there."

Chuck said, "Please tell me you're joking, Bob. I don't think even Martin would stoop so low."

"Well, Chuckles, my boy, you are free to believe as you may, but I know the truth. The man would stoop to count your poop."

"Whatever. Look, Bob. I have to get to work. We'll talk later."

Chuck returned his cell phone to his shirt pocket and began his work. Chuck had trouble keeping his mind focused on his tasks as he worked. He kept drifting off course, thinking about the image he believed he had seen. How had it been that he was sure he had seen some goat creature walking upright in front of his house on the video, yet now it was gone? This wasn't a one-time occurrence either; he had seen something the previous day as well . . . hadn't he?

Then he recalled the screenshot he had taken. He might have accidentally advanced the video beyond the goat's appearance, but the still photo should show the beast. But he was wrong. There was no goat creature in the image either. What the Hell was going on? Chuck began to wonder if he was having a mental breakdown, seeing things that didn't exist.

He decided to do some research, so he got onto Google and searched for "Goats walking upright." He expected to find a few videos of goats that people had trained to walk on their hind legs for entertainment, and of course, he did see many of those. But then he found a link that said, "Wild goat-like creature terrorizes New England village." He clicked on the link and read a brief article about various sightings of a giant creature described as being goat-like in appearance, walking about on hind legs in a small New England town. It always seemed to be spotted in the early morning hours.

Many attempts had been made to capture the creature on film, but most had failed. However, one videographer with a high-resolution night-vision camera managed to catch a shot of the beast. It was a short 20-second video of the creature walking through a farmyard. There were a lot of comments about the video, saying it was faked and staged. They claimed the photographer had used a man in a goat suit because of the size of the monster. However, no attempts to invalidate the film had been successful. Chuck knew it was authentic, as he had seen the same thing on his doorbell cam.

So now, what was he supposed to do, he wondered. Did he have a goat monster walking around his neighborhood? Was the creature dangerous? Should he report it to the police or animal control? But how could he? He had no proof. The video he thought he had was essentially blank, at least as far as any creature was concerned. Was the beast even natural? Was it a real goat, a mythical creature, or perhaps some demonic apparition? Chuck realized he was starting to have thoughts that might border a bit crazy. Yet, as bizarre as they may seem, the ideas made some sense to him.

Perhaps that would explain why almost no one had filmed the monster previously. Maybe this creature was some demon-like being that could only be caught on film if it was unaware. Chuck watched the video again and noticed the goat-thing never looked into the camera as it had done with his doorbell cam. The creature didn't know anyone was filming it.

Chuck couldn't believe what he was thinking. In just two minutes, not only had he decided the creature was some mythical, Hell-born goat monster, but he had even started setting down a list of rules he suspected the beast must follow. What made him imagine that any laws of man or science would apply to such a demon? Just because movie monsters had rules to follow didn't mean this goat creature did.

It only appears when the moon is full. Nope, not true. That was a werewolf thing. It can't come out in daylight. Nope, that's a vampire. You have to shoot it in the head. Nope, that's zombies. You can't feed it after midnight. That's a gremlin thing. Silver bullets? Werewolves. Stake through the heart? Vampires. Rules. All monsters have rules. So why shouldn't this goat demon have similar laws?

Chuck answered his question by saying, "Because it's likely I imagined everything." Work had become quite stressful over the previous weeks, and he might have unknowingly succumbed to that stress. He would be the first to admit the stress was affecting his sleep. Chuck often woke up several times a night in cold sweats after having frustrating dreams of various things going wrong on the job. Would it be a stretch to conclude that the same stress and sleep deprivation might be causing him to imagine something as well? Chuck didn't think so. However, he couldn't argue with facts. His doorbell camera had shown nothing.

Although that was not entirely true, his camera initially recorded the creature. Chuck had seen it. But now, the image was gone from the video and his screenshot.

Realizing this train of thought was getting him nowhere, Chuck decided it would be better to put the event out of his mind and do his best to dig into his work. That was what he did.

After work, Chuck headed straight home. While he was eating dinner, he suddenly had an idea. Perhaps the problem with capturing a permanent shot of the creature was that his photographic media was digital. Maybe if he reverted to old-school analog, things would be different. He didn't know why, but he believed he might be correct about this.

He had what he considered a very old video camera that used video cassettes. Fortunately, it wasn't one of the ancient varieties that were huge, clunky, and had to be carried on your shoulders. His was fairly compact and used the mini-cassettes. He knew he would need the camera's night vision capability. It was powered by a rechargeable battery that he probably hadn't used in a decade, and he had no idea if it would still work. All he could do was let it charge overnight and then test it in the morning. If it still worked, then he could try his idea.

Chuck didn't experience restful sleep that night, as horrifying visions haunted his dreams. In one, he found himself alone in a dark wooded area, in a clearing dimly lit by moonlight. Chuck was terrified and uncertain of where he was or how he had gotten there. There was an unpleasant scent in the air, that same feral, woodsy odor he had smelled on the piece of fur he had found. But now, the smell was much stronger and far more unpleasant. It was accompanied by the foul stench of rotting meat and burning sulfur.

Chuck heard a chuffing sound like a bull or an animal snorting. Looking out into the darkness of the forest, he saw two glowing red-rimmed yellow eyes staring out at him from between a copse of trees. The eyes began to move closer as Chuck heard the crunching of dried leaves and small twigs breaking under the feet of whatever was approaching. When the thing came out into the moonlit clearing, the sight made Chuck feel as if his heart would stop.

The horrid creature stood more than eight feet tall. It was naked and covered from head to toe in gnarly, thick, slimy, matted fur. Its arms were long and muscular with a roadmap of bulging ropey veins. The beast had massive hands that at first appeared human-like, save for the long claws on its fingers. The thing's legs were equally muscular and tattooed with veins; however, they ended in wide, cloven hooves.

The monster's face was probably its most disturbing feature. It was almost human in appearance, resembling a wild bearded man. But that was where the similarities ended. Its ears were pointed, and it had a pig-like snout with wide nostrils that puffed mist into the cold night air. The creature had a mane of long, greasy black hair slicked back and trailing down from a broad Neanderthal forehead, which created a thick furry shelf over top of the deep-set glowing eyes.

Two long ram-like horns curved back from both sides of the monster's skull, ending in sharp, pointed tips. The beast opened its massive mouth to reveal rows of large, yellowed, sharp teeth as streams of bloody drool dripped from its continuous salivation.

Then, the monster howled with a sound like the mournful cry of a wounded animal. The roar sent icy chills down Chuck's spine. Moments later, Chuck heard the clicking of more leaves crackling all around him. He looked out into the forest's darkness and saw many more sets of glowing eyes coming forward. He heard snorting and chuffing sounds behind him and knew he was surrounded. Then he felt the first of the claws digging into the back of his neck.

Chuck awoke the next morning, trembling and panting in a cold sweat. He sat bolt upright in bed, his head darting back and forth as if searching for something. What that might be, Chuck had no idea. The memories of his horrible nightmares were already fading into the void that separates the realm of dreams from the waking world. Yet the anxious feeling of discomfort that only bad dreams could create remained.

Chuck stumbled into the bathroom to begin the ritual of another day. As he was getting his shower, he recalled his video camera idea. He believed he was on the right track and couldn't wait to put his theory to the test. As soon as he was dried and dressed, Chuck headed to the kitchen, where the camera battery was charging.

Everything seemed in order, so he loaded the battery into the camera, made sure there was a cassette in the appropriate port and shot his kitchen counter quickly. When he was finished, Chuck rewound the cassette and pressed play. On the small screen of his recorder, he saw a perfect playback of what he had just recorded. He switched his camera to night vision mode and was ready for action.

Chuck pretended to get ready to leave for work as normal. He started his car, left it running, and then slipped out the door, quietly shutting it behind him. Then Chuck crawled around the front of the car, eventually positioning himself near the right side of the front bumper. He pointed his camera toward the back of his car and started recording. He had about an hour's worth of recording time on the cassette but suspected he might not need that much. Besides, he had to get to work, limiting his available time more than the camera.

The early morning sky was clear, and the almost full moon was still high in the sky, casting an eerie glow in the driveway. Chuck figured this would only help with the recording process. Now, all he had to do was wait. Before long, he heard a clip-clopping sound like an animal's hooves on the blacktop. It was coming from the area at the rear of his car. What Chuck saw next nearly caused him to drop his camera.

A large goat-like creature was walking behind his car, oblivious to the filming. The beast was over seven feet tall, walking on its hind legs, and covered with coarse brown hair from head to toe. Chuck's stomach clenched with terror, and cold sweat streamed down the cleft of his back.

One thing Chuck hadn't noticed when he looked at the original doorbell video, and something for which he was ill-prepared, was the monster's huge pendulous breasts. They hung down-pointing due south while swinging to and fro as the beast walked slowly forward. Miraculously, the creature seemed to be still unaware of either Chuck's presence or his videotaping.

A female, Chuck thought. Then a strange thought hit him, *I don't recall that original screenshot being female.* He was certain he would have noticed something so obvious, but perhaps he had been too shocked to notice previously. He suddenly realized since she was a female, there must be others like her.

She must have a mate somewhere. Chuck thought. Suddenly, his nightmare of the previous evening popped back into his conscious mind, and he realized he had made the worst mistake of his life. That was when he heard a deep chuffing sound, smelled a deep woodsy feral stench, and felt hot breath against the back of his neck.

VINES

"If you don't want to do it, Bob, just say so, and I'll call Jean and see if her son, Chad, is available. He'll be happy to make some extra cash."

Bob Harman and his wife Sheryl were discussing his pulling out some troublesome, invasive vines creeping up the side of their home. It was a hot July afternoon, and both of them had already put in a long day of yard work.

Regardless, they knew it was far past time to remove these vines. It was an annual ritual Bob tried to perform every year and had usually done so in the past two decades. But he realized he had skipped the previous couple of years, and the wretched things had gotten out of hand.

"I didn't say I wouldn't do it, Sheryl. I wish you'd stop putting words in my mouth, for Pete's sake. You know I try to do this every year."

"Emphasis on try," she chided.

Bob explained, "I was just commenting on the futility of the chore, not to mention the irony."

"Well, it sounded to me like you weren't interested in cleaning out those vines. It seemed like you intended to let them continue to creep up the brick and get under our siding. They'd eventually push the siding out and ruin it. Besides, I fail to see this irony and futility you're so keen to point out."

"The futility comes from the fact that no matter how many times I trim back or rip out these stupid vines, they always return with a vengeance. The irony is that we planted them deliberately, all those many years ago, thereby creating a self-inflicted perpetual problem."

"But, Honey. We both agree they make an attractive ground cover for the raised flower bed. You even commented that it gives our house great curb appeal."

"Of course, it does or did, until they start crawling up the front of the house like a nest of rattlers. Then I have to come out here and yank a bunch of it out. This stuff never dies either."

"That's true," Sheryl agreed, "It always grows back, often thicker than before. In fact, I can't recall it ever looking so lush before."

"See? Ironic. Just like the front lawn."

"Excuse me? What do the vines have to do with the lawn, Bob?"

"Well, I suppose at first glance, nothing. That is until you take the time to think about it."

"Enlighten me, dear husband."

Bob said, "It's like this. We pay that guy, Scott, to treat and fertilize our lawn, right?"

"Right."

"Well, because of that, our grass looks great, but it grows almost twice as fast as normal. So when I'm out there in the hot sun, sweating like a pig, cutting the grass twice a week, and cursing the lawn for growing so fast, I should be cursing myself. I'm the one paying someone to have our grass grow faster. Like the vines, it's a self-inflicted problem. Now, do you see what I'm saying?"

"Pigs don't sweat, Husband."

"What?"

"Pigs . . . they don't sweat. They have no sweat glands, so saying you sweat like a pig is an inaccurate statement."

"Ok, pigs don't sweat . . . but I do. Regardless, do you understand the point I'm trying to make about irony?"

"Well, now that you mention it, I suppose 'ironic' does describe it quite nicely."

"Well, Sheryl. Ironic or not, the job of removing these invasive, practically alien lifeforms once again falls upon my elderly shoulders."

"Oh, Bob. You're not that old. I mean, sixty-six might be a bit long in the tooth, but elderly? I don't think so."

"Maybe not. But tonight, when I'm aching from head to toe, at least I'll know why."

"If you forget why, then I'll be sure to be a good wife and remind you," Sheryl said. Then she looked at her husband with concern and asked, "Bob, Honey. Are you sure you're up for this? Seriously, I can still call Jean and see if Chad could come up to do this."

"No, Sweetie. I'll be fine," Bob said.

"If you say so."

"I say so."

"Well then. I'm going to go back inside and start working on preparing dinner. It should be ready in about an hour or so."

"Good idea, Sheryl. By then, I should be finished here and should even have time to shower before dinner."

"Um . . . yeah . . . I should think a shower might be in order after working up a sweat out here."

"Haha. Very funny. I'd better get to work."

Bob went around to the side of their split-level home, retrieved one of the six plastic trash cans he kept there, and used to haul yard waste to their local organic recycling center. Bob realized he probably should have brought two large tubs with him as he suspected he would easily fill several.

But one thing Bob learned a few years earlier was that once a man passes 60 years old, he had better start pacing himself. He had lost several close friends to the Grim Reaper over those past six years. Every one of them suffered from the same ailment. They apparently seemed to think they were still twenty-year-olds. That was a fatal mistake as far as Bob was concerned and one he had no intention of making.

He recalled something some older one-liner comedian, possibly Rodney Dangerfield, once said, "The only exercise I get is being a pall-bearer for my friends that exercise." Unfortunately, that joke wasn't so funny in real life, as Bob had filled that pallbearer role more times than he cared to mention.

This is not to suggest that the couple didn't get their fair share of workouts. They were both avid gardeners; they took walks together, cleaned the house, and did small home improvement projects. Since they both still worked full-time, their gardening took on weekend warrior status.

The key point they learned was to pace themselves. There was a time years earlier when Bob would start a weekend outdoor project at seven in the morning and not quit until it was finished, or else if he ran out of daylight.

Now, he and Sheryl might work for a few hours, take a lunch break, run to the store or take an afternoon nap. He had mastered the fine art of not overdoing it, which may have contributed to why he had not yet joined the ranks of the formerly living.

However, today, neither Bob nor his wife had followed that golden rule of the sixty-plus generation and had already pushed themselves more than was normal. It was long past the time for him to take his break. And yet, now he was preparing to tackle yet another strenuous job.

The weather forecast for the next several days was extremely hot and humid. Bob knew what that meant. Seniors stay inside in the air conditioning and relax. Therefore, he had decided to remove the infernal vines once and for all today while the air was still somewhat cooler.

Bob firmly believed in getting even the most distasteful job done when the time was right. He began tearing out the vines, first dealing with those climbing the house. To his surprise, the job went very well, and before he knew it, he had filled one of the trash tubs.

He took the container to the side of the house where he stored them and brought two empties back with him. As he got close to the front of the house, he stopped in his tracks.

"Wait a minute," Bob said, "What the Hell is this?"

If he hadn't known how many vines he had just ripped off the house and out of the ground, Bob would have wondered why he hadn't started yet. The vines, the same vines he had just destroyed, were back. They had completely filled in the area Bob had left bare and had even crawled back up the side of the house.

That was impossible. Maybe the work was getting to him. Perhaps he was exhausted and should call it quits for the day. Maybe he never pulled out the vines and only imagined he had. Bob walked back to the side of his house and removed the lid from his plastic tub, certain he would find it empty. But the tub was filled to the top with broken vines.

Bob shook his head in confusion, then grabbed two more empties and brought them with him. He now had four tubs waiting to be filled, and he had no intention of leaving the area until his job was completed. Bob still couldn't explain what had actually occurred versus what he might have imagined, but he was going to make short work of these invasive vines and do it now.

Lining up his four empties in a tight row, Bob began to pull out more vines and fill each container. Sweat streamed from every pore in his body, saturating his clothing. His back hurt badly, and his arthritic hands screamed from the exertion. Bob stood back to examine his work when all the tubs had been filled. He was well pleased.

An area across the length of the front of his house and about three feet deep had been cleared of all vines. That is to say, cleared as best as Bob could do. He knew there would be a few stragglers, including roots that would likely mature into new vines by Spring. But Spring was a long way from now, and as far as Bob was concerned, his work was finished.

He caught a slight movement in his peripheral vision off to his right. Bob turned but saw nothing. Then, he saw another low-to-the-ground motion to his left. He walked toward the area he had just cleared and was sure it seemed to have less bare space than when he had finished.

Bob knew that was impossible. There was no way the vines had grown back that fast. Yet in his heart, he knew, somehow, they had. He ran to the cleared area and placed his back against the house. He stared down at the vines, trying to catch even one movement.

He shouted at the trimmed vines, "No. You don't! You can't come any closer. I forbid it."

Bob realized that anyone strolling down the sidewalk listening to him screaming at weeds would likely assume he was gardening with an empty tool shed. Or perhaps sniffing the herbicide. Or maybe he was a weed wacko. Regardless, he didn't care because something was very wrong in his garden, and he was determined to get to the bottom. That was when Bob saw movement from his right.

Before he could react, Bob felt something wrap around his right ankle and tighten so severely that he felt like his flesh was being flayed from his bones. He looked down and saw that one of the accursed vines had grabbed him. Crimson liquid ran down the length of the vine, forming ruby puddles in the dirt.

It took Bob a moment to realize he was looking at something the likes of which he could never imagine. The pools were immediately sucked into the soil, and new vines instantly sprang up. It was as if his blood was stimulating the rapid growth of these strange weeds.

These new vines rapidly crept up Bob's leg while others wrapped themselves around his wrists, pulling him downward. He fell face-first onto the dirt bed, rapidly refilling with creeping vines. Bob felt other vines crawling over him as he lay helpless on the ground. The weeds tightened their grip on him, squeezing the air from his body.

He wanted to scream out for help but couldn't. The pain he was experiencing hindered his ability to breathe, and making matters even worse, several vines had found their way into his mouth, traveling down his throat and searing it with white-hot agony. He could no longer breathe at all. Then Bob felt his bones splinter and break as the blanket of vines pulled him further down into the cold, damp ground.

When Bob's wife came out to call him for dinner, he was nowhere in sight. She checked the four plastic waste tubs and found them full to capacity with broken remnants of pulled vines. Yet the flower bed remained overgrown with the invasive nuisances. It looked as if Bob hadn't touched the weeds. Still, she couldn't explain the full containers.

Sheryl called the local police and reported her husband missing. Perhaps he had a minor stroke, became confused, and was roaming around the neighborhood. Maybe he had been kidnapped. Or perhaps the reason was simpler than that.

At first, she found it difficult to imagine after so many years of what she considered a happy marriage. But eventually, Sheryl came to the sad conclusion that, for whatever reason, her husband had decided to leave her.

As the weeks passed, she began to accept he would never return. But why would he just up and leave? Sheryl knew that she tended to be sometimes demanding, perhaps too much. Maybe that day, she had pushed him too hard, and he simply couldn't take it anymore.

Eventually, she had no choice but to sell the house and move away. It was too much for her to handle alone, especially the yard work. She figured it was best to unload the place and let someone else, maybe someone younger, deal with the troublesome vines.

TAIL GUNNER JOE

Author's Note: Although this story could technically be classified as a sci-fi/ horror story, you will quickly notice it is also my attempt at creating a light, somewhat humorous tale. I feel it's a good idea to occasionally break things up a bit to give your soul a rest. I wrote this for my friend and fellow author, Mark Slade, based on a rough idea he came up with. It was for a spoof men's magazine called Rumble. *Enjoy.*

The man began to wake slowly, in a stupor, feeling like 200 lbs of soggy elephant dung. He had far too many questions running through his mind, "Where am I? What happened to me? Who am I? If God and Superman fought, who would win? So, so many questions. All he knew was he seemed to be lying in a bed in a dimly lit room.

"Uh oh!" he thought to himself, "Not again!" A faint memory began to form in his mind. The last time he had felt like this was a few months earlier, in early 1950, when he had awoken one morning, naked, on a straw mattress in a thatched hut. He was in bed with an equally naked, toothless sixty-some-year-old Korean grandmother, a very contented-looking female dog, two ducks, and a spilled plate of pork dumplings, complete with dipping sauce. He was glad he had no memory of the previous night but was sorry he couldn't recall eating the dumplings. He really loved dumplings.

Then, another memory relating to that one popped into his mind. He and his squadron of B-29 Superfortress flyers had landed in South

Korea. His job was tail gunner, and his somewhat uncreative nickname was Tail Gunner, something or other. Tail Gunner Pete? Tail Gunner Frank? No, that didn't seem quite right. It would probably come back to him eventually. It was his name, after all. The only thing he could remember was that he and his buddies had decided to go out and have one last bout of hellraising before they had to begin their bombing runs, which were scheduled to take place later that week. He had no idea how much he had to drink or how he'd ended up in that bizarre situation with madam gum-flapper and her barnyard menagerie.

That was how he felt now: confused and disoriented, yet at the same time, he was surprisingly quite strong, perhaps stronger than he had ever felt. He tried to sit up but found himself strapped to the bed. Wherever it was he happened to be, the great strength he now felt wasn't going to do him any good. He couldn't move his head and couldn't see anywhere but the ceiling directly in front of him. He was relieved that the roof was not thatched but appeared to be some sort of metal roof, perhaps a hospital or laboratory. A thatched roof and restraints might signify something much worse than that previous embarrassment.

Whew. Dodged that bullet again, he thought, recalling the morning after the incident with the old woman. Much to his dismay, her dog had followed him back to the base, constantly rubbing against his leg. He obviously had made an impression. He had to chase her away and then felt a bit sorry that he didn't even get her name: the dog, not the old woman.

There was a bad smell in the room, like wild animals, like the stink of a zoo. Was he being held captive in a zoo somewhere? He felt the air in front of his face flutter as if a bird had flown close enough for him to feel the flapping of its wings. He heard a wild chittering sound made by a squirrel, and it was also frighteningly close to his face.

He realized he was hungry and was having strange cravings. It was not his typical need for cheesesteak sandwiches or pizza but for food and fruit, which he usually hated. He wanted a salad, a really big, really leafy salad. He also had an unexplainable craving for bananas, not just one, but an entire bunch of bananas.

Then, a soft voice came out of the darkness, saying. "Ah, so I see you're awake."

"Y . . . yeah . . . I'm awake," the confused man said slowly, intending to say more but shocked at the sound of his voice. It was deeper than normal and somewhat raspy, catching him by surprise. It sounded like a female impersonator making a bad impression of Cher. He also noticed that his head felt like John Bonham and Keith Moon had a drum-off inside his skull. "Where . . . where am I? What the Hell is wrong with my voice?"

"Oh yes. Questions, questions, so many questions, I'm sure," the other voice said, sounding surprisingly cheerful. "I assure you all your inquiries will be answered in due course. I, too, have plenty of questions, my new friend. For example, what's your name?"

The man thought for a bit, trying to fight through the thick cotton candy fog clouding his mind. Then it came to him, "J . . . J . . . Joe. I think my name is Joe. That feels right. Yeah . . . they call me Tail Gunner Joe."

"Hum," the voice said, "I suppose that makes sense, all things considered. However, I would have pegged you for a Waldo or maybe a Wendel. Then again, I suppose Tail Gunner Waldo doesn't have a very good ring to it. Well, Tail Gunner Joe, do you happen to know your last name?"

Joe replied, "Of course. Sure, it's . . . it's . . . huh? I got nothin'. Maybe it's Smith."

"Really? Smith? That's the best you can come up with, Smith? Not the most creative sort, are we?"

"Forgive me all to Hell and back, but I'm not feeling quite myself here. You know what I mean?"

"Oh yes. I most definitely know. More than you may realize. Well, I suppose we have to call you something; how about Simian? Joe Simian. That feels right to me. How do you like that name?"

"Simian? Why does that name sound familiar? Well, I suppose it's ok for now, but how about you tell me where I am and why I'm strapped down? Say . . . you're not some weirdo pervert who's been doing dirty sexual things to me while I was asleep, are you? Because I'm not into kinky crap, no matter what you might have heard. Well, there was that time with the dog and the ducks, but let's not bring that up."

The man sounded like he had been caught off guard, "Why . . . why no, of course not. I'm not that sort of . . . absolutely not. I'm a man of science."

Joe asked, "You mean, like a doctor or something?"

"Yes . . . a doctor . . . or something," the man replied vaguely.

"Well, how's about you get me off this table so I can get out of here."

"I'm afraid that's not quite possible at this time. You're strapped down for your own protection as well as mine," the doctor said.

"Protection. What are you talking about? I'm an American soldier; I'm one of the good guys. I can't see you; it's too dark in here. But you aren't Korean, are you? You sound American to me, and your voice has no trace of any accent. Look, I promise I wouldn't hurt you."

"Don't be so quick to make promises when you have no idea whether or not you can keep them," the doctor said; then, he hesitated for a moment and reluctantly said, "Here's the deal, Joe. Several weeks ago, your plane came down as it was leaving a bombing raid over North Korea. I believe it might have been shot down or had some sort of mechanical malfunction. The bottom line is it crashed, and everyone on the plane was killed."

Joe was even more confused, "Um . . . excuse me. But I'm pretty sure I wasn't killed, or else I wouldn't be here talking to you. Right? Isn't that how those things usually work."

Hesitantly, the doctor said, "Well, yes. But that's where things start to get a bit tricky, or perhaps hairy would be a better word." He let loose an insane-sounding chuckle, "You see, you were barely alive when I came upon your downed plane. Your body was crushed beyond repair, and I managed to keep you alive just long enough to take a few significant corrective measures."

"Corrective measures? But how could my body be crushed? I feel very strong, like I have the strength of a gorilla."

"Interesting choice of words," the doctor said, once again giving that crazy chuckle. "Well, Joe. As things worked out, I had to make a choice. I had to decide whether to let your brain eventually die as your body had done or try something else, something risky but also revolutionary."

"Something else? Revolutionary?" Joe asked, beginning to get worried.

"Yes, well, I suppose there is no good way to say this. I had to take your brain and transplant it into the head of a gorilla."

Joe said calmly, "Oh, is that all . . . I was afraid . . ." Then he shouted, "Hey! Wait a minute . . . did you just say gorilla?"

"Why, yes. Specifically, a western lowland gorilla; scientific name, Gorilla gorilla gorilla; phylum, Chordata; class, Mammalia. It's a relatively small gorilla with dark brownish-black hair and a large skull. Its average size is about 200 to 600 pounds, with males being about twice the size of females. They tend to be herbivorous and have a lifespan of about 35 years. The one whose body your brain now occupies was about five years old, so you should be good for another thirty years, give or take."

"G . . . g . . . give or take?" Joe said in shock.

"Why, yes. No one can be sure of such things. Then again, without the operation, your lifespan would be zilch. You'd be el-dead-amundo."

"So, that's why you have me strapped down. You're afraid I might go, pardon the expression, ape, and tear you apart."

"Well, there is that," the doctor replied.

Joe shouted, "You sick and twisted bastard. Why didn't you just let me die? How am I going to survive inside the body of a gorilla?"

The doctor said, "Oh, Joe, I'm sure you'll adapt."

"Adapt? Adapt? Adapt to being in the body of an ape? How the Hell do I adapt to being a monkey?"

"Forgive me for correcting you, but a gorilla and a monkey are different. For example, monkeys are primates that belong to the Haplorhini suborder and Simiiformes infraorder, whereas Gorillas belong to the Hominidae family and Gorilla Genus. Gorillas are considered the largest primates by physical size. Monkeys have long tails that can be used to help them balance, while Gorillas are tailless. There is also a significant difference between monkeys and gorillas in terms of evolution when it comes to diet and posture as well. It is also interesting to note that gorillas are the closest taxonomical relatives of humans in the animal world, that is, after chimpanzees and bonobos."

"Bonobos? Bonobos? What the Hell is a Bonobo?" Joe asked.

The doctor started to speak, "A bonobo is . . ."

Joe shouted, "Never mind. I don't know and don't care. Look, Doc, give me a break here. Ok, look. You don't have to release me yet, but could you at least turn on the lights? I need to see what I'm dealing with here, you know?"

"Very well," the doctor said as he turned on the laboratory lights. Harsh fluorescent illumination seemed to scald Joe's overly sensitive eyes.

"Jeeze, Doc. You're killing me here!" Joe shouted.

"Just relax, Joe. Close your eyes and slowly open them until they get used to the brightness."

Joe squinted his eyes, gradually opening them, and eventually, he could clearly see the ceiling and some of the area around. He was in a metal building like an airplane hangar or a Quonset hut. He wanted to get a better idea of just how bad his situation was. If his brain really was inside a gorilla, what would his life be like from this day forward?

"Come closer, Doc, so I can see you, and please, explain to me how I'm supposed to live my life trapped in the body of a gorilla?"

An odd-looking little man in his sixties, bald, with just a fringe of wild, bushy white hair and equally bushy eyebrows, came into view. His eyes were large and showed an extraordinary level of intelligence, coupled with what looked to Joe like an equal amount of insanity. Then again, he realized it would take a combination like that to do what this man had done to him.

Something was sitting on the doctor's shoulder. It looked like a parrot or some other large bird, but its head was that of a squirrel. Joe asked as calmly as he could manage, "Um, excuse me, Doc, but there's some kind of weird bird-squirrel thing perched on your shoulder. Care to tell me what that's all about?"

The doctor glanced over to his shoulder, then raised his hand, extending one finger, and said, "Oh, that. That's Carl. He was one of my first successful experiments." The bird-squirrel creature fluttered from the man's shoulder to his outstretched hand, preaching on his extended finger. "He's a sweet little thing and completely trained."

As he said those last words, the Carl creature took flight from the doctor's finger, leaving a runny blob of bird/squirrel crap in his wake.

The doctor explained to Joe about Carl while simultaneously flicking the errant turd off his finger and onto the floor. He. said, "Like yourself, Carl was one of my success stories. You wouldn't want to see my failures."

Joe realized what the doctor said was true. He was certain he didn't want to see himself in a mirror. Then he realized he never got an answer to his previous question, "Anyway, Doc, as I asked earlier, would you please explain to me how I'm supposed to live my life trapped in the body of a gorilla?"

The doctor stared down at him and then said, "Well, I hadn't really had much time to think about that. I was quite busy saving your life. I suppose you'll have to learn to make the best of it. I mean, you are still alive and have your human mind and intelligence, and as a gorilla, you'll have great strength."

Joe knew the doctor was right, as he was already feeling much stronger. Then he said, "I suppose that's true. Gorillas are strong, and that's probably a good thing. Right?"

Then his eyes grew wide as he suddenly had an epiphany, "Say, Doc, do gorillas have big schlongs? That would be awesome if this body had a foot-long kielbasa. Whoa, think about it! Wait till I get back to the States and my girlfriend gets a look at my tallywacker of terror. I'll be able to run a three-legged race by myself. It'll be awesome. Maybe I can get into making stag films. I could bill myself as the human tripod. Please tell me I got a monster dong, Doc."

"Well, about that . . ."

"Oh boy, more bad news is coming. I can feel it," Joe said with frustration.

The doctor released, sighed, and said, "Unfortunately, you're right. You see, the only gorilla I had available was a female."

"What? Now, wait a cotton-pickin' minute there. Are you seriously telling me you put my brain into the body of a female gorilla?"

"Well, Yes, I suppose I am."

"Not a big, strapping savage, chest-pounding, schwantz-swinging male gorilla, but a namby-pamby, no-nuts, frail, delicate little female gorilla."

The doctor said, "To be honest, she was not so frail or delicate. She was well over three hundred pounds of solid muscle. I'm sorry, but I don't see that it's all such a big deal."

"You don't, do you? So, not only do I not have a foot-long war wanger, but I have no wanger whatsoever. Is that what you're trying to tell me?"

"Yes, I suppose that's correct."

"You suppose? Well, I suppose you supposed correctly. What am I going to do now? I'm a pitcher, Doc, not a catcher. I like women, not men. What am I supposed to tell my girlfriend when I get home? Well, Honey, not only am I now a gorilla, but it seems I'm a lesbian gorilla."

The doctor thought for a moment, then said, "Perhaps your girl would not be opposed to a bit of girl-on-girl gorilla action. Do you suppose she ever tried, as they say, playing for the other team?"

"Of course not. My girl is 100% woman." He hesitated for a moment, then said, "Then again, there was that time she told me about when she was away at girl's summer camp, but I'm pretty sure that was just experimental. But what about my squadron? What the Hell am I supposed to tell my commander? Sorry, Captain, but now that I'm a gorilla, I'll be too big to sit in the tail gunner seat, so I'll have to be assigned to the motor pool with the rest of the grease monkeys."

"As far as the Air Force is concerned, you were killed in action."

"But they won't find my body, will they?"

The doctor hesitated, then said, "Well . . . yes, they will. It's just that it will be a mess, what with the accident and the removal of your brain. Messy business, all that. I'm sure they will chalk that up to scavengers having their way with the corpses. Lord knows, I barely beat the blighters to the bodies."

"OK, so I can't go back to the military. And my girlfriend back home won't be an issue since if I'm dead, I can't go there either. So, to summarize, everyone thinks I'm dead. My brain and essence occupy the body of a chick gorilla, complete with gorilla gina. I can't go live in the jungle unless I'm prepared to be used as a love pin cushion being assaulted by every male silver-back gorilla within sniffing distance. I can't stay here with you since, for one thing, I have no idea who you are. And for another thing . . . there are probably a million other things. So, Doc. What do you recommend I do?"

The doctor seemed to ponder this question and then said, "I know some people who are active in the black market. It's how I get most of my lab supplies. I've heard that they always look for others to work with. I think if we shaved your face, arms, and hands, we might be able to pass you off as a human. Not the most attractive human, but human nonetheless. After all, apes are our closest relatives in the animal kingdom."

"Man, oh, man! This is all so uncool. It's probably the least cool thing I've ever heard of. But what choice do I have? I don't suppose you'd consider shooting me and ending it all."

The doctor said, "I would prefer not to. But if that's what you want, I'd be willing to euthanize you." He reached over to his metal worktable and picked up a syringe filled with a clear liquid. It was only water, but Joe had no way of knowing that.

"You mean, you'd really do that?"

"Yes, if that's what you really want."

Joe thought for a moment, then said, "Nah! Forget about it. I guess I'll have to make the best of this. Hey, Doc, how about you unstrap me and let me get up and get a feel for what it's like to have this new body?"

Reluctantly, the doctor said, "OK, Joe. If you promise to behave yourself."

"I will. Look, Doc, I've been thinking about all this. And although I'm not thrilled with being a gorilla chick, you're right about one thing. At least I'm still alive and can still think with my own brain."

"I'm glad to hear that," the doctor said as he released Joe from his straps.

Joe sat up and slowly got off the table, surprised at how quickly he was getting accustomed to this strange, new body. Looking around the room, he saw many wooden cages occupied by various animals. Then Joe realized that the animal stink he had been smelling was coming from himself; he'd have to do something about that. In fact, he had to do something about a lot of things very soon.

"I've been thinking, Doc, maybe that job with your black-market pal is worth considering. Do you have his name handy?"

The doctor walked over to his desk and returned with a piece of paper covered in barely intelligible scrawl. Joe took the paper in his hairy black hand, read it, and then memorized the name, address, and phone number. He looked at the doctor and asked, "Say, Doc, don't you have an assistant, nurse, or somebody who works with you?"

"Heavens, no!" He said with great surprise. "My work is far too secret to risk having anyone steal my ideas. All my information, skills, and right here." The doctor pointed to his head.

"Sweet," Joe said, "that's exactly what I wanted to hear." With one quick swipe of his massive hand, Joe promptly removed the doctor's head from his body, leaving a bloody neck stump pumping blood for a few seconds before the corpse collapsed to the floor. The bird/squirrel thing tried a divebomb attack, and Joe plucked it out of the air, bit its head off Ozzy-style, and spit it onto the floor. Then he ambled over to the cages and released all the animals.

He looked into a nearby mirror, and although shocked, he gently rubbed his chin and said, "Well, it appears I have some serious shaving to do and have a date with my new career."

BLOODSHOT

The storm was one of the worst to hit the area in decades, more severe than Frank Burnett could recall. The previous week had been especially brutal, with dark, gray skies and harsh, cold winds that seemed to blast through even the heaviest clothing. This day was no better; even now, it looked as dark as a late evening at one o'clock in the afternoon.

Frank waited in the restaurant lobby for the storm to break or at least for it to subside enough for him to run to his car without getting soaked. The valet would be bringing his Mercedes around any time now. A minute later, Frank saw his car pull up to the curb. The valet got out of the driver's seat, opened a large, black golf umbrella, and came around to help Frank stay dry on his way to the car.

"Thanks, man, I appreciate it," Frank said to the valet.

"Not a problem," the valet replied. His polite voice was pleasantly smooth with . . . what was that . . . a hint of a southern accent? Frank hadn't remembered seeing this particular worker before. He assumed the man must be new, especially since he had gone further to assure Frank's comfort. None of the other employees would have done such a thing, even hoping to get a generous tip.

The valet wore a dark blue or black rain slicker with a hood that hid most of his face. Frank could tell that the man was in his mid to late thirties, somewhat older than the previous valets he had seen at the restaurant. Then, again, times were hard, and he supposed a fellow down on his luck might try to find employment wherever he could. Frank had to give the guy props for his resourcefulness. The valet escorted Frank to his car, under cover of the umbrella, opened the door, then waited until Frank was behind the wheel. Frank turned and handed the man a twenty-dollar bill, grateful for the special service he had provided.

The man smiled, reached out with his gloved left hand, and then put the twenty in his coat pocket. Then he pulled a pistol with a sound suppressor from his right pocket, placed it against Frank's temple, and pulled the trigger. The "pfft" sound the .22-caliber pistol made was barely discernable in the pouring rain and howling winds. The valet leaned Frank's corpse back against the headrest, closed the door, and began slowly walking away down the street.

He hadn't needed to remove his gloves and risk leaving fingerprints to check the body for a pulse. He had done this many times before and knew the small caliber hollow-point round had done its job, bouncing around inside Frank's skull and turning his brain to cottage cheese. He tossed his gloves into two separate storm drains along the way and continued for several blocks to where he parked his stolen car. The valet smiled, knowing that the final payment for a job well done was just a few hours away. Now, it was time for him to make a call.

/ \ /

James Stevens sat behind his mahogany desk in his opulent office, sipping his coffee and nervously tapping his fingers on his old-fashioned desk blotter. He had no idea why he still used such a thing in the 21st century when ninety-eight percent of his work was done on a keyboard and displayed on his six large, flat-screen wall-mounted monitors. He supposed it, along with his green banker's lamp, was his way of keeping in touch with a simpler time, a time before his life got so damned complicated. Jim could see his secretary, Joan, through the window of his closed office door, working feverishly at her desk. Joan seldom left her desk, even for lunch. She would usually gobble down a sandwich she brought from home while working. Sweet, innocent Joan, unknowingly, would be one of his alibis.

A disposable cell phone sat on the desktop in the middle of his green felt blotter, seeming to stare at him and mock his right to exist. Jim recalled the name "burner phone," which he had often heard on television detective shows. Now, he had his own burner and waited for the call, which greatly increased his wealth. Of course, it would also cost him a bit financially, but he could afford it. He had a safe in his office with more than triple the cash he would require. Besides, he planned to do some renegotiating once the call came. Negotiating was, as a successful businessman, what he did best.

He had contracted to have his business partner, Frank Burnett, killed. Jim could hardly believe he had the testicular fortitude to do such a thing, but he certainly had. Any minute now, he would find out if his efforts were rewarded.

I actually put a hit on someone, Jim had found himself thinking on more than one occasion. Yet, even hearing himself say it aloud in the privacy of his office, Jim could scarcely believe it. He was simultaneously filled with a sense of incredible relief and mounting anxiety. After all, this was all new territory for him to be exploring.

It had all started innocently enough at a get-together several days earlier. It was held at a local bar, and the place was packed with revelers. Jim had drunk too much and had started mouthing off a bit too loudly about problems he had been experiencing with his business partner. Alcohol always did have a way of loosening Jim's tongue.

The next morning, as he awoke with a killer hangover, Jim had little memory of the previous night's rant and had no idea what he might have said in his drunken stupor. But apparently, someone at the bar had been paying attention.

When Jim went out to the mailbox to retrieve the morning newspaper, he was surprised to find a small box in the newspaper tube with no address, only the message "open me" printed outside. The words were constructed of individual multi-colored letters cut from different print sources, resembling ransom notes Jim had seen portrayed in movies.

Jim was uncertain if he should open the box because of its unknown origin. His active imagination envisioned a bomb hidden inside the box that might trigger as he tried to open it. However, it seemed too small to house any incendiary device. Then, again, who would want him dead? Maybe his partner, Frank, would, especially if he was as unhappy with their business arrangement as Jim was. But Frank was far too civilized to think of such a thing.

Frank had been born into money and had never had to work hard for anything in his life. On the other hand, Jim came from a poor family and had to work his butt off for everything he had gotten from life. Frank was the company's golden boy and could afford to be every-one's friend. He was the one everyone loved, while Jim had to carry the autocratic burden and run the business with an iron fist. But Jim needed Frank's capital to start the company, so he had to live with the situation. Now that the company had grown and become so successful under Jim's guidance, the need for a partner with money had become unimportant.

As he held the box in his hands, Jim tried again to remember The details of his rant from the previous evening and who might have heard him. But try as he might, Jim could not. The bar had been packed with strangers, any of whom could have overheard his drunken ravings.

Perhaps it was because he was so badly hungover and not firing on all cylinders, but eventually, Jim gave in to his curiosity, took the box into his home office, and opened it. To his surprise, the box contained a disposable cell phone with a similarly constructed note reading, "Call recent."

"Call recent?" Jim said aloud, "What the Hell is that supposed to mean?"

He selected the icon for recent calls and found a single number listed. He hesitated for a few seconds, unsure this was a rabbit hole into which he wanted to venture. Once again, his curiosity got the better of him, and Jim selected the number and called it.

The phone rang twice, and then a smooth male voice with a slightly Southern accent said, "Good morning, Mr. Stevens."

/ 2 /

"How are you this fine morning, Mr. Stevens? I hope you don't have too much of a headache upon awakening. That was quite a performance you gave at the bar last night."

Jim was confused at first, wondering who was on the other end of the line and how the man knew his name. Surprisingly, he became angry with the man on the phone, likely due to his throbbing head and upset stomach. "What's the meaning of this? Who the Hell are you, anyway?"

"Woah, now. Easy there, Jim. May I call you Jim?"

"No, you most certainly may not. I have no idea who you are or what you want with me."

"Well now, Jimmy boy. I can't exactly tell you who I am now, can I? You see, that would prove substantially detrimental to my ability to earn a comfortable living and thereby enhance my financial portfolio, as it were."

Jim thought, "Substantially detrimental?" He recognized this man's manner of speaking, as he had encountered it many times over the years. It was typical of uneducated thugs trying to sound smarter than they were by filling the air with unnecessary words.

"Look, whoever you are. I don't have time for your stupid games. I think perhaps it would be best if we just ended this ridiculous conversation immediately."

He got ready to hang up when he heard the voice say in a disturbingly calm but direct voice, "So, do you want Frank Burnett dead or not?"

Jim hesitated for a moment, dumbfounded and uncertain about what he had just heard. The caller hadn't peppered that last sentence with flowery words. He had gotten right to the point.

"Wha . . . what did you just say?" Jim asked nervously.

"Ah, so it appears I've gotten your attention, Jimmy boy. And we both know you heard me the first time. So there's no need for me to repeat myself."

"But . . . but, why would you ask me such a horrible thing?"

The smooth, southern voice said, "You see, Jimmy. This is how I earn my keep, so to speak. I solve the problems of others like yourself . . . for a fee, of course."

"A fee? What sort of fee?"

"May I assume from your question that you're interested in procuring my humble services?"

Jim hesitated for a moment, then said, "For the moment, let's just say I'm hypothetically curious."

"Hypothetically curious? Humm . . . that's a rather interesting way to approach this discussion. However, unfortunately for you, Jimmy boy, I don't deal in hypotheticals. The last time I checked, hypotheticals don't bring home the bacon, as they say. However, if you are willing to speak factually, mano a mano, then all you need do is provide me with a mere ten thousand dollars in cash, and all your troubles will be over."

Jim was beside himself, "Ten thousand dollars? You must be out of your goddamned mind. What makes you think I could afford to pay you that kind of money?"

The voice on the phone chuckled slightly, then replied, "Oh, Jimmy. We both know you're quite rich and can easily afford such a payment. I know you could afford much more and never even miss it. However, I am not the greedy sort. I'm just out to earn daily bread. I also know that if your partner we're to, shall we say, cross over to that great corporate conglomerate in the sky, the operation of the company and its subsequent profits will all be yours. This means your finances would more than double, actually triple, once you take your company public."

"How . . . how did you know that?"

"Due diligence, Jim, my man. Due diligence, plain and simple. I like to know who I'm fixin' to partner up with; it's just smart for business. By the way, Jimmy, don't let this country bumpkin accent fool you none. This book has a lot more to it than its cover might suggest. In other words, my new friend, underestimate me; I dare you. It'll be so much fun."

A cold chill ran down Jim's spine. One of those gut-based red flags screamed at him to hang up the phone, destroy it and forget it ever arrived. Yet another part of his body, his reptilian business-savvy brain, told him the man might be the answer to his problems despite his uncertainty about the caller.

"Ok," Jim said, "suppose I did want to hire you to perform that unmentioned task. How would I go about doing it?"

"Well, now. Isn't that so much better? When two like-minded people come together in a lucrative business arrangement for both parties . . . well, things just seem right with the world. Don't you agree, Jim?"

Jim wasn't so certain he agreed with the caller's sentiments. He just wanted to get this over with as soon as possible. "Please tell me what I have to do?"

"You will have just about done all you have to when you accept the terms of this agreement. Here's how this will work. After our conversation has ended, I'll send you a text message. It'll contain a nondescript drop box location where you will put the cash. You can pay half upfront and the other half upon fulfillment of the contract. When I complete the assignment, I will call you on this phone and say, 'It's done.' Then, you will drop another $5k into the drop box by 5:00 pm. Once that has been done, you and I will part company as gentlemen, never to speak again."

"But I need to know when it will happen to set up an alibi for myself. Surely, as soon as something happens to Frank, the police will be here to question me."

"That is quite correct on both accounts, Jimmy boy. If you tell me to proceed, the event will occur tomorrow after lunch. I have already checked, and I know that Frank has lunch alone every Thursday at that fancy-pants restaurant over on Bleaker Street. So, all you have to do is be at your desk during that time and make sure many people see you there. Maybe even be sure to have one or more of your employees stop by for instructions. Anything to ensure that you are seen diligently working at your desk."

This was the moment of truth. Jim had a chance to rid himself of Frank and have everything he always wanted. All he had to do was give this stranger the go-ahead. Then he wondered, what if this character wasn't really who he said he was? What if he was an actor hired by Frank to see if Jim would consider such a proposal? Or worse, what if he were a cop Frank asked to entrap him into attempting to hire a contract killer? If he told the guy on the phone to do the deed, would he find himself under arrest and thrown into jail?

Jim asked, "How do I know this is legitimate? How do I know you're not some cop or private security guy hired by Frank to entrap me?"

"Well now, Jimmy boy. Those certainly are good questions. I'm glad to see you are thinking that way. That means you're giving serious consideration to our proposal."

"Maybe not, maybe so. But I need some guarantee you are who you say you are."

"Not a problem, Jim, old pal. Here's what I'm gonna do for you. Listen carefully because this will guarantee that I am not entrapping you, at least from a legal standpoint. I am offering to blow the brains out of your business partner, Frank Burnett, for the fee of ten thousand dollars. I am guaranteeing he will be dead meat by tomorrow at 1:30 pm. There you go, Jim. I just put all my cards on the table. If I were a cop offering this service to you, a good lawyer could get this thrown out of court in no time. Now, to keep you further protected, all you have to do is say, 'agreed.'"

Jim had no idea if what this mysterious stranger said was true or not, but it sounded like it might be legitimate. He had a good head for business law but knew nothing about criminal law. He knew cops could lie to people during interrogations to get them to confess or turn on their co-conspirators, but he thought it would be entrapment if they tried to set someone up in advance. Jim believed when the caller spelled out exactly what he planned to do, that guaranteed he was not a cop.

"So what's it gonna be, Jimmy, old boy? Agreed? Or disagreed?"

Jim asked, "This is all so strange. I'm not sure. I don't even know what your name is."

"Oh, Jim. Don't be silly. You don't need to know my name. But hey, if it makes you feel more comfortable, you can call me Bloodshot."

"B . . . B . . . Bloodshot?"

"Yeah, it kinda has a nice ring, doesn't it? So what's it gonna be, Jimmy?"

Jim hesitated for a long moment, then said, "Agreed."

The phone went dead.

/ 3 /

It was now Thursday at 1:10 pm, and Jim was waiting for the call to come. He had deposited five thousand dollars in the designated drop box earlier that morning. He had five thousand more in an envelope in his briefcase, although if things went according to plan, he would never have to part with it.

Jim was surprised to find himself more relaxed about the pending call than he thought he ever would be. He felt confident and in control, probably because he had a plan to renegotiate his deal with the caller. It was his prerogative as the customer, after all. Besides, what would the guy do, run to the police? The caller would have no other choice but to be content to agree to Jim's new terms.

Suddenly, the burner phone rang, and despite his previously relaxed demeanor, Jim practically jumped out of his leather office chair. Maybe he wasn't quite as comfortable as he thought he was. The important thing was not to let the caller notice. Jim believed in the adage, "Never let them see you sweat." He picked up the phone and answered it.

"Hello?" Jim inquired.

A smooth, calm voice on the other end of the line said, "It's done."

Jim took a deep breath and said, "Good, very good. Thank you."

"Sorry, Jimmy boy. I do not need your thanks. All I want to know is that my money will be there by 5:00."

"How do I know the job was done? What guarantee do I have?"

"I told you it was done, Jimmy boy, and my word is golden."

"So you say. But I need proof."

"You'll get your proof shortly . . . as soon as a valet discovers his dead body in the car parked in front of the restaurant. You will no doubt get a call from someone shortly. Now, let's not waste any more time, Jimmy boy. I look forward to receiving the rest of my money and parting ways with you."

"About that," Jim said, trying to sound more confident than he felt.

"What about that, Jim?" The caller said, sounding noticeably uncomfortable with the conversation's direction.

"I've changed my mind about the payment we originally agreed to. I think ten thousand might be a bit high for the job. I think perhaps the five thousand dollars I already paid you would be more in line for the service you provide."

The caller chuckled, "Oh, you do, do you? That's quite a pair of balls you have hanging there, Jimmy boy."

"I didn't get rich by accident. I know how to negotiate a deal, and that's what we're doing right now."

"Well, just look at you gettin' all high and mighty all of a sudden. I have to admit you surprised me, Jimmy. I didn't think you had it in you. But if you insist on having a negotiation, then, by all means, negotiate away."

"I think I made myself clear already. Five thousand dollars, take it or leave it."

"Oh, Jim. You hurt my feelings. I just made you one hundred thousand dollars, not counting the additional money you will make with your company."

"One hundred thousand? What are you talking about?"

"Jimmy, oh Jimmy. You see, I know about the insurance policies you each took out at the start of your partnership. If either of you should die, the other is the beneficiary of the hundred-thousand-dollar payout. So now, getting back to the negotiations you so desire . . . the new fee is twenty thousand."

"Twenty thousand? Are you insane?"

"The jury is out on the insanity thing, Jim. But if anyone in this conversation is crazy, I suspect it must be you. You see, five minutes ago, I would have been content with ten thousand until you decided to get all uppity. You insisted on negotiating, so that's what we're doing. The new number is now $20k, and you have until 5:00 pm today to put it in the drop box as you did earlier."

"And if I refuse?"

"Oh, Jimmy boy. You cut me to the quick. I pegged you for being a lot of things, but stupid wasn't one of them. What to do, what to do. How about this? Let's try a different approach. I have something to say to you, James, my new friend, Amanda Lynn Stevens, and The Chelsea Elementary Education Center."

"What? What are you saying?"

"You know what I'm talking about, Jimmy. That prestigious private elementary school where your baby girl Amanda is presently studying. It is quite an expensive school, and I must admit, quite a lovely building. You see, I'm looking at it right now. I was just thinking how tragic it would be if someone were to get inside the building and start randomly shooting teachers and students until they eventually got to your precious blonde-haired, blue-eyed baby girl. But you needn't worry, Jimmy. I wouldn't kill your daughter, not outright. Oh no. I would have much better plans for her, involving taking my sweet old time and having great creative fun in the process."

"I . . . no . . . please . . . don't . . . not Amanda."

"You now have until 4:00 to transfer the remaining $15k. As you can see, I have math skills, too, Jim. But now, these negotiations are officially over." The phone went dead.

Jim lowered his head to his desk and began to shake. Then he forced himself to regain control, went into his office safe, and withdrew $15,000 in cash. Then, noticing the burner phone sitting on his desk blotted, Jim tossed the blasted thing into his trash can.

/ 4 /

Jim began to have many other concerns now. He knew, eventually, the police would come by to question him. After all, he had been Frank's partner in business and now ran the entire company. Then there was that life insurance policy. It suddenly seemed apparent that Jim had more motives for murder than most people.

Over the next fifteen minutes, Jim used his personal smartphone to call Frank's cell phone several times and left messages asking Frank to return his call and, sounding like he and Jim needed to discuss some important business as soon as possible. He included a few references to different business issues and clients for authenticity.

Then, he decided to take a stroll through the office again. Jim had done so a half-hour earlier, but it never hurt to allow more corroborating witnesses to see him in the office. After all, there was no way he could be at work and be several miles away, killing his partner.

He stopped by the break room and saw one of the interns he and Frank had interviewed a month earlier. Jim searched his memory for the girl's name but came up empty. He thought her name might be Jill or Janet or maybe some name that didn't even start with "J." For all he knew, her name could have been Priscilla.

He had not wanted to hire the girl as he felt she didn't project a professional enough image. Her skirts were too short, and her low-cut tops were far too revealing. This, however, was not to suggest she didn't have the body and looks to wear such outfits. The truth was, she was a knockout. Still, at the risk of appearing prudish, Jim felt she didn't belong in a business office in that manner of dress.

These feelings resulted in another heated argument between him and Frank. In the end, Frank insisted on hiring the bimbo, and Jim reluctantly conceded. For all Jim knew, Frank might be secretly banging the doors off of her on the sly. Jim had noticed the pair seemed way too chummy when they were together. Well, that love train had just run off the rails, and Jim was the engineer driving that train. He planned on kicking that worthless tramp to the curb as soon as the dust settled on this Frank murder thing.

"Hi, how's it going?" Jim asked, figuring if he initiated the conversation, he could do so without using her name, which still escaped him.

"Oh, hi, Mr. Stevens. Everything is going great. I love working for Frank . . . I mean Mr. Burnett. I feel like I've known him forever."

Jim did his best to conceal his feelings about her while simultaneously trying in vain to smile cordially without looking like a raving lunatic. Pleasant interactions and friendly smiling were not Jim's strong suits. Most of the time, his face bore a permanent scowl. As a result, he felt he looked like a psycho killer when forcing a smile. Now that he thought about it, that analogy was no longer so far from the truth. He may not have pulled the trigger that killed Frank, but he had done the same thing indirectly.

Jim asked, "Um, so where is Mr. Burnett? I wanted to ask him something, but I can't seem to find him."

"I believe he went out to eat lunch at that place across town he likes so much. Did you ever go there with him?"

"No. I seldom go out for lunch. I have too many pressing matters to take care of here and usually eat at my desk like I did today."

"Yes, I saw you in there working away." Then she gave him a coquettish smile, ran her finger down his tie, and said in a sultry voice, "You know, Mr. Stevens, it wouldn't hurt you to go out at lunch and have a little fun. I'm sure I could take you somewhere that would, shall we say, satisfy you."

Jim was taken aback, "Um . . . yes, I'm sure you could. Now tell me, do you know when Mr. Burnett will return?"

"Actually, he should have returned by now. I don't know what's taking him so long."

Jim looked confused, "Me either. I tried calling him several times a few minutes ago, but he's not answering his cell phone."

Suddenly, the girl looked concerned and said, "I hope Frank . . . Mr. Burnett is ok. You don't think anything bad happened to him, do you?"

"Heavens, no," Jim replied, "I'm sure Frank is relaxing and having a nice drink with his lunch. As you said, sometimes it's good to relax. I may have to try it sometime, but not today. I have too many problems to take care of at the moment. I must get back to it. Enjoy the rest of your day."

With that, Jim returned to his office, content that he had covered all his bases and established a sufficient alibi. Then he recalled the burner phone he had tossed into his trash can. He had to get rid of it and eliminate any trace of it. When he returned to his office, he closed the door and lowered the blinds.

Then he grabbed the phone from his trashcan and, using a letter opener he kept in his desk drawer, he began disassembling it to the best of his ability. When it was broken down into five pieces, he tucked the fragments into his top desk drawer and went to the company's mailroom.

The mailroom was empty, as the attendant must have taken a late lunch. Jim found a bin containing small bubble wrap envelopes. They were blank, with no corporate logo or address on them. He took five of them and put them into his sports coat pocket. When he returned to his office, he used his handkerchief to wipe any fingerprints off each phone piece and then placed each into a separate envelope, careful not to touch them with his fingers. He smashed any parts that resembled a SIM card before putting them into its envelope. He didn't know if burner phones had SIM cards, but he assumed they might. Again, using the handkerchief, he wiped down each of the envelopes and put them inside his briefcase, covering them with several papers. Later, on his way to the drop box, he would put each envelope into separate trashcans at various fast-food restaurants and mini-marts he passed.

/ 5 /

At 2:15 p.m., with his door open and his blinds again pulled up, Jim was in his office pretending to be hard at work while thinking about what he had done. More importantly, he thought about what he would do and how he would react when the police came. He was sure their visit would be inevitable. Jim tried to imagine two hard-nosed detectives grilling him about his whereabouts at the time of the murder.

Before the cops came to give him the third degree, they would, of course, research him, his family, and his company and dig into his private life. They'd likely talk to his subordinates, who would confirm his alibi. However, some had witnessed heated arguments between him and Frank, and they might mention something to the cops. He would have to dampen any suspicions they might have by explaining it away as friendly arguments between business partners.

Jim looked at the clock and saw it was 2:30. Although he usually stayed in the office until 6:00 or sometimes later, Jim needed to head out to bring the rest of the money to the designated drop box. If the police wanted to track him down afterward, they could catch him at home. Besides, he had to get rid of the burner phone fragments along the way to the drop zone. He closed his briefcase, checking to see if the envelope containing the money and the smaller envelopes containing the cell phone parts were still there and readily available.

He looked out his office window at the continuing storm, put on his raincoat and hat, and grabbed his umbrella from the stand at the base of his coat tree. He stopped by his secretary's desk and said, "Joan, I'm going to be heading out early today. I have a few stops to make on the way home. I've been trying to reach Frank for some time but haven't had any luck. If he comes back in later, please ask him to call me on my cell."

"Will do, Mr. Stevens," Joan said, scarcely paying attention to him. Jim always marveled at what an old-school, super-efficient secretary Joan was. She was a no-nonsense, nose-to-the-grindstone older worker, the kind he knew were a dying breed. He often wondered what his company would do when employees like Joan were all either retired or dead. He had little faith in the younger workers like Jill, Janet, Precilla, or whatever the Hell her name was.

"Very good, Joan. I'll see you tomorrow morning."

Frank left the office and took care of everything he needed to do on the way home. He felt as if an enormous weight had been lifted from his shoulders. As usual, Jim had dinner with his wife and daughter and only felt guilty when he looked at his happy little girl and recalled the threat the killer had made earlier that day. His stupid attempt at negotiation nearly cost him his daughter's life. Jim did his best to put that out of his mind. Then, to his surprise, he slept soundly that evening and never thought again about the previous day's events.

/ 6 /

The next day, he awoke, took care of his morning routine, and went down to have breakfast. His wife, Barbara, prepared his typical pancakes, eggs, sausage, and toast. When he entered the kitchen, he took in the incredible smells.

Barbara said, "Jim, your secretary, Joan called. She said it was urgent and sounded very upset."

Jim looked at his watch and said, "It's only seven o'clock. She's in early."

"She's in early every day, Jim. You just don't notice. Sometimes, I think you take that poor woman for granted."

"You are probably right, Barb. I truly do appreciate her dedication, and I suppose I should show it more often. I think I'll talk to Frank today about giving her a raise. I'm sure he'll agree." Jim figured it never hurt to keep solidifying his alibi. Now his wife could tell police her husband had no idea about Frank's death as he planned on discussing Joan's raise with him.

"I'll keep your breakfast warm while you call Joan," Barbara said.

Jim barely heard her as he was busy trying to determine the best approach to take when he got the news from Joan. He knew Barbara would be eavesdropping, and he had to make his reaction believable for Joan and his wife.

He said into his phone, "Joan, this is Jim. Barbara said you have some sort of emergency at the office. What's up?"

"Oh my God, Jim. Don't you know? Didn't you hear?" She cried into the phone. Jim could tell she was upset because she had never called him by any name other than Mr. Stevens.

"I'm sorry, Joan. I don't understand. What didn't I hear? What's the problem?" He replied, sounding genuinely concerned. Barbara looked over at him, more curious than ever.

"Frank . . . Mr. Burnett is dead."

"Wa . . . what? Frank? Dead? Oh my God, Joan! What happened? Was it a heart attack? Jesus, Joan! What was it?" Jim looked at his wife with as much false concerned surprise as he could muster. She looked back at him in stunned shock. She mouthed the word, "Frank?" Jim nodded his head.

Joan said, "No, it wasn't his heart. He was killed. Someone shot him?"

"Shot him?" Frank said, "What do you mean, shot him? Was it a robbery or something?"

"I don't know. I haven't heard anything official yet. It might have been a mugging or a carjacking gone wrong. All I know is he was found dead in his Mercedes outside of the restaurant yesterday after lunch. The police said he was shot once in the head."

"Police? Were they at the office? Are they still there? Can I talk to someone about this? Oh, my Lord, this is terrible!" Jim was amazed at his improvisational acting skills. He never knew he had such talent. He was actually starting to tear up a little bit.

"Yes, they're still here. They won't tell me any more than they already did. The police are questioning everyone in the office as they report to work. They asked for you as well."

"For me? Jim said, sounding surprised.

"Yes. As I said, they want to speak to everyone."

"Of course, yes . . . of course, they do. Forgive me. I'm a bit upset. I'm obviously not thinking clearly. Look, Joan. Please tell them I'm on my way in and should arrive within half an hour."

She said, "Yes . . . yes, I will. I'll tell them you're on your way."

"And, I'm sorry, Joan. I forgot to ask: are you ok? Is there anything I can do for you?"

"Thanks, Jim . . . Mr. Stevens. I'm doing as well as can be expected. All of us are in shock, as I'm sure you are. We'll be better once you're here."

"I'm on my way," Jim said and hung up the phone.

"What is it, Honey? What happened to Frank?"

"I don't have all the details, but Joan said the police told her Frank was shot in his car outside the restaurant yesterday at lunch . . . he . . . he's dead."

"Oh my God, Jim! That's horrible! It's unbelievable."

"I know. I'm beside myself. I don't know what to do. The police are at work questioning all of our employees. They want to talk to me as well. Look, Sweetie, I'm sorry about breakfast, but I have to go right in."

"Are you going to be ok to drive? Do you want me to drop you off?"

"No, no, I'll be ok. I need time to process all of this. The drive will do me good, I think."

"Just be careful and try not to be too distracted. And call me as soon as you get to the office. You have your cellphone, right?"

Jim reached into his jacket pocket, half expecting to find the dreaded burner phone in there, but was relieved to feel his smartphone right where it was supposed to be. He said, "Yes, I have it right here."

"Good. Now, please be careful, and don't forget to call."

"I won't forget," Jim said as he kissed his wife goodbye and headed for the door.

"Jim?" She called out to him. "You forgot your briefcase."

"Oh crap!" He said, "I'm sorry. I'm so scatterbrained sometimes."

Barbara realized she would have to give her husband a half hour to get to work and then call or text him to make sure he made it in safely. As justifiably upset as he was, there was no way he would remember to call her.

/ 7 /

As Jim drove to the office, he was amazed by the performance he had just given. Both his wife and his secretary would be able to testify to his shock and grief over the loss of his partner. Now, he had to figure out the best approach when questioned by the cops. He had to be careful not to be too over-the-top with his theatrics yet not too unfeeling. The police were not his wife or anyone close to him that he could easily fool. They were professionals trained to watch for signs and tells that indicated untruths and pointed them to suspects.

He had to remember that he had an alibi; he was at his desk at the time of the murder. Jim had paid with cash from his personal safe that no one, not even his wife or secretary, knew anything about. He had left the killer's fee at an obscure location where there were no cameras, in a drop box only known to the killer. He destroyed the burner phone and spread its remains throughout the city. Even the cardboard box the phone had come in days earlier was gone, burned in the fireplace in his home office. Nothing tied him to the crime except for the killer's word.

This gave Jim pause for a moment. Maybe he had less to fear from the police than he did from the hitman. The killer knew all about Jim, and he knew nothing about the killer other than that stupid name, Bloodshot. Jim suddenly wondered if perhaps the murderer had recorded their conversation. What then? What if he came back looking to extort Jim for more money? The killer couldn't go to the police, but he could send them any digital file he might have recorded. The man had mentioned Jim by name. He had mentioned Jim's business dealings as well as his daughter's. Perhaps the police could use voice recognition to identify Jim as the man who had ordered the hit. If he were being honest with himself, Jim had felt the twenty-thousand he paid the man was fairly cheap, considering the act could bring the killer the death penalty.

A cold chill ran down Jim's spine. What if this killer had set him up? Maybe the man had planted a seed he planned to use to harvest a money crop from Jim for the rest of his life. Jim cursed his stupidity for drinking so much at the bar and spouting off with his big mouth. Then, he was so foolish as to agree to the hit while suffering from one of the worst hangovers of his life. Why hadn't he thought of this potential complication earlier? And why think of it now when he had to focus all of his energy on answering very important questions from some very serious police officers?

Jim pulled over to the side of the road, feeling as if he were about to have a panic attack or perhaps throw up all over himself. He got out of the car and walked carefully over to the side of the highway. Jim leaned against the passenger side of his car, staring down at the ground and taking deep, cleansing breaths. He kept repeating in his mind, "You're ok. You can do this. Stop thinking about problems that don't exist. Focus, dammit, focus."

After a few minutes, Jim regained his composure, got back into his car, started his engine, and headed to work with one final sigh. As he pulled into his executive parking space, Jim expected to see his building surrounded by a dozen police cars with lights flashing and maybe a swat team ready to storm the building. Then, realizing he wasn't in a TV cop show, he looked again and saw three nondescript sedans parked in the visitor's parking space. Of course, this was how they would come. There would likely be three teams of two detectives that would take turns interviewing everyone and checking alibis. One would ask the questions while the other would stare a hole in the subject with his cop eyes, waiting for a flinch or sign that the person was lying.

Jim took another deep breath and got out of his car. If he let his imagination get away from him, he was toast. He kept reminding himself that he had a solid alibi, and there was no way they could ever tie him to Frank's death. He slowly walked to the building and took the elevator to his office floor. When the doors opened, he saw his employees standing in small groups waiting to be interviewed. He looked at the large conference room and saw that new girl whose name he couldn't recall yesterday, crying and speaking with two stern-looking detectives. He saw that the small conference room was likewise occupied by a junior executive, Charles Desmond, questioned by two other officers.

Joan came running up to Jim and, to his surprise, wrapped her arms around him, sobbing into his sports coat, "Oh Mr. Stevens, Mr. Stevens, what are we going to do? Who could do such an awful thing to Mr. Burnett? And why would anybody want to hurt him? Everybody loved Mr. Burnett."

Jim did his best to comfort her, spreading a bit of extra manure in the process, "I honestly don't know, Joan. Frank was one of the best. I feel like I have lost a brother. It had to have been some sort of random, tragic mistake. Frank didn't have an enemy in the world. Hopefully, the police will be able to get to the bottom of this."

"Mr. Stevens? Mr. James Stevens?" A voice said from Jim's right. Jim turned and saw a man in an off-the-rack, slightly rumpled suit looking at him with . . . with . . . yep, there they were . . . cop eyes.

"Yes, I'm Jim Stevens. And you are?" Jim said as he extended his hand for a handshake while releasing Joan and doing his best to look like his world had just come crashing around him.

"I'm Chief Inspector Joe Logan. I'm in charge of this investigation."

"Thank God, Inspector Logan. I'm so glad you and your men are here. I just heard about my friend's death this morning at home when my secretary, Joan here, called.

Joan said tearfully, " I'll leave you two to talk. I have to go back and sit down for a bit."

Jim said, "Yes, Joan. Please do. I'll be back to talk to you as soon as I can."

Joan started to walk away.

"She's taking it pretty hard," the detective said.

"Yes, we all are. I'm still trying to take all of this in. I'm still in shock. I only got the call a half-hour or so ago. This is . . . well . . . it's impossible . . . I can't wrap my head around it . . . Frank . . . Frank was my partner, my best friend."

"Look, Mr. Stevens. I'm so sorry for your loss, but please understand we have to speak to everyone and ask questions if we're ever going to get to the bottom of this."

"Yes, of course. I understand completely. What can I do to help? Anything, just name it?"

"Can we go into your office and chat for a bit?"

"Um . . . sure, most certainly. Please follow me." Jim felt like he was handling things pretty well so far. He played the role of a grieving partner while not going overboard with his emotions. After all, he was the president of this company, and he had to be the shepherd of his grieving flock and appear that way to the police.

Inspector Logan made himself comfortable in the guest chair while Jim placed his briefcase on his credenza and sank into his leather executive chair, heaving a deep sigh and shaking his head as if in disbelief.

"Tough start of an even rougher day, I'm sure," Logan said.

"Yeah," Jim replied, sounding as if he would rather be anywhere than there, which was truer than, hopefully, anyone realized. "So, Inspector Logan, what can I do to help?"

"Please call me Joe. You've been through quite enough today without worrying about formalities."

"And Joe, you can call me Jim. I suppose we should get this thing started so we can help you figure out who did this to my friend . . ." Jim hesitated, then swallowed as if holding back his emotions. He cleared his throat and finished, ". . . Frank."

"Yes indeed," Logan said, "But we already know what happened to Mr. Burnett, and we even have a good idea and are pretty sure who was responsible."

For a second, Jim felt as if he might throw up all over the top of his desk; he did his best to hide his initial reaction, hoping the cop didn't detect anything out of the ordinary from his behavior. Jim said, "You . . . you do? That's fantastic news. Have you caught the murderer?"

Logan hesitated, then said, "No, not yet."

Jim looked perplexed, "I'm sorry, Joe. I'm a bit confused. My secretary told me Frank was shot outside a restaurant yesterday at lunch. And if you already know who did it, why haven't you arrested him? And why are you bothering to question my employees? What do you hope to get from them when you seem to already have all the answers you need?"

Logan said, "Well, Jim. It's like this. We know who killed your partner, Frank, because we have seen his M-O before. Well, I should say we haven't seen his M-O before, but other police in other parts of the country have seen similar Motis Operandi."

"Ok, I suppose. I think I'm following you, Joe. Are you saying this guy is a serial killer of some sort?"

"Yes and no. If the killer is who we think he is, he has killed before, many times, and in the same way. But unlike a serial killer, he doesn't do so for psychological gratification, although we're fairly certain he enjoys his work."

"Work?" Jim asked, feeling bile rise in his throat.

"Yes, work. You see, Jim. This character is a contract killer."

"You mean . . . a hitman, like on TV?"

"Yes, but unlike on TV, this killer won't be caught by the end of the hour and, in fact, has never been caught. No one knows his real name or what he looks like. From what we have been able to gather, the killer learns everything he can about people who want to have someone killed. Then, he contacts them through various means, ensuring they can never identify him. He does, as I said, learn everything he can about them, usually enough to intimidate them into never crossing him. He convinces them to use his services, which he performs flawlessly, and then he disappears."

Jim was silent.

"Is everything ok, Jim?" Logan said. Jim could feel those cop eyes burning a hole in him again.

"Yes, sure. I'm just still perplexed. Are you saying someone in my company hired a hitman to kill Frank? Why the Hell would someone do such a thing? We all loved Frank. Hell, everyone he ever met loved Frank. He was just that sort of guy. So even outside of this company, I can't imagine anyone wanting to hurt him."

"Yet someone obviously did," Logan said.

Jim asked, "Could it have been a mistake? You know, a case of mistaken identity? Could the killer have killed Frank thinking he was someone else?"

"Hum . . ." Logan said as if he hadn't thought of such an idea before. "Perhaps. But unlikely. This killer has never made a mistake so far. It's also possible we are completely off base here, and the killer might be someone else entirely, but someone with a similar M-O."

"Seriously. You think that's possible?" Jim asked.

"I suppose anything is possible," Logan said, "Actually, we hope for the sake of whoever hired this guy that the killer isn't who we think it is."

Suddenly, Jim had a very bad feeling about where this conversation was going. He felt his mouth go dry as he asked, "Why is that, Joe?"

Logan smiled and said, "Remember I said the killer kills for money and doesn't kill his contract victim for personal gratification?"

"Yes, I recall."

"Well, he has another way of getting his, shall we say, psychopathic rocks off. He kills his contract clients directly by shooting them once in the head. However, he is also a butcher who likes to make his other victims suffer for a long time. I'm talking about raping and killing family members in front of each other. He's been known to flay the flesh from his victims while they beg for death."

"Oh my God, that's horrible. You said his other victims. What does that mean?"

"As strange as this may sound, I suppose your partner Frank had it easy, being the contracted victim. You see, this killer never leaves witnesses of any sort, even if he is sure they know nothing about him. That's also part of his M-O. And, of course, it's the part he loves best. Remember I said he learns all he can about the people who hire him?"

"Um . . . yes, I do," Jim said, dreading what was coming next.

"Well, this guy usually takes on a contract for a very small fee from someone he knows can afford to pay much more. Then he carries out the hit as he was hired to do."

"Ok, but why do I feel there is more to this story?"

Logan said, "Because there is. Once the contract is completed, the killer returns and forces the person who hired him to cough up a lot more money. Then he kidnaps the person and all of his loved ones. He eventually tortures and kills them in the sick manner I described earlier."

"Oh my God! You have to catch this psycho, whoever he is."

"We hope to, but as I said, we know very little about him. All we know is he goes by the name Bloodshot."

THE NURSE

I'm a great believer in karma, and the vengeance that it serves up to
those who are deliberately mean is generally enough for me."
—BETH DITTO

"Vengeance is in my heart, death in my hand.
Blood and revenge are hammering in my head."
—WILLIAM SHAKESPEARE

"Revenge is the sweetest morsel to the mouth
that was ever was cooked in Hell."
—WALTER SCOTT

Joe Montero slowly began to claw his way back to consciousness. He
was feeling disoriented; he was not certain if he was awake or asleep. He
had no idea where he was or what had happened to him. His brain felt
foggy and unable to focus. He suspected he might have been drugged.
If he had been, the drugs were not doing a very good job of numbing
his discomfort.

His body was cold; his lips shivered involuntarily from a sudden
chill, which seemed to work its icy fingers from the top of his head to
the tips of his toes. His body ached, and he felt as if a truck had run
over him, and then it decided to back up and run over him several
more times for good measure. Surely, something bad must have happened to him; what exactly that might be, Joe didn't know. He may
have been in an accident, though he couldn't recall.

The air around him stank of dampness, mold and sulfur, and something like rotting meat. His lips felt dry and cracked; his throat parched and on fire. Joe cautiously opened his eyes to tiny slits, trying to focus but not succeeding. He noticed the room was dismal and barely lit with a haunting green light, unlike anything he had ever imagined.

With his eyes still mostly closed, Joe tried moving his arms and legs, discovering he couldn't. He thought he might be paralyzed because of his lack of ability to move, but if so, why did he feel so much pain? Didn't paralysis bring the inability to feel? His head ached, and his back felt like a thousand daggers pierced him. Moving his eyes from side to side, He tried to use his peripheral vision to learn what he could about his surroundings.

Looking straight up toward the ceiling, he saw old wooden joists, cross beams, and rusty pipes. The structures were rotted in places and glowed with the same eerie green light as the rest of the room. Dozens of spider webs stretched from pipe to beam. Directing his gaze downward, Joe saw stone walls glistening with moisture and covered with mold. There were places in the cracks between the stones where moss grew freely. He couldn't be sure, but Joe thought he saw some large insects, like oversized centipedes, slithering from stone to stone.

An eight-panel metal-framed window was positioned in the center of the wall, blackened out with paint. Joe thought he might be in some old cellar, perhaps part of some industrial building. As his senses continued to awaken, the foul stench of the place became even more nauseating.

Looking toward the ground as best as his limited vision would allow, Joe saw a six-inch drainpipe mounted to the wall and a bunch of debris littering the ground. He even saw a road sign on its side that read Speed Limit 45. Once again, Joe wondered what this place was. Why was he hurting so badly, and what happened to him?

He tried to call out for help but could only utter a dry, faint "heh" sound. As he lay in the bed, virtually helpless, Joe vainly tried to focus and caught some slight movement off to his right. He strained through the foggy vision to see whatever it might be. After a few seconds, he thought he could make out the faint shape of some movement down low to the ground.

As the blurry figure crawled closer, he saw it was definitely a woman, wearing a white nurse's uniform, the style with a short sleeve top and dress combination of the variety he remembered seeing in old movies from the 1960s but never saw anymore. He was pretty sure most nurses now wore what they called scrubs.

Looking closer, trying hard once again to focus, he realized his original assessment of the nurse wasn't quite accurate. The hairs on the back of his neck began to stand on end as he realized something appeared very wrong, something so horrid and unearthly his mind could barely come to grips with what his eyes were seeing.

The nurse—if she actually was a nurse—was crawling along the ground. Her uniform yellowed, worn, and was soiled and bloody. Her arms and legs were bruised and scored with open bleeding lacerations. A network of red and blue veins formed a hideous roadmap on her ghostly pale, almost transparent skin. Her face was scrapped and scared with only one eye, her left, still appearing to function. Her blouse was ripped open, revealing two ample breasts, and her short hiked-up skirt left little to the imagination. Her legs were long and disturbingly shapely, traveling upwards to a short, tattered dress.

The most frightening thing about the woman was her teeth. They looked razor-sharp, and in her angry face, they seemed ready to tear the flesh from his body. What Joe found most disconcerting was his conflicting emotions. He was terrified in this horrible place and in more pain than he had ever imagined. He was revolted by this woman, yet he also became aroused by her haunting sexuality. He was disgusted and ashamed of his inability to control these sensations.

While Joe struggled with his jumbled emotions, the woman began to get to her feet. The nurse creature didn't walk into his line of sight but shambled awkwardly, leaning severely to her left, dragging her right leg behind. Her left shoulder likewise hung downward, and her entire body seemed to wrench and twitch spasmodically with every step she took.

As she came further into view, Joe saw that her uniform was stained with blood, urine, dark black soot, and quite possibly excrement. The nurse carried the vile, putrid, sickening, sweet stench of decay.

The woman's ratty nurses' cap was a filthy, crumpled mess hanging askew, barely staying on top of her twitching and trembling skull. Looking at the back of her exposed head, David could see her hair; that is, what remained of her hair was dyed a ridiculous shade of yellow. Bald, pinkish patches of scab-covered flesh covered her twitching head, which was scarred and smeared with what appeared to be dried blood.

Where clumps of the greasy, matted hair had fallen out, her scalp looked like those historical pictures Joe had seen of victims of radiation poisoning. The woman continued to shamble forward, and Joe understood everything about the woman was very wrong. As the nurse turned toward his bed, Joe realized he couldn't even say he was certain the thing he saw might still be considered human. The deeply furrowed gashes on her face streamed blood.

The nurse creature's one good left eye bulged from its dark ringed socket as if in a fury. As Joe watched further, he saw the thing had to move its battered head slightly to see him better since that eye was its only means of vision.

The top few buttons of the creature's uniform were missing, and her massive breasts, mapped with unsightly veins, swelled from her tattered bra as if ready to explode. When she stumbled about, the nurse's short skirt rose, giving him a disturbing view of her most private area. Once more, Joe was hit with the same conflicting sexual sensations he had experienced when he first saw the nurse. Suddenly, his formerly dry mouth and throat were filled with moisture.

As the demonic creature turned in Joe's direction, he saw she gripped a long, sharp sword, a Katana blade, in her right hand. The thing was rusted and coated with crimson-brown clotted blood. Joe hoped he might be dreaming, having some sort of terrible nightmare. He opened his eyes a bit more and was shocked to see the twitching, convulsing nurse thing had reached the center of the bottom of his bed and had turned in the direction of his helpless, prone body. He could feel his heart race with uncontrollable fear and pound like a drum in his chest. Then the horrifying monstrosity spoke in a quiet, robotic monotone that hissed snake-like as each word passed over her cracked and bloody lips.

"Joseph Rocco Montero. Known to friends and enemies alike as Mad Dog Montero, a professional assassin and boot-licking lapdog for Antonio Dominguez and Los Asesinos drug cartel."

Joe couldn't believe what he was hearing. How could this creature know such things about him? Then he realized there was no way she could know. He must be having one of those bizarre nightmares where everything seemed real, no matter how impossible. Yes, that must be it. He was probably at home in his bed, sleeping in an uncomfortable position. That would explain why he felt pain in this dream world. Of course, the discomfort would seem magnified by the nightmare landscape of this nocturnal Hell.

The demon nurse said, "Ah, yes. Denial. I can see it on your face. Almost always, after confusion, comes realization, followed by denial. You subconsciously realize the extent of your dilemma, but your mind refuses to accept the reality. So, you try to convince yourself you're dreaming. Sorry, Mad Dog. You're not asleep, and this is your new reality. She brought the point of her blade down, sinking it deep into his leg and scraping along his ankle bone.

Joe screamed in agony as the pain shot up through his body. He bellowed through his sobs, "Why? Why are you doing this to me?"

The nurse thing came closer, placing her huge breasts against his face as she whispered in his ear, "Like what you see, Joey boy?"

The stench surrounding her was like roadkill baking in the July sun. Her breath was even more disgusting, if that were possible. In the green glow of the room's eerie light, Joe had an up-close and personal look at this demon's swelling breasts. They no longer made him feel in any way sexually aroused. Besides the network of veins and tributaries, something was crawling beneath her gray and mottled flesh. It looked like thousands of tiny worms creeping around inside her, raising the thin skin as they slithered over each other.

As the nurse backed away and pulled her blade from his leg. Instead of the gush of blood, Joe expected to see there was nothing. That is to say, nothing but the agonizing pain. As he watched in horror, the wound at the point of entry slowly began to heal itself, leaving a small puckered scar in its wake. One thing that didn't change, however, was the pain. It hurt as much as if the blade had just been slid into him.

"Does that seem familiar, Mad Dog? Does it bring back any memories? How about the time you drove your own blade down through the ankle of that low-level drug dealer in Cincinnati? Remember how he screamed? He sounded very much like you just did. But back then, you laughed and found it all so amusing. It's no longer funny, is it, Mad Dog?"

Joe didn't reply; he was too busy dealing with his pain. Yet, in the back of his mind, he recalled the situation she had been referring to. Joe had been sent to Cincinnati to deal with a street corner dealer who had been skimming money from the cartel. Joe eventually killed the punk, but not before having some fun with him. The knife in the ankle was just the start of things. Then Joe trembled with terror when he realized what he had done next to the dealer was stab him in his thigh.

Joe screamed as the nurse pierced his thigh with her Katana blade. He heard her maniacal laughter through the fog of his pain and realized how much it sounded hauntingly like his own had been back when he had been the one wielding the blade.

"Are you starting to understand yet, Mad Dog?" The hideous nurse thing asked with a horrible smirk.

Joe screamed like the wounded animal he had become. Again, there was no blood, and the wound healed itself in seconds, but the agony remained. Crying like an injured child, Joe pleaded, "Please, please, I don't understand. Why are you doing this to me?"

The nurse smiled a particularly evil grin and reminded him, "That's the same question many of your victims asked you, isn't it? Little did they know just how merciless you were. Remember that accountant secretly working with the FBI to nail your boss, Antonio Dominguez? You made him write his suicide note before you drugged him, then slit his wrists. The cops never figured that one for murder, did they? You were sure you got away with that one, but we were watching Mad Dog. Oh yes, we were watching very closely."

"What do you mean by 'we'? Who was watching me?"

The nurse didn't answer, but instead, she made two slices, one down each of Joe's wrists, and he screamed with the pain as the bloodless gashes healed themselves once again. The nurse creature grinned with those razor-sharp teeth and walked to the center of the room, where she began to move about in a macabre series of disturbing sensual poses. All the while, she spoke in a sing-song voice, albeit harsh, raspy, and serpentine.

"Oh, my Joseph. Oh, my Mad Dog. You were always such a fool, and apparently, you still are. You don't even recognize me, do you?"

Joe said angrily, "Recognize you? Of course not. I've never seen you before in my life. Surely, I would have remembered seeing someone as . . . someone like you."

"Go ahead and say it, Joe. Someone as ugly as me. Someone as hideously deformed as I am. I wasn't always this way. Once, I was quite beautiful. But no, it's obvious you don't remember me. Then again, why would you? You never knew me. I wasn't one of your planned assignments, one of your hits. I was what you liked to refer to as collateral damage, just an innocent bystander who happened to be at the wrong place at the wrong time."

"I don't understand," Joe said through his pain.

The nurse creature became angry and swung her blade in a sharp arc, slicing through Joe's throat and practically decapitating him. His head fell backward on a hinge of flesh, then quickly returned to its original position, and the gash began to heal.

"That was what you did to that rich old man, Mr. Wallenstine, when you came into his bedroom and decapitated the poor sick man in his sleep. As you fled the scene, his live-in nurse, who was sleeping in the next room, made the mistake of coming out into the hall. You stabbed her through the heart with the same Katana blade you used to kill her employer. Do you recognize the blade, Mad Dog?"

She held out the sword for him to examine closer. Joe was stunned to realize he did recognize the blade. It had originally hung on the wall in Mr. Wallenstine's study. Joe had removed it and used it to kill the old man. Then, he used it on a woman he had encountered in the hallway. But that had been so long ago, and so many killings have occurred since then.

Then, a realization struck him. This woman must be the same woman he thought he had killed. Maybe she had survived his attack and had been planning his capture and torture for years. But that didn't explain how his wounds were suddenly able to heal so quickly. How could this be that woman? Why had she been damaged and horrid?

"But how did you get so . . ."

The woman laughed and said, "So hideous? We all have our own crosses to bear, and mine have been dealt with for a very long time before you decided to join us."

"Join you? But none of this makes any sense. You can't be that woman. I killed her, I'm sure."

The nurse smiled and said, "That's right, Mad Dog. You did kill me, just like you killed so many others. And that is the cross that you must bear. What you seem to have forgotten is the last hit you planned backfired, and you were the one who was killed. That's right, Joseph. You're dead now, and you're in a special place where I have been given the honor and pleasure of torturing you repeatedly for eternity. Welcome, Mad Dog Montero, to your own special Hell.

DOORS OF DEATH

"In the universe, there are things that are known, and things
that are unknown, and in between, there are doors."
—WILLIAM BLAKE

The man and the woman sat on the cold, filthy concrete floor among
the reeking stench of urine, vomit, feces, death, and decay. The man
stared silently at the woman, whose gaze was distant and unfocused.
Something would happen soon. Something had to happen. And when
it did, one of them would probably die, and one might have a chance
to live.

Their number had initially been five. Three men and two women.
Five strangers, thrown together with one common goal: survival. Now,
only these two remained. Byron wondered how long he could hold out
before he was forced to make an impossible decision.

Under other circumstances, he might have been attracted to the
woman, but not now. Because now she was a wretched shadow of what
she once was. Her hair was greasy and unwashed. She stank from vomit
and from soiling herself on many occasions. This was not to suggest
that Byron was much better himself since he was every bit the stinking,
filthy wretch the woman was.

Byron was an engineer by profession and believed any problem
could be solved by logic and scientific reasoning. He felt if he could
just last a bit longer, the woman might give in and take her chance. If
so, Byron might yet make it out of this mess alive.

He couldn't recall the circumstances by which he had ended up in this situation. He wasn't even from this part of the country. Byron had been on a business trip, having flown east several days earlier. Then he realized his original estimation of time was likely no longer valid. If he was accurate, he had arrived several days before his abduction. He had no idea how long ago that had been. However, since he was dehydrated and starving, he suspected it had been for at least two or three days.

He knew people could survive a long time without food, but what about going without water? He didn't know, but he suspected not much longer. He had not yet reached the stage where he was willing to drink his urine. Then again, he couldn't recall the last time he needed to relieve himself. No input, no output, he assumed.

As far as how he had ended up here, the last thing Byron remembered was stopping by a local restaurant and ordering dinner. Since breakfast, he hadn't had time to eat, so he ordered the most significant steak dinner on the menu. He had started with a drink and an appetizer. The server had also brought out a small basket of hot, fresh bread.

Brandon recalled the alcohol in his drink had been strong, and now that he thought about it, the beverage did have a slightly different taste. At the time, he assumed the whiskey had come from a local distillery, which often was the case and could account for the somewhat unusual flavor.

After taking only a few healthy swallows while enjoying his bread, he was surprised to realize that he had already started feeling drunk. It typically took several strong drinks to do him in, even on an empty stomach. But how could it be possible that only one drink could take him down? Byron decided he had most definitely been drugged. But for what purpose? The amusement of some psycho?

He wished he could have been able to eat the meal he had ordered. To the best of his recollection, he had only had time to nibble on that single piece of bread, and it was lights out. When he awoke, he was in this horrible place with four equally confused strangers. Byron was hungrier and thirstier than he had ever been. How long had he been out? Hours? Days? As famished as he felt, it could have been days.

The room where he awoke was a giant hexagonal structure more than thirty feet across. It was painted black from floor to ceiling and illuminated by small, dimly lighted candle-style bulbs positioned in sconces, one on six adjacent walls. Also, on each wall was a door. The doors had numbers from 1 to 6 scrolled on them with dripping red paint. Byron suspected the color was to project the illusion of blood to screw with their heads.

The message was painted in large florescent yellow letters above the doors, lit by a series of blacklights. It wrapped entirely around the room. The statement read, "Welcome to Doors of Death. One door leads to freedom. The others lead to death."

"What . . . what the Hell . . . is this all about? And who . . . who are you, people?" One of the strangers mumbled in his sleepy confusion as he stood staring at the glowing words.

Byron had been the first to respond, although doing so in his still foggy mental state was difficult, "I . . . I don't know. I don't understand. One minute . . . I was eating dinner . . . and the next, I woke up here. I have no idea why we're here or who you people are. But apparently, we've been here for a while. I'm Byron, by the way, Byron Addison." The man who had initially spoken didn't respond. Instead, he strolled around the room, examining the walls and doors.

A slim, confused-looking middle-aged woman extended her trembling hand and said, "I'm Sarah Jenkins, and I don't mind saying I'm quite terrified."

Byron gently shook her hand and replied, "As am I, Sarah. As am I. This is a strange place; unfortunately, I think we all have good reason to be scared."

The other woman in the group came forward and introduced herself. "I'm Janice Parker. I have no idea what's going on here, but I don't like it. This is highly irregular."

"Wow, that's profound," the young man said as he walked from door to door. "Such an incredible overstating of the obvious."

"There's no need to be like that, buddy," a well-built man appearing to be in his early sixties said. "None of us wants to be here and have no idea how or why we are. This has to be some sort of misunderstanding.

Incidentally, I'm David Slater." The man shook hands with the others except for the young man, still examining the six doors.

"Well, aren't we all just one big happy freaking family?" The cocky young man said with more anger than seemed warranted, "I'd tell you all to call me Chuck if I was going to hang around long enough to get all buddy-buddy you, but I'm not. I have places to go and people to see. This isn't one of them, and you folks aren't either."

Byron had no idea why this Chuck fellow was so hostile and rude, but he suspected the young man was just as frightened as the rest. This abrasive false bravado was apparently how Chuck dealt with his fear.

Many days later, as Byron sat on the cold floor, the image of that young man's face was as present in his mind as it had been on that first encounter. Byron suspected that look, Chuck's name, and what eventually happened to the man would remain ingrained in his memory for as long as he lived, however long that might be.

Byron instinctively knew this Chuck fellow would be the first to try a door. The man was young, strong, impatient, and likely believed he was immortal as all foolish young people did. If there was one thing Byron had learned in his fifty-eight years on Earth, it was to take his time before making a decision. What was that old saying—Fools rush in where angels fear to tread? Yeah, that was it. Byron had little doubt that Chucky boy would be the first. However, it had happened even more quickly than Byron realized.

Chuck looked around at the four strangers and said, "You can't take any of this crap seriously. Can't you see we're being punked? This is some idiot's idea of a joke, a prank, or a gag. Don't you get that?"

"Someone drugged us and brought us here for some purpose," Byron tried to reason with the man. "I think that's rather extreme for a practical joke, don't you?"

"I agree with Byron. Something nefarious is happening here," David added.

"Nefarious? Did you actually just say nefarious? What are you, like a hundred years old or something? Jesus!" Chuck complained.

"Easy, Chuck," Sarah said, "there's no need to be like that. We're all frightened here, but we're all in this together. We have to figure a way out of here."

"We? We? What's this 'we' crap? Do you have a mouse in your pocket or something? Wee wee wee! There ain't no we, Babe. There's me, and there are you bunch of losers. And I ain't no part of your little band of bozos. As far as I'm concerned, you morons can stand around looking like lost sheep until the cows come home, but I'm outta here." With that, Chuck made a beeline for the door with the number three painted on it. Before anyone could stop him, his hand turned the knob, and the door swung open.

What happened next was something Byron could not explain with either his beloved science or logic, although later, despite his distress, he couldn't help but wonder about the mechanics behind it.

From the darkness behind the door came what sounded like the whirring of a dozen circular saw blades. In the few seconds that followed, the young man Chuck turned briefly to look back at his companions. The finality in that accepting look on his face spoke volumes in its simple comprehension. In his silence, it said, "I'm a dead man."

His head was separated from his body in a spray of blood and buzzing saw blades. Simultaneously, the rest of him exploded into fragments as dozens of rotating razor-toothed circles of steel tore him to bloody bits. A few passed right through him, then ricocheted off the remaining doors and flew into the group of strangers.

Sarah was slightly wounded as one of the blades skimmed across her forearm. David only marginally missed getting neutered by a whirring blade that passed between his legs. Everyone was screaming and diving for cover.

When the chaos was over, Sarah grabbed her arm through blood-soaked fingers and cried hysterically. What remained of Chuck was scattered in pieces all over the room. The concrete floor was awash with his blood and gore. The stench of his death filled the room, and the reek of vomit when several of the group threw up upon themselves and on the floor. That was when Byron suddenly realized there was no toilet in the room and no sink or source of water whatsoever.

Byron kneeled and examined the wound on Sarah's arm. It wasn't deep, and it wouldn't need a tourniquet. However, it would leave a nasty scar, and if untreated in this unsanitary environment, it would most definitely become infected. Then again, Byron suspected fear of infection was the least of their immediate problems. He had managed to stop the bleeding with a bandage he made by removing and ripping his outer shirt. Afterward, he wished he had found another way to make a bandage. The room was quite chilly when all he had to wear was an athletic undershirt, known in modern times as a wife-beater tee.

When things calmed down, the strangers sat huddled in the middle of the room as far away from the splattered remains of Chuck as possible. They were all stippled with crimson castoff from Chuck's bloody demise. Sarah had stopped sobbing and had collapsed into a mentally exhausted sleep.

"Oh my God, did you see that?" Janice whimpered, "That Chuck guy . . . he was . . . Oh, Jesus!"

David put his arm around the young woman and said, "It's ok, Janice. Let it out. There, there."

Byron watched David console Janice as Sarah slept nearby. His thoughts began to blur as he felt the effects of an adrenaline crash overtaking him, and soon, he, too, collapsed onto the floor asleep.

He was startled awake by the sound of an explosion. He had no idea if he had been asleep for a few minutes or hours. All he knew was he was hungry and thirsty. As his eyes regained focus, Byron saw another of the doors standing open. It was the door labeled number five. He walked on trembling legs over to see what had happened.

In front of the door lay the bloodied remains of what was once that woman, Janice. Her torso was separated from the lower half of her body by what appeared to be a shotgun blast. One of her hands still twitched in what Byron hoped was only a nervous reaction. The idea of her still alive and in agony was more than he could imagine. He felt his stomach turn, and then he vomited what little remained in his stomach onto the bloody floor. Byron felt weak and dizzy. How much time had passed? He returned to the center of the room and lay down on the cold concrete floor, unsure if his wobbly legs would support him.

"Why are we here?" Sarah cried. "Why is this happening to us, Byron?"

Byron didn't answer. He lay silently in the fetal position on the floor, trying futilely to make sense of everything happening. He could smell the sharp scent of urine and realized some of his companions had been soiling themselves rather than exposing themselves to the others. It was dark in the room, dark enough to hide any wet stains but too light for complete privacy. As he lay, Byron listened to his two remaining companions discussing their plight.

"I think it's the government. You know, some sort of scientific mind game. It's probably the military," David suggested.

Sarah said, "I agree. I read a lot, and the government is always screwing with people in my books. You know, using us in their weird experiments."

David said, "Mind games, I tell you. They're killing us one at a time to see how we react. They're making us wallow in our filth and the rotting remains of these poor dead souls."

Then David stood on his weakened legs, raised his fists to the ceiling, and screamed, "What the Hell do you people want from us? If you want us dead, then kill us now. Don't drag this out any longer. Either let us go or kill us."

David's tirade was met with silence. Sarah began weeping, which echoed pathetically in the tomb-like quiet of their prison.

Byron said quietly from his prone position, "You might as well blame space aliens while you're at it." Then he sat up and chastised them, "It's obvious, Sarah, that you read a lot of fiction. But you must understand something. That crap in books is all made up. That's why it's called fiction. Nerdy writers put these stories together, sitting at their computers typing and lying their collective butts off. That's what they do."

David said, "But even fiction has elements of truth in it. So, this actually could be a government thing."

"It most certainly could be," Sarah agreed.

"I don't know what government you two are talking about. But any government I know about in this country couldn't conduct a one-car funeral successfully. I don't understand what's happening here any more than you both do. I can't pretend to know who is doing this or why. And to be honest, neither of those things matters anyway, as they won't change our situation."

"Meaning what?" David asked. "Are we just supposed to give up? Do you want us to bend over, spread our cheeks, and tell them to have at it?"

Before speaking, Byron waited for a beat, then said, "We're helpless here. Four doors remain, and there are only three of us. Sooner or later, we will have to open a door and die or find our way out of here. I assume once the door to freedom is found, all of us still alive will be free to go. But sitting around trying to figure out who's responsible won't help us one little bit. Honestly, I don't know what will help us at this point. So, for now, why don't you both please keep the volume down, relax and try to rest and save what little strength you have left? Lord knows I need to get some sleep."

With that, Byron lay his head back onto his arms, and before he realized it, he was fast asleep. Sometime later, he awoke to the sound of a blood-curdling scream. As his eyes focused, Byron saw Sarah whaling like a banshee. Before asking her what had happened, he saw David in the distance. It took a few seconds for Byron's mind to comprehend what he was witnessing.

The door numbered six was standing wide open. David was standing in front of the open door with his waving arms as if trying to maintain his balance while simultaneously having trouble comprehending what had just happened to him. All the while, Sarah screamed like her last piece of sanity had just shattered. Perhaps it had. After seeing David, Byron wondered how long he could hope to keep his mind from splintering into a million insane pieces.

David stood with an eight-foot-long, six-inch around shaft penetrating his abdomen. It not only had entered through his stomach and now extended a foot out of his back, but after skewering David like a human shishkabob, the front of the massive spear had opened up like an umbrella. But this umbrella was made of eight razor-sharp blades. The edge of each blade arched back toward David, and in the few seconds remaining, Byron understood what was coming next.

An unseen force, the same one that had sent the projectile outward, now retracted the weapon at unimaginable speed, pulling the impaled David with it into the darkness beyond the door. The horror was all over in seconds.

Sarah had mercifully stopped screaming. She had also stopped sobbing. Then Byron realized the young woman had become like a clock whose spring had been overwound to the point of breaking. Sarah had shut down, falling into some self-preserving catatonic state. She sat silently on the floor, staring at nothing.

That was when Byron saw the small urine stream seeping from under the woman. It wasn't much; they were both too dehydrated for that. Nor was it the first time she had soiled herself. Hell, they all had. In addition, they were weak, thirsty, and starving. So, when they deemed it necessary, they went in their clothes. Now Sarah sat in her most recent filth, never moving or reacting to what she had done.

Now, God only knew how much later, Byron sat on the floor across from Sarah, waiting to see if she would eventually rejoin him in the land of the barely living. So far, she had shown no signs of recuperating from her silent state.

"Sarah? Can you hear me in there? I need you to come back, Sarah. I can't do this on my own. Look, Sarah, we're both starving and dying of thirst. I don't know how much longer we can go on like this. I'm not ashamed to say that I'm terrified, Sarah. I don't want to die like this, but I can't find the courage to open one of those doors either.

"Look, I'm going to lay down and sleep. If I'm lucky, I won't wake up. There are worse ways to die, as you've seen first-hand. If I don't wake up again, I just want to say how sorry I am. Not only for not being more helpful to you but also for leaving you behind. I don't want to give these sick bastards whatever they seem to want from us. I only want it all to end. So, I suppose this is goodbye, Sarah. Stay strong."

Byron lay down again on the cold, chilled concrete floor of their prison among the stench of his fallen comrades' rotting, tattered remains. He wanted nothing better than to die in his sleep and hoped his final wish would come true. He closed his eyes and let the darkness of sleep envelope him.

His wish was not granted, however. Byron awoke sometime later. He had no idea how long he had slept, but judging by how weak he felt, Byron knew it had to have been a significant amount of time. His stomach was cramped with hunger. His mouth and tongue were dry, and his lips cracked and bleeding. It took a while for his dry and pasted eyes to gain focus. That was when he saw Sarah was gone.

He looked over and saw the door marked with the number two was standing open. There was no sign of Sarah, so Byron hoped against hope that perhaps Sarah had found the door to freedom, even if it was pure chance. He stumbled over to the open door and was stopped dead in his tracks. A trail of blood led from just outside the door into the blackness within.

This was no safe exit, no door to freedom. It was another death trap set by whoever orchestrated this bizarre experiment. Byron heard the sound that resembled the noise made by a ball rolling. It was coming from inside the blackness of whatever world lay beyond the threshold. Seconds later, he saw Sarah's severed head rolling into the main room. A scream caught in his throat as his stomach clenched. Her hair had all been shaved off to give it a more spherical ball-like appearance. This violation only served to make the scene more repulsive.

Byron had had enough. He knew he had to end this no matter what. He was near death, and his mind was on the verge of shattering if it hadn't already done so. He stumbled toward the door marked with a bloody number 1. He thought about a bumper sticker he had seen on the back of a truck hauling portable toilets that read, "We're #1 in the #2 business."

He chuckled insanely to himself as he grabbed for the handle, and without taking another moment to consider the consequences, he yanked open the door. Byron was not prepared for what awaited him inside. He assumed he would be blown to bits by some explosive device or sliced into a dozen pieces as his companions had been, but that was not the case.

This door opened to a three feet wide and thirty feet long hallway. Byron thought he must be imagining things, but the hallway seemed to lead to the outside. Byron could see a beautiful afternoon through the window at the far end of the hall, complete with sunshine, grass, trees, and even a stream.

He had done it. He had picked the right door. He found it ironic that the door to freedom would be the first of the six they had to choose. Perhaps whoever was orchestrating this twisted experiment had understood that it would be human nature to try any door but the most obvious. Had Byron reasoned more coherently and taken the time to think about it, he might have chosen the other remaining door rather than one. If he had done so, he would be dead by now instead of heading to freedom.

Byron used what little strength he had remaining to trudge slowly down the hall. He already knew the first thing he would do. He would head right for that stream and take an enormous cleansing drink. Then, he would crawl into the water and wash the filth of his captivity off of him. Byron didn't know if there would be any fruit trees or vegetables nearby, but he didn't care. He was going to be free. He would find food somewhere or find a road that would lead him back to civilization.

As he approached the outer end of the hallway, Byron hesitated for a moment as he looked at the scene of the beautiful day awaiting him. Something wasn't right with the image he was seeing. Upon closer examination, Byron noticed that a small fold appeared in the upper left-hand corner of the scene. He realized he was looking at a picture or painting but not the world outside. He reached out and touched what he thought was a stream and felt the hardness of a wall behind the scenery.

He heard a noise like a door opening behind him and, at first, could not gather the courage to turn to see what it was. Then he heard a deep guttural growl of an animal coming from the darkness behind him. As he forced his back helplessly against the outdoor scene blocking his exit, he stared at the two glowing eyes as the creature made its way toward its dinner.

THE CARDINAL

The old woman stood at the kitchen window, a washcloth in her hand, cleaning up the few remaining dishes from the previous evening, brushing away a few errant hairs from her eyes with the back of her hand. It was a beautiful, sunny Saturday morning. Daylight savings time was about to go into effect that very evening. She tried to recall how she would have to change her clocks, remembering the little ditty she had been taught as a young girl in the 1960s.

"Spring ahead, fall behind," She whispered to herself as she gazed out the kitchen window.

Looking out into her raised garden area, Madeline thought about the spring cleanup she would have to begin soon to remove winter's fallen leaves and broken twigs. The garden was only beginning to show signs of new growth. Cleanup should be relatively easy as she had thoroughly removed the dead plants and weeds the previous fall. Then she sighed, realizing she would face a summer of continuous weeding and maintenance. Despite the anticipation of future work, she loved her garden. It was probably the most beautiful garden in the entire neighborhood, but she knew it just didn't get that way on its own. It took a lot of work to make it lovely, maintain it, and keep it looking great. And this year, she would be tackling the job alone for the first time.

She didn't consider herself old yet but most certainly was getting older. At sixty-six, she knew the weeding, raking, digging, and planting would result in many sore, stiff muscles. Then she rationalized that the exercise would probably do her good, painful or not. However, it would do little for the onset of arthritis she was starting to feel in her hands. Her over-the-counter pain pills did little to relieve the creeping soreness.

Looking up into the sky, Madeline saw a turkey vulture flying overhead. She shook her head and wondered what the hideous thing was doing over her house, but she assumed it might simply be scrambling around looking for a morning snack. For some reason, over the past several years, the population of turkey vultures in her small Pennsylvania subdivision had grown from a handful to well over a hundred. They nested in some of her neighbor's tall pine trees. She assumed they had no natural enemies since they seemed to flourish.

Madeline's neighborhood was located at the base of a large mountain range, and there were lots of woods and trees along the ridge, which meant there were all sorts of woodland creatures about, such as deer, possums, and groundhogs, squirrels, and a variety of birds. She supposed, at one time or another, something was likely to be dead somewhere in the neighborhood, and it was the job of the turkey vulture cleaning crew to take care of such things.

Then her heart leaped as she saw something wonderful. Perched on the branch of her maple tree was a bright red cardinal, the first one of the Spring. It filled her with joy, knowing the bleak winter was over and summer was just around the corner. The cardinal was nesting, which meant baby cardinals in a short time. Madeline couldn't wait till the time when she could open the back door and listen to the songs of the many birds that populated her garden. Over the years, her husband had made and hung over twenty new birdhouses to accommodate their feathered neighbors. Some structures appeared worse for wear, but there was little she could do about that; the birds would have to adapt.

She saw the male cardinal fly from the maple branch and down to the ground. Only the top of his bright red crown was visible. He was standing behind her raised garden. A wall of stacked flat stones surrounded the feature. The cardinal seemed to be pushing or nudging something with its beak. Something seemed very wrong with what he was doing.

Putting on her jacket and walking out into the backyard, Madeline went to see why the bird was acting so strangely. As she walked toward the garden, she looked up and noticed two more turkey vultures had joined the first, circling and floating high above her. She was amazed at how they seemed to have no fear of humans. She recalled driving by a group of scavengers munching on a deer carcass along the side of the road. When she had slowed down her car to see what they were doing, the birds simply gave her a suspicious glance, then ignoring her, they returned to their feast.

As she rounded the back of the garden, Madeline's heart sank as she saw the body of a beautiful female cardinal lying dead on the ground. It was obviously the mate of the male bird. He had been pushing at her with his head, trying to revive her as if from sleep. But this was a sleep from which she would never awaken. It was a pitiful sight. Seeing this tragic scene, she recalled something she either heard or read, stating cardinals mated for life. She didn't know if this was true, but she needed to believe it was. Madeline knew the pain this poor fellow felt, having lost her husband of forty years to cancer the previous year.

Seeing Madeline approach, the male cardinal fled to a nearby tree branch for safety and perhaps to watch this strange human to determine what purpose it had with his mate. The bird obviously couldn't understand the concept of death. Living in the wild, the bird had seen death, but the reality and comprehension of the end of life escaped him. The only thing he knew for certain was that his mate was lying motionless on the cold ground, and this human was paying too much attention to her. He gave his loudest and most frightening cry, hoping to frighten the human away, but to no avail.

Madeline looked down at the poor, dead creature. Her heart was heavy with grief for the male sitting on a tree branch shouting what she supposed were avian threats and curses. She was not surprised to realize tears were freely flowing down her cheeks. It seemed Madeline had spent the last year doing far too much crying. The tears came when they chose to, and she had little control over them. She walked to a nearby utility shed and returned with a small shovel and an orange plastic pail.

She looked up at the crimson bird and said, tremblingly, "I'm so sorry, Mr. Cardinal. I don't know what happened to your wife, but she's gone now. I have to do something I know you won't like or understand. She can no longer be your mate. And I can't leave her out here, or her beautiful little body will be torn and eaten by those scavengers up there. I have to take her now. I hope you can forgive me."

Madeline placed the shovel in the grass as flatly as possible and gently slid it under the already stiff body of the female cardinal. Lifting the shovel, she tilted it over the top of the bucket, allowing the bird to slide down and drop inside with a barely audible thud. The cardinal in the tree was squawking loudly, making a most unpleasant situation even worse. Madeline began walking back to the house, still uncertain about what she would do next.

This dead bird was not the first she had found in her yard, which was, after all, abundant with trees, plants, and flowers. She and her late husband had dedicated countless hours and labor to create this incredible paradise and habitat for nature and its many animals.

In the past, when she had found dead birds, her husband had simply scooped them up, placed them into a plastic bag, and put them out for her weekly trash pickup. But Bob was gone, and the heavy responsibility now fell on her shoulders. She felt that sort of disposal was undignified for such a special bird. In the back of her mind, Madeline realized she had no idea if this bird was special or not. She supposed the whole "mate for life" thing and the loss of her life mate was responsible for making her feel that way.

She carried the bucket out to her garage and set it on the floor, deciding she would take a few minutes to determine how best to handle things. She walked into her living room and sat on her recliner to contemplate her dilemma. Perhaps she would dig a hole in her garden and bury the bird there. She wondered if she should first put it into a zip-lock bag to keep the bugs and scavengers from getting its scent. Then she realized she would be going against nature.

"Ashes to ashes," she whispered as she recalled saying the same thing while she had spread her husband's ashes in their garden. It had been his wish, and she had carried out his request as painful as it might be. Now, it comforted her that when her garden was growing and flourishing, Bob would still be helping in his own way. She decided she would bury the bird and let nature take its course.

Madeline heard a thumping sound that stirred her from her thoughts. It was coming from the kitchen. As she walked through the doorway, her breath caught in her throat as she saw the male cardinal flying repeatedly into her kitchen window. She ran to the window shouting, "Stop it! Stop it now!" but the bird continued its charge. She knew if the bird didn't stop soon, it would die because the glass was heavy, triple-pained, and insulated. There was no way the cardinal could do anything but hurt itself. By now, Madeline was in full panic mode and, through uncontrollable tears, shouted, "Stop it, you stupid bird. You're killing yourself." A small area of crimson blood appeared on the outside of the window.

Madeline grabbed a towel and rushed down the steps and out into the backyard, hoping to scare the bird away. She ran toward the window waving her towel, looking like a mad woman to any curious neighbors who might have heard her and peeked out to investigate the disturbance. But Madeline didn't care. As she got to the window, she was horrified to see the male cardinal dead on the ground, its neck visibly broken by repeated crashes into the window.

Amid tears of sadness and frustration, Madeline wrapped the towel around the broken bird and carried him inside to join his mate in the orange plastic bucket. She knew she would have to deal with both bodies sooner rather than later, but for the moment, she was far too emotionally distraught to consider it. She closed the door between the house and the garage and decided it wasn't as lovely a day as she had originally thought. The truth was everything seemed rather hopeless and without purpose.

Madeline poured herself a glass of wine, something she had been doing quite often since Bob's passing, and drank it quickly before poring and drinking two more in rapid succession. She sat at the kitchen table, staring bleary-eyed at the red blotch on the window. She'd have to get around to cleaning that off, another chore she would have preferred to do without. Life was so much simpler when Bob was alive.

He would have taken care of all these unpleasant things for her. But no longer, now all the responsibility was Madeline's. With a sigh of resignation, Madeline stood on wobbly legs and retrieved the orange pail from the garage.

She looked down at the bodies of the two cardinals, pressed against each other. Madeline was surprised to find herself envious of the dead birds. They were together again in death. She wondered if someday she and Bob would be reunited in death. She wanted to believe this more than anything else but was uncertain. It had been something she had been taught since she was a child in Sunday school. There was an afterlife, a place after death where we reunite with our loved ones who had gone on before us. But she was having doubts after seeing her husband suffer and die the way he did and seeing his lifeless body before his cremation.

What if this was all there was? What if she was never to see her Bob again? She often spoke to him when she was out in the garden where his ashes were spread, but she never got any response. And why should she expect one? Bob was dead and gone, and she was stuck here on Earth alone to try to carry on with a life that was no longer what she thought of as a life. She was simply plodding along, putting one foot in front of the other. Madeline realized she was slipping into the familiar territory of self-pity, usually brought on by alcohol. She shook her head in frustration the headed out to the garden to put the two birds to rest.

Using the same shovel she had used to pick up the female cardinal, Madeline began to dig a hole in the garden. As she did, she spoke in her usual one-sided conversation with her husband.

"Well, Bob. It looks like I have some company for you. I hope you don't mind too much. They are two really pretty cardinals. Their story is tragic, not much different than our own. The female died, and the male decided he couldn't live without her. I can sympathize with him completely."

Madeline found that the soil in her garden was much harder than anticipated because it had been a dry winter and an equally dry spring. She realized if the rain didn't arrive soon, her gardening would be even more challenging. As she struggled to dig deeper, Madeline broke out in a cold sweat, and her muscles ached with the effort. She knew her arthritic hands would pay the price for her labor the next day. Finally, she placed the birds in the hole and recovered them with dirt, patting the soil down with the back of the shovel. When satisfied she had done her best, Madeline returned to her house, plopped down in her recliner, and quickly fell asleep.

After a time, Madeline awoke to the sounds of people shouting outside. The commotion seemed to be coming from her backyard.

"Get the hell out of here, you disgusting beasts!" a male voice shouted. It sounded like her next-door neighbor, Frank Ortiz.

A woman's voice cried, "Oh my God, what should we do?" That one sounded like Mable Johnston, the woman in the house behind hers. Still, others joined in with a chorus of, "Oh my God," "Sweet Jesus help us," "that poor woman," and even a voice that sounded like a teenage boy saying, "Woah! That's so freaking cool."

Still wobbly from her wine consumption, Madeline stumble-stepped to the kitchen window and saw a sight that looked like something from a horror movie. A woman's body lay sprawled across Madeline's garden. Obviously, the woman was dead, but who was she, and what was she doing in Madeline's yard? And to make matters worse, the corpse was surrounded by turkey vultures that were busy picking away at the poor woman's flesh with their sharp, hooked beaks. Several neighbors she knew, and a few she didn't were inside the yard.

Mr. Ortiz kicked at the buzzards, and they hopped away from the dead woman but didn't yet take flight. One of the birds had something stringy with a tiny ball on its end dangling from its mouth. Madeline realized with disgust the thing was an eyeball. *That poor woman*, Madeline thought, *to suffer such indignities, even in death*. Then, when more of the neighbors started waving their arms and charging the birds, the vultures opened their large wings and took flight.

That was when she looked at the clothing the dead woman wore and saw it was identical to hers. "What in the world is going on here?" She wondered aloud.

"It takes a little while to wrap your head around, Maddie," a familiar voice said from behind. Only one person called her Maddie, and that was her husband, Bob.

"Bob?" She asked, turning around to confront the owner of that voice. She knew it couldn't possibly be her husband, but she had to know. To her dismay, her dead husband was standing behind her in their kitchen. This version of her husband wasn't the frail and broken man ravaged by cancer but the young and vibrant man she had fallen in love with. She said, "Bob? Is that really you?"

"Yep, Maddie, it's me, and you're you. Look at your hands."

She looked down expecting to see old, arthritic fingers, but instead, she saw the hands of a young woman, those she hadn't seen in decades.

"But . . . but . . . how?" She was quickly becoming overwhelmed, unable to form the words she wanted to say.

Bob replied, "I don't know, Maddie. It just is. I always figured all my questions would be answered once I crossed over, but I was wrong. I now have more questions than before, but you know what? None of them matter to me anymore, especially now that we're together again."

Madeline said, "But . . . what about?" She pointed out the window to the commotion in the backyard.

"That's not our concern anymore. Someone will take care of things. Let's go," Bob said as he took Madeline's hand, turned, and walked away, vanishing as they did.

THERE ARE NO GHOSTS

"I just don't want to believe in ghosts, ghouls, and spirits."
—SADIE SINK

"Monsters are real, and ghosts are real, too. They live inside us, and
sometimes, they win."
—STEPHEN KING

"Ghosts are all around us. Look for them, and you will find them."
—RUSKIN BOND

"Why fear imaginary ghosts when we have living humans to fear?"
—THOMAS M. MALAFARINA

The sparse crowd of onlookers strolled casually by, not quite ignoring his table, doing their best to glance over without making eye contact. Harold was used to this. He had been a published horror author for over a decade and had done more than his share of book shows. During that time, he had grown to accept his place in the pecking order of "serious authors." Sadly, that place was the proverbial bottom of the literary heap.

Book shows were usually divided into sections featuring authors of various genres such as historical non-fiction, biographical, mystery, romance, young adult, etc. These disciplines tended to get the ideal spots within the general flow of pedestrian traffic. This favorable placement meant they were in the best area to sell their wares.

Then, of course, there were the horror authors. These less-than-desirable folks often found themselves stuck in an out-of-the-way corner near the back of the event venue. To make matters worse, they were usually located next to the authors of erotica, literary porn, in Harold's mind. He gained a bit of satisfaction in believing that even though his genre might be considered bottom-feeding by the book-reading elite, at least it wasn't erotica.

Harold always did his best to decorate his table in a way that would leave little doubt about what genre of author he was. In addition to having his books with their terrifying covers prominently displayed, he used a variety of Halloween-type props, such as skulls and severed hands. The purpose of this was not simply to attract the horror-loving public to his table, but it also served as a bit of an in-your-face proclamation to the world that he was proud of his chosen genre.

Few high-brow literary snobs ever wandered back into this dark den of iniquity and sexual depravity. If they did, it was usually by accident while looking for the restrooms, to which Harold often found himself unfortunately located much too close. If he were to describe how these giants of intellectuality looked at him and his table of wares, he would have to say that demeaning and condescending didn't quite cover it. It was more like the way some rich person might look at a homeless drunk lying in an ally, wallowing in a pool of his own vomit and excrement.

Fortunately, Harold found a way to cope with this blatant subbing. He chose to ignore the people walking by. He often would be busy writing another story or book while the crowds passed. Harold felt that if he didn't see their looks of disgust, then they weren't there.

As a result, he inadvertently gained the reputation of being "aloof and unapproachable." This reputation couldn't be farther from the truth, as Harold was quite a friendly individual under favorable circumstances. Unfortunately, book shows were not the ideal situation, more often than not.

The other problem Harold faced came from some of the people who actually did stop at his booth. He liked it when true fans of horror fiction books came by because they could discuss the genre with like minds. These people might even buy a book or two. However, whether they purchased one or not, he did enjoy spirited conversations with these horror enthusiasts.

The fans of horror movies, however, were another story. Harold had run-ins with this breed of fan, usually at horror conventions. One would think such a gathering would be crawling with horror reading enthusiasts, but not so. These strange fans often proudly proclaim that they loved horror movies but didn't read. Harold never quite understood how someone could proudly announce that they didn't read. Who do they think came up with the stories for the horror movies?

Then, of course, there were the true believers. More often than not, Harold thought they were by far the most bizarre. Although these folks were big fans of the horror genre, they didn't quite think of it as fiction. They spoke about fictional characters and fabricated horror story plots as real.

As the crowds of book enthusiasts passed by and Harold did his best to ignore them, he noticed some movement at the front of his table. He glanced up to see a peculiar-looking, pale-skinned man staring down at his collection of books.

The man was over six feet tall, although his stovepipe-styled hat and gaunt frame made him look even taller. Long, grayish-white hair hung down from below his hat, flowing over the shoulders of his dirty black overcoat. Harold could see the man's dingy black pants and worn dark shoes extending from below this crypt-keeper-look-alike's coat. The man's corpse-like cheeks were hallowed, and his coal-black eyes were sunken deep into dark-rimmed sockets.

What Harold found most disturbing was the man's smile. He stood silently in front of the table, first looking at a book displayed there, then looking at Harold, giving him a yellow-black grin that Harold felt worthy of any psychopath depicted in any slasher film.

The man's behavior reminded Harold of another reality of book shows. That was, sometimes, the people eager to approach a horror author's table could be downright wacky. This gentleman might be one of the craziest Harold had encountered so far. Harold ignored the weirdo for a moment, hoping he might leave. Then, realizing he hadn't sold a book all day, Harold wondered if this character might be ripe for picking.

"I see you're checking out that book, *Ghostly Mansion of Death*. It was one of my earlier novels. If you're interested in buying it, I'd be happy to sign and personalize it for you," Harold offered.

The strange man stared at the book's cover, depicting a dark, dilapidated, abandoned house backlit by moonlight. Then he looked at Harold, giving him that disturbing yellow-tooth grin, and asked in a somewhat monotone voice, "Is it a real ghost story?"

Harold was momentarily taken aback; then he questioned, "What do you mean by 'real' ghost story?"

The man looked at him, somewhat perplexed, and said, "You know. Is this a story about real ghosts, or is it fiction?"

"Of course, it's fiction," Harold responded.

"Of course?"

"Of course. What else could it be? Especially since there are no such things as ghosts."

The man hesitated momentarily, then said, "I beg to differ. Many people worldwide have reported encountering visits from spirits—many more who have reported sightings and hauntings."

Harold countered, "Many people in the world are crazy, and others simply need some form of attention or anything to distinguish them from the rest of the world. They find camaraderie by flocking together with like-minded people, even if those people are somewhat deranged."

The man said, "Many individuals spend great sums of money buying sophisticated equipment to locate and record ethereal presences."

"I think they would be better off spending a few bucks and buying one of my books, which are much more entertaining."

"But you do write horror fiction. Do you mean to tell me you don't believe in ghosts?"

"That's exactly what I'm telling you. There are no ghosts, demons, zombies, ghouls, or anything. Do you honestly think I could write such stories if I believed beings like this actually existed? That's why it's called horror fiction because it's fiction about horror."

"So, in your opinion, there are no ghosts?"

"Isn't that what I just said? Now, how about you do us both a favor and either buy a book or please move on."

Suddenly, a voice came from Harold's left, "Hey, man. Who the hell are you talking to? I know writers can be a bit odd, but dude, are you nuts or something?"

Harold turned slightly and saw a young man in a horror-themed tee shirt looking at him as if he might be afraid to approach his table.

"I'm having a discussion with this gentleman," Harold said as he turned back to the subject of his debate. To Harold's horror, the strange man was becoming translucent and beginning to fade before his eyes.

Harold stared in shock as the dissolving image raised his hand, wiggling his fingers in a "Toodle-doo" style wave, still giving Harold that hideous rotten-toothed grin. Harold could see the man's lips moving but couldn't hear any sounds. In a few seconds, the man was gone. A moment later, he heard the man's voice in his mind saying, "So, do you still believe there are no ghosts?"

IN HELL, EVERYONE CAN HEAR YOU SCREAM (AND THEY LOVE IT!)

"A good many dramatic situations begin with screaming."
—JANE FONDA

"It's not tough at all as long as the fans are yelling,
screaming, and hollering."
—BILL LAIMBEER

"I sort of went into the TV thing kicking and screaming."
—CANDICE OLSON

"Screaming is bad for the voice, but it's good for the heart."
—CONOR OBERST

"Welcome everyone to another exciting evening with Hell's number one game show, 'Scream Like The Devil.' I'm your congenial demonic host, Gragnar Dargon Zark, welcoming all of you demons in our studio audience as well as those of you watching from your lairs on Hellivision," a tall, handsome man in a black tuxedo with a white shirt, red cumberbund and matching red bowtie said from center stage.

His long, coal-black hair was slicked back from his overly tanned face. His gleaming white teeth, dimpled smile, and hypnotic dark eyes could charm the pants off of any girl and had done so often during his time as a Hollywood star while among the living. If it weren't for the two ram-like horns on the sides of his forehead and the four fangs—two up, two down—most people would say he could pass for human. However, his days of being a living human had gone long ago.

The stage on which Zark stood was large, round, with three hundred and sixty-degree visibility. The platform rotated slowly and continuously, guaranteeing the studio audience a good view of everything happening on stage. In addition, huge curved screens surrounded high on the walls of the massive circular arena and were fed with stage images from more than a dozen cameras. There were no bad seats on the "Scream Like The Devil" show set.

In the center of the stage, sitting on a three-tier series of round rotating platforms, was a large, heavy chair appearing to be constructed of some shiny metal. The monstrosity resembled the electric chairs used in the early days of death row electrocution back in the living world. The metal skull cap and wires typical of that chair were missing, but thick metal wrist and ankle clamps were present. In reality, these methods of securing a victim weren't necessary, as the power of Hell would be enough to confine anyone. However, they were present for visual effects. It was a showbiz thing.

Surrounding the stage was a huge round arena filled to capacity with an array of hundreds of seats occupied by demons of every shape and size imaginable. The front rows held spots for the most prestigious of Hell's rulers. Only one seat remained empty. It always remained open. That seat was reserved for the numero uno big man, who seldom showed up for these events. Still, the place was secured, just in case he decided to make an appearance. Zark had no desire to see that seat be anything but empty. He knew what it meant when Mr. Big did choose to attend. It meant something had displeased him, and nothing good ever came of that, especially for the show's host.

That was how Zark wound up in his current job. The last host of the show displeased the master with his lackluster performance and low ratings. That poor character was enduring tortures beyond comprehension and would be doing so for many millennia. Zark's ratings, fortunately, were very high, and he intended to keep them that way. He would not give the master any reason to remove him from this plumb job, and he refused to think about what would become of him if such a thing did happen.

Zark continued his monologue, "As you may have guessed, we have another fantastic show for you tonight with two brand new unsuspecting arrivals!"

The audience went wild, screaming, howling, clapping hands, and stomping feet. This din was exactly what the studio execs wanted to hear. As always, per Zark's instructions, the audience was hand-picked from some of Hell's worst and rowdiest demons. This made for excellent Hellivision. Gragnar Zark knew how to please his viewers.

When the audience quieted somewhat, Zark continued, "You folks know the rules of the show. We have two unsuspecting new souls. So fresh that they may not even realize they're dead yet."

Again, the audience went wild with raucous laughter.

"We'll be choosing two random members of our studio audience to come up and do their best to make the victims scream. Each contestant will get three attempts with their subjects. Their screams will be measured on our scream-o-meter."

Zark pointed to an oversized prop that resembled a giant thermometer well over ten feet tall. The thermometer was composed of a glass tube filled with a crimson liquid, which happened to be blood. Various levels were designated by colors along the meter's path, from low to high, with bright white lettering. On the bottom-most section, colored blue, was written, "You gotta be kidding." Next was the yellow section labeled "Getting Better." The third section was green and said, "Yeah, baby!" And on the final segment in blood-red was written in a creepy font, "That's what I'm talkin' about!"

Zark continued with his introduction, "The victim that screams the loudest and longest will determine which contestant wins the competition. That winning contestant will take home this week's fantastic prize package."

He turned and pointed to the giant curved screens surrounding the arena and said, "And our lovely hostess, Delemina Gronk, will show us what that prize package is . . ."

Suddenly, all the screens lit up with the image of a gorgeous, curvaceous, scantily-clad woman standing in front of a curtain. As the curtain opened, the audience gasped with predictable surprise as the grand prize was revealed.

". . . That's right, my demonic friends, it's an all-expense-paid trip for two to Las Vegas. Our winner and the guest of their choice will spend a week of unbridled debauchery in beautiful Sin City, USA. They, of course, will be disguised as humans and, as such, will be free to do whatever they choose. The more havoc they can wreak, the better. Gambling, drinking, fornication, robbery, murder, you name it, nothing is off-limits. I mean, what's the worst that can happen? They get killed and just end up back here sooner than expected."

The audience was worked up into a frenzy now. Everyone wanted to be chosen and have the opportunity to win such a wonderful prize. Most of these demons had been in Hell for thousands of years, and just the idea of being able to return to Earth was more than any of them could imagine. But a week of complete debauchery in the capital of sin sent them into fits of ecstasy.

Zark said, "OK, Delemina, tell us who our first contestant will be."

On the huge video screens, Delemina was spinning a large circular wire cage filled with slips of paper. Zark said, "As I have said many times before, this drum contains the names of everyone in our studio audience. If your name is selected, I want you to make your way to the stage as soon as possible. Delemina, do we have a winner?"

Delemina said, "Well, Gragnar, we most certainly do. Our first contestant is from the southern district of the sixth circle. He likes to call himself a 'Master of Mayhem.' Let's give it up for Dratzap Kronkhart."

"Dratzap Kronkhart, come on down!" Zark shouted into his stage microphone."

A squat, almost naked demon wearing a loin cloth that did little to hide his massive swaying manhood waddled down the aisle, making his way to the stage. Because of his short stature, the demon couldn't step up the platform levels. He had to climb up to the top, and by the time he reached the host, Dratzap glistened with sweat.

Zark looked down at the dwarf and said, "Master of Mayhem, you call yourself. Seriously?"

Winded, the demon managed to puff out, "Just you wait and see, Gragnar Zark. Dratzap will bring screams from the victim, the likes of which have never been heard anywhere in Hell before!"

"Well," Zark replied, "That's quite a declaration. Let's see if you can back it up. Our first victim, Robert Wellington, a new arrival, is a former accountant from Pennsylvania. He managed to embezzle millions of dollars from the small company he was supposed to help manage. His actions resulted in the company going bankrupt and its owner committing suicide. Our boy Robert was later caught and sentenced to twenty years in jail. However, he never made it past day one, as he was gang raped and beaten to death shortly after his arrival. Hopefully, that experience will help prepare him for what's to befall him shortly. Send in Robert Wellington, please."

Suddenly, a form began to take shape on the large metal chair at center stage. It was a naked man who was secured tightly in place. He looked confused and disoriented. The crowd roared with pleasure.

"Where . . . where am I? What is this?"

"Welcome to Hell, Robert. More specifically, Welcome to the latest installment of "Scream Like The Devil," the show that turns pain into pleasure."

"But . . . but I don't understand!"

"Not a problem, Robert. Ok, Dratzap, do your worst. You get three screams on the scream-o-meter, starting right now."

The little demon went right to work. A pin more than eight inches long, resembling a hat pin, materialized in Dratzap's hand, and the tip burned with white-hot fire.

"Very nice," Zark said, adding commentary, preventing any dead air or slow spots in the show. "Excellent choice."

Dratzap shoved the pin under the man's big toenail, pushing in all eight inches. The bound man let out an ear-piercing howl of pain reverberating throughout the studio.

"Delemina . . . show us the scream-o-meter."

The giant thermometer appeared on the curved screens, and the red bubbling liquid rose just past the blue area marked "You Gotta Be Kidding" into the lower portion of the yellow area labeled "Getting Better."

"Not a bad start, Dratzap. But it's a bit shy of what I'd expect from a so-called Master of Mayhem. What say we give it another try?"

The demon twirled his fingers in the air, held his hand out palm-up, and a swirling ball of flames appeared. Dratzap hurled the ball of fire at the bound victim, and as it flew, its consistency changed to a liquid resembling Napalm. However, this was living Napalm. When it landed on Robert Wellington's lap, the liquid fire spread down his legs, up his chest, and down his arms. The vile concoction spread and caused the victim's flesh to bubble and smoke. The man screamed even louder and longer than before.

The studio audience roared with delight as the red liquid in the scream-o-meter soared past the blue area, past the yellow, into the top portion of the green zone, labeled "Yeah, baby!" It was just shy of the red and final area, which read, "That's what I'm Talking About!"

"Excellent improvement, Dratzap. You almost made it to the top," Zark said. "You get one more try."

Dratzap looked at the badly damaged Robert Wellington as his flesh began healing, as things in Hell always did. After all, you couldn't have eternal, never-ending torture if the soul couldn't regenerate itself. But Dratzap knew it was time for him to make his final play before the victim had self-healed. He stretched out his stunted arms as far as possible, pointed his fingers at the victim, and wiggled them.

Rain began to fall on Robert Wellington, but this was no ordinary rain. The liquid was laced with a super-concentrated salt-like substance designed to seek out damaged flesh, adhere to the open soars, devour the tissue and cause unimaginable agony, which it did quite well. The victim howled and thrashed about to the best of his limited ability. That did the trick. The scream-o-meter raced upward into the read, "That's What I'm Talking About" area, within a few inches of the top.

"Yes!" Zark shouted, "That is what we're talking about! Excellent job, Dratzap! Now go over there, take a seat off stage and watch the next contestant. Speaking of which, Delemina, who is our next contestant?"

Once again, she spun the giant wire drum, and when it stopped, she drew the name and said, "Our next contestant hails from the savage outer lands, and his name is Horgroth Rogg."

"Horgroth Rogg, come on down!" Zark shouted.

Suddenly, a roar came from the back of the studio, and the sound of thunderous footfalls echoed through the air. Zark looked to see a massive muscle-bound demon trudging purposefully toward the stage. Zark almost signaled his security staff to intervene for a moment or so. The monster looked like a wild and savage creature. The demon was more than ten feet tall, dressed in a hand-made tunic, obviously sewn together from dozens of pieces of human flesh. The top portion was sleeveless to allow space for the gigantic biceps to have room to flex. The bulging muscles glistened with sweat.

Likewise, the lower portion of the tunic stopped just above the creature's knee, and the muscles in the beast's legs were equally huge, hairy, and sweat-covered. The demon's eyes were large, bulging, and visibly insane.

"So . . ." Zark said, "You're Horgroth Rogg."

The monster bellowed, "I am the great and magnificent Horgroth Rogg! I am a master torturer and will bring screams louder than imaginable." The crowd began to holler and stomp their feet.

Zark replied, "I certainly hope so. Now, Delemina, please bring forth our next soul." As Delemina began to speak, a new form began to take shape in the huge metal chair.

She said, "Well, Gragnar, our next tortured soul comes from New York City. His name is Byron Maddocks, and in life was a high-priced defense lawyer representing various organized crime figures. Although a lifetime of defending these scumbags would have guaranteed him a one-way ticket to Hell, Byron managed to find himself a ride on the Hell Express train after successfully defending a child molester and getting him his freedom. The irony of ironies is that the same degenerate eventually raped and murdered Byron's little girl. This drove Byron over the edge, and after murdering his former client, Byron committed suicide."

The crowd shouted, "Woo! Woo! Woo!"

Zark added, "Just so you know, that child killer is currently being treated to some of the best torture the seventh circle has to offer. But on with the show. Ok, Horgroth. You're up. Give it your best shot."

The giant demon approached the bound man, took a deep breath, and exhaled a storm of molten fire with an ear-piercing roar. The defenseless Byron never knew what hit him. In milliseconds, his entire spiritual body was engulfed in flames so intense that he was instantly disintegrated. He never even had the chance to scream. When the fire died, the metal chair was covered in a thin coating of sparkling dust. Horgroth stood stunned, looking as though he had no idea what had happened, which was true.

The audience was furious, shouted boos and cat calls, and pummeled the hapless demon with an assortment of trash and whatever they could find. For a moment, Zark worried that a full-scale riot might occur. But eventually, the crowd returned to normal.

Zark stood shaking his head, waited for the audience to get quiet, and then said, "Oh, Horgroth, now you've gone and done it. Not only didn't you get a single reading on the scream-o-meter, but you vaporized Mr. Maddock's soul. Good thing our chair was protected from such an attack. Not good for you, however, my huge friend, not good for you at all. You see, it will take many millennia to reconstruct poor Byron's soul so it can be properly subjected to the agonizing torture it deserves. That means we'll miss all those millions of opportunities to inflict pain on him. That might throw things off balance unless someone else takes his place. So it is written, so it shall be."

The audience replied, "So it is written, so it shall be."

"Gentlemen," Zark said, waving his arm, "please remove Mr. Rogg."

Rogg looked around the stage, confused. He had no idea what was to happen to him. Four demons dressed in dark suits, white shirts with black ties, and dark sunglasses approached with their arms outstretched. The stage began to rumble, and Rogg looked down to see the cracks forming in the floor.

The cracks widened as smoke, steam, and flames billowed out of the openings. Long serpentine tentacles emerged from the crevasses, quickly encircling the body of the still-stunned Rogg. With his body trapped inside the array of vine-like creatures, Rogg could not move. The crowd was going wild, shouting with delight for more. Then Rogg began to scream. The encircling snake creatures were glowing with an eye-blinding white light, and everywhere they came into contact with the giant demon, his flesh was bubbling, melting, and sloughing off his body. The sound coming from the monster was ear-piercing, so loud that the audience had to try to mute it by covering their ears in protection. Several demons in the first five rows fell to the ground, screaming in pain from the noise.

The large round screens surrounding the stage displayed the scream-o-meter and showed how the blood not only had reached the top of the thermometer but also shattered the top bubble and was shooting all over the place like lava from an exploding volcano. Delemina was screaming as well and running for cover from the falling liquid. The entire studio was thrust into chaos, with the audience members running in all directions for exits.

On stage, the tentacles had separated Rogg's various body parts into melting mounds of bubbling flesh and dragged them down into the cracks, never to be seen again. To his surprise, Zark saw Dratzap sitting calmly off to the side of the studio. The stunted little demon stood up and hobbled over to the host.

"Rogg is disqualified. That means I win, right?"

Zark thought for a moment, then said, "Sorry, Dratzap. As you saw, Rogg's screams literally exploded the scream-o-meter. It looks like he won."

"But he's been dragged off to who in Hell knows where. I think I should get the prize."

Zark looked into the audience and saw that the studio was empty except for a few security guards. He noticed the cameras were no longer filming and said, "Look, Dratzap. I explained that you did not win. Now, either you get lost, or I'll call security, and you can join Rogg on his less-than-pleasant journey to the seventh circle."

The demon shook his head in disgust as he hobbled away, mumbling, "It's not fair; it's just not fair."

Zark shouted after him, "This is Hell, Dratzap. By now, you should know that nothing in Hell is fair."

The studio seating area was suddenly thrust into darkness, and Zark was alone on center stage. The floor cracks had mended themselves when the serpentine creatures were gone. The only thing still needing repair was the scream-o-meter. Fortunately, there was a spare in the warehouse so that the show would go on. Zark heard a solitary clapping sound from somewhere in the darkened spectator area.

"Excuse me. The show is over now. Can I help you?" Zark asked into the darkness.

"Great show tonight, Gragnar, probably one of your best," the voice said.

Zark was both flattered and concerned. Everyone liked a compliment, but there was something in that voice he didn't feel good about. Then, a spotlight appeared from nowhere and shone down on the only occupied seat in the auditorium. It was the seat Zark had never seen filled before and dreaded seeing filled now.

The man appeared middle-aged, dressed in a black suit, black shirt, and blood-red tie. His skin was white as a sheet, accentuating his crimson lips fixed in a disturbing smile. His coal-black hair was long and slicked back in a fashion similar to Zark's, and he sported two small red horns, one on each side of his forehead.

If Zark still had blood in his ethereal body, it would have run cold as ice. The man in the seat was him, numero uno, the master, the great deceiver, himself. Zark was certain his appearance could mean nothing good. He thought again of his predecessor, suffering unimaginable agony somewhere in the same seventh circle Rogg was occupying. If the big man was here, Zark was certain things would not end well. He fell to his knees in a posture of supplication.

"Oh, it's you, oh great one. Forgive me. I hadn't expected you to be here. I'm so sorry for the way the show ended. I had no idea Rogg would cause so many problems. As you know, I have no control over who gets picked to participate. Yet I am the host, and I must take full responsibility for the fiasco that ensued."

The guest smiled further with a mouth full of razor-sharp teeth and said, "Fiasco is not a strong enough word, I'm afraid. Perhaps chaos, anarchy, madness, mayhem, or pandemonium might be more accurate."

"As you say, Master," Zark humbly agreed.

"In all the millennia of this show's existence, I don't believe I ever witnessed such carnage on live Hellivision. It was most certainly a first."

"Again, Master. I am so very sorry."

"Sorry? You insist on saying you are sorry?"

"Yes, your greatness. Please forgive me."

"Forgive you? Do you want me to forgive you for creating the best Hellivision anyone has ever imagined? There's nothing to forgive, Zark. This is Hell. Hell is chaos. Hell is madness. Hell is exactly what you demonstrated on stage tonight. Did you see the demons run screaming from the auditorium? Several were trampled and crushed almost out of existence in the stampede. I was ecstatic with joy."

"You were?" Zark could feel his confidence returning.

"Yes, I was. I must admit that lately, things have been getting boring and mundane around here. Existence was becoming a type of Hell and not the kind I liked. You, Zark, have raised the bar and brought mayhem back to a ho-hum existence. I just wanted to say, "Well done, my good and faithful servant.""

"Th . . . Thank you, your eminence," Zark managed to stammer. This was a boost to his ego he had not expected. Zark realized he was the man. He was probably the greatest Hellivision host the dark world had ever seen. He was unstoppable. He had gotten praise from the highest and most powerful being in Hell. It simply didn't get any better than that. He had arrived.

Then the master said, "You can count on me to be front and center for all your shows from this day forward. I should point out, however, that since you have set the bar so high, I'm expecting bigger and better things from you every show. Get those creative juices flowing, Zark. And just so you remember, I'm sure you know what happens if I'm ever disappointed."

THE LAST GHOST WALK
(A NOVELLA)

"It is with true love as it is with ghosts; everyone talks about it,
but few have seen it."
—Francois de La Rochefoucauld

"I like the influence of the macabre, but I don't believe in ghosts."
—Sophie Ellis-Bextor

/ PRELUDE /

"Do it! I command you! Do it Now!"

The unearthly voice screamed inside Jacob's skull. He stood in the darkened hallway, bent over with his palms pressed tightly against his ears. However, this futile act could do nothing to stop the dreaded voice screaming inside his skull. He could smell his sweat, which seemed to stream from every pore in his body as he struggled to fight for control. Whoever, whatever this voice was, it was wrestling away his willpower. Unfortunately, he realized far too late that the voice was not in his ears but was reverberating deep in his brain. It was destroying the last shattered fragments of his self-control, forcing the part of him that was Jacob to step helplessly aside and let the other take over.

He was dressed in his summer pajamas, a white athletic tee shirt, and blue cotton shorts. His feet were bare. He felt the soft, comforting texture of the hall carpet between his toes. This feeling of comfort directly contradicted what he knew he was about to be forced to do. A thin beam of moonlight shone through the hall window, reflecting off the razor-sharp edge of the butcher's knife he had let fall to the hall carpet when he had tried one final time to drive the demon out of his skull.

Through the open doorway to his left, he could hear his wife, Suzie's peaceful, rhythmical breathing as she slept, unaware of the war of wills taking place just a few feet away. He saw the Amber glow of the digital clock on the oak end table on her side of the bed. It read 12:34.

But I can't! Jacob thought, trying yet another time to suppress that maddening, strangely accented voice slowly and methodically robbing him of his free will over the previous nights, "She's my wife, and I love her."

But the entity within him would have none of his protestations. It howled at him in a ragged, inhuman growl, "She is a sow, you fool. She is nothing more than a breed hog that has been bending over for every rutting swine passing her way. She does not love you. She's incapable of love, you fool. You do not even matter enough for her to hate you. That is how insignificant you are to her. She loathes the very sight of you. She finds your touch repugnant while she craves the caresses of others. She mocks your very right to exist with her never-ending fornications. You have no choice. She needs to die right this minute, and you must be the one who does the deed."

Still, in the bent position, Jacob's hands had dropped to his bent knees for support because as his mind swam, he sensed he might vomit or pass out at any minute while his body reacted to the devastating conflict within him. There was simply no way he could kill Suzie.

"I don't believe you. I don't know who you are or why you're doing this, but I know you're lying to me. I tell you, my Suzie would never do such a thing." Despite the conviction in Jacob's voice, he felt his resolve wearing down; he felt himself losing control.

"Of course, she would, and she has, so many times with so many other men! Your Suzie, you say? Your Suzie? She has never been your Suzie, you gullible fool. Oh, but she has been everyone else's Suzie, over and over and over again," the voice insisted.

Jacob felt the pull of the horrible voice, now stronger than he had ever felt before. He could feel that its commands would soon be too powerful for him to resist much longer. He wished he had recognized the voice's evil intent much sooner before it had become so strong. But now, it was far too late for any such lamenting.

"Do it, I tell you. Now is the time!"

"But I, I . . ." Jacob's mind tried one final time to resist.

Then, before he even realized it, Jacob was standing in the bedroom doorway holding the glimmering dagger tightly in his right hand, although he couldn't remember picking it up. The Jacob who had been was gone, replaced by a flesh puppet helpless to anything save what the voice commanded.

"But I must," Jacob now whispered in a voice so distant, robotic, and unfamiliar that no one, including himself, would ever have recognized it as his own.

He slowly shuffled into the bedroom with his knife at the ready and then stood silently next to the sleeping woman. Gone was the husband who had been Jacob. Gone was the loving wife that had been Suzie. Now, all that remained was a walking sack of meat with a knife and the sleeping slut in the bed. It no longer mattered whether the accusations the voice made were true or false. Whoever Jacob had once been was no more. Whoever Suzie had been to him was equally a thing of the past. They were now the couple condemned by the voice still screaming inside his head.

The man standing by the bedside with the knife gripped tightly in his hand knew what he must do, what he had to do. The voice had made that clear. He raised the knife high above his head as the moonlight reflected off the blade in the otherwise darkened room.

The woman's even breathing stopped as she suddenly called out in the darkness in a sleepy voice, "Jacob? Honey? Is everything all right?"

In that strange disembodied voice sounding nothing like he had once sounded, Jacob Lightner, holding tightly onto the knife's handle, bellowed, "Everything will be all right now . . . PIG!"

"What?" Was all the helpless Suzie managed to get out before the screaming started as the blade came plunging into the soft flesh of her abdomen? A moment later, the knife struck her again and again in the chest, stomach, face, neck, and everywhere. She let out a few final weak moans of anguish amid the insane blows before finally surrendering to the blessed blackness.

The man with the knife stood panting in the darkness. His arms, hands, and wrists ached from the force of his repeated strikes, especially when the blade slammed into and through the woman's ribcage. He turned and walked robotically from the bedroom, out into the hallway, then down to the bathroom.

He switched the overhead light on and lifted his head to look into the mirror above the vanity. What he saw was horrifying enough to snap Jacob out of his trance and return him to reality. The eyes looking back at him from the blood-drenched face were wide and blazing with white-hot madness. His hair was caked with gore and fragments of torn flesh. Blood and sweat plastered his hair to his skull. His once-white tee shirt was now nothing but crimson splatter, resembling some macabre attempt to create modern artwork.

The being controlling Jacob now allowed him to return to semi-consciousness as he stood staring at his reflection with mixed measures of confusion and horror. Then Jacob was forced to recall every detail of what he had just done to the woman he loved more than life itself. Grief and remorse swept over him like a blanket of blackness. Then he heard that terrifying voice in his head again.

"There is just one more thing for you to do, and you know what that is."

"Yes," Jacob whimpered, "I know what that is, and after what you made me do, I'll welcome it."

He lifted the knife and held it in front of his face, studying the blood-coated steel in the light and the mirror. It was surrealistic like he was watching a movie of himself. He slowly directed the tip of the knife toward his face, stopping it just a fraction of an inch away from his right eye. He switched his left hand onto the handle leaving his right free to do what must be done next. With all of his might, Jacob slammed the heel of his right palm against the back of the handle, driving the blade in through the soft gel of his eyeball and then deep into the spongy mass of his brain.

The body that once housed Jacob Lightner's soul stood momentarily before its legs gave way, and it collapsed to the bathroom floor. A blood-red marble-sized glowing orb of light floated an inch above the corpse's lips, then flew away at an immeasurable speed, returning to its home.

/ \ /

"I'm hoping this will be a good one," Terry said to his wife, Jolene, "the last one was sort of lame."

"Actually, Babe. If you put things in perspective, they've all been lame and not just sort of either," she replied.

"Ah, come on, Honey. You liked that one we did in Williamsburg, remember? Am I right?"

"It wasn't too bad, but it certainly wasn't all that scary either."

Terry and Jolene Monroe were discussing what was to become the ninth or tenth ghost walk in which they had participated for almost as many years. Every time they vacationed in an area of historical significance, there was a ghost walking tour of the area. Often, there were several competing ghost tours, each of which claimed to be the best. On one vacation, they experimented and tried two different ghost walks. Still, the presentations were so similar they decided not to waste time or money doing more than one walk in one area again.

"They're not always supposed to be scary, Jolene. Sometimes, they're meant just to be tools to find an entertaining way to teach us about their local history, which I think most of them do very well. Remember how much we learned on the Virginia Beach tour?"

"Yeah. That was a good one, for sure. And the one we took in Savannah, Georgia; that was pretty cool," she agreed.

Terry said, "It was, but there we were, in what is touted as the most haunted city in America, and we didn't see anything even remotely scary. That is unless you count our tour guide. Remember, she was that beefy chick who wore yoga pants and no underwear? I saw sights no man should have to endure."

"Terry! That's an awful thing to say."

"Maybe so, but it was the scariest sight I saw in Savannah."

"Whatever, Terry. Anyway, remember that picture you took of that house the day before we took the ghost walk? The one on Abercorn Street."

"Oh yeah. That was the infamous 432 Abercorn, supposedly the most haunted building in Savannah. I honestly thought I might have caught something in that window, but it was just the reflection of clouds."

"Too bad. I was hoping that place had potential. Do you remember Williamsburg? Remember how that tour guide missed a fantastic opportunity to scare the crap out of everybody?" Jolene asked.

She referred to a lantern ghost tour they did when visiting the Colonial Williamsburg settlement in Virginia. The tour was typical. It was heavy on historical information but lacked ghosts or a general fright factor. During that particular walk, the tourists were standing in the dark outside the building known as the Peyton Randolph House. It was a stark, two-story, wood-sided structure painted blood red, which looked quite ominous in the glow of the guide's oil lantern.

As the guide gave her presentation, trying her best to sound as scary as possible, the group was captivated, focusing on the many darkened windows along the length of the building, just begging for some ghostly apparition to manifest. Suddenly, a white light appeared in one of the second-story windows and then slowly moved to the next window.

Several people in the group saw the apparition, and a collective gasp came from the onlookers, followed by lots of whispering and pointing and the unexplained and possibly terrifying sight. This would have been the perfect time for the guide to play on the group's fear and have a bit of ghostly sport at their expense. But instead, she told the crowd not to be concerned and that it was nothing more than a security guard on his rounds inside the building.

"She could have really turned that into something special," Jolene said, "but she just blew it all off as if we weren't even interested in being scared. Hello? This is supposed to be a ghost tour. We wanted to be scared."

"Yeah, I know what you mean, Babe. But seriously, if you think these ghost walks are lame, then why in the world do we pay good money to go on them? I thought you liked them."

"I do like them, especially the historical aspect. I don't know. Maybe it's like when we go to a casino or something."

"Huh. You lost me, Jolene. I have no idea where you're going with that. What does us gambling in a casino have in common with our taking ghost walks?"

"Ok. Think of it this way. When you go to a casino and gamble, you pretty much know ahead of time that you're more likely to lose than win. Right? But somewhere in the back of your mind, there's a feeling that there's always a very slim chance you might beat the odds and actually win big. You know what I mean?"

"Ok. I'm following you so far. And to tell you the truth, that's the sort of logic that turns casual gamblers into addicted gamblers."

"Yes, I know all that. And that's why whenever we go to a casino, we decide how much we're willing to lose before we get there. Anyway, the way I see it, ghost walks are kind of like that. I mean, we both know there are no such things as ghosts. I mean, even though you like to write horror stories featuring monsters, demons, ghosts, and such, you'd be the first to agree there are no such things in the real world. Right?"

Terry was a part-time published horror fiction author with more than thirteen books to his credit. He never seemed to make any money or win any significant notoriety from his work, or how Jolene referred to it, his hobby. Yet he loved the thrill of seeing a new book published with his name on it, and no matter how many times he held a new book in his hands, the excitement never lessened for him.

"Yeah, sure," Terry agreed, "if I did believe in ghosts, I could never write the sort of stuff I write. I'd be too scared. But again, what exactly are you getting at with the casino analogy?"

"I'm saying we know before we go on one of these tours, we're not going to see any ghosts. Sure, we'll hear stories of mysterious sightings and unexplained moving of furniture and stuff, but that's about it. The presentation might be a little creepy or even disturbing if we're lucky. But seeing or photographing actual paranormal activities? No,

I don't think so. But it's still a lot of fun. And maybe, just maybe, one of those ghost tours might actually turn up something to make even non-believers like us sit up and take notice."

"A big payday is like a big win at the casino, right?"

"Exactly."

"But you don't really believe any big payoff is ever coming from any of these tours, do you?"

"Of course not. But half the thrill is in the anticipation, wondering what we'd do if we actually did see something."

They both stood smiling at each other with mutual understanding. Then Jolene suggested, "It's 7:45, and the tour starts at 8:00. So, we'd better work our way over there."

/ 2 /

The tour they were taking that evening in historic Plymouth, Massachusetts, was called "The Dead Ringer Ghost Tour." The couple had been visiting the Plymouth area for the previous week and had finally made time for their traditional vacation pastime. The tour originated just to the left of the world-famous circular arched structure, which housed the legendary albeit underwhelming Plymouth Rock.

The tour staff worked out of an old hearse, which seemed appropriate since part of the tour took place on Plymouth's Cemetery Hill. The thing was about as cheesy as any prop could be, and Terry was sure the meat wagon probably no longer ran and had been towed to what was likely its permanent residence. The company probably leased the spot from the city for an exorbitant fee. It was black with rusty chrome bumpers and curtained back Windows with what appeared to be a real casket. The outside of the hearse was adorned with bright white letters in a creepy gothic font screaming the name "Dead Ringer Ghost Tours," along with a phone number.

Terry and Jolene had called ahead of time and made reservations, although Terry seriously doubted any latecomers would be turned away, especially at twenty bucks a head. They approached the hearse, paid their fees, and waited patiently for the tour to start.

They were issued authentic-looking oil lanterns, which they were supposed to carry on the tour. Terry suspected if he turned the lantern upside down, he might see "Made in China" stamped on the bottom, but he decided he didn't want to spoil the illusion. Their tour guide, a man named Bob, also encouraged them to take as many pictures on the tour as they wanted. He requested that if they found anything out of the ordinary after examining their images, they could email the photos to the Dead Ringer website. The site was where the staff displayed various pictures of unexplainable phenomena captured by visitors.

"Some of the best shots we've ever gotten have been from people just like you," Bob told them. Then, he showed the group pictures he had mounted on a large piece of double-sided cardboard. The quality of the pictures left a lot to be desired. They looked to Terry as if they had been sitting in the sunlight for too many years and had become faded and discolored. He doubted even if he had walked up to within two inches of the shots, he would be able to see anything interesting.

Bob said, "I know some of you probably don't believe in ghosts or spirits, but by the end of this tour, we hope to either completely change your minds or, at least, maybe you will consider the possibility of their existence."

Terry looked around and noticed several participants wearing tee shirts with the logos of different paranormal investigative groups. He realized he was among a crowd of believers, so he'd have to be careful about the questions he might ask. He had no desire to have the tour marred by any potentially negative interactions with this group of weirdos.

The first stop on the tour was at a place known for a supposed high degree of paranormal activity. It was a monument high on a hill overlooking Plymouth Harbor known as Cole's Hill. It was where several dozen original Plymouth Colony settlers had been buried in a mass grave.

In September 1620, 102 pilgrims and a crew of about 30 sailors set sail on the *Mayflower*, heading to the New World. Only one person died during the two-month journey, and one baby was born. They were originally heading to Virginia to a location north of Jamestown but became lost at sea.

Eventually, they set ground on what would become known as Cape Cod and set up camp not far from Plymouth Rock. During the winter of 1620-1621, the Mayflower colonists suffered greatly from diseases such as scurvy from general unsanitary conditions. As a result, 45 of the 102 pilgrims died and were buried on Cole's Hill.

Because relations between the remaining settlers and the Native American tribes had become strained, the colonists chose to use a mass grave rather than individual markers because they didn't want the natives to realize how depleted their numbers had become. So, under cover of night, the settlers buried their dead in the mass grave. The tour guide showed the group the memorial to the deceased.

"This is a great place to take pictures," he suggested. "We've received many shots of both glowing spirit orbs as well as actual shadow shapes around this monument."

Terry took several pictures using his smartphone, as did Jolene and the rest of the tour group. After a cursory examination of his phone, Terry couldn't see anything out of the ordinary on any shots. He looked up to see Jolene looking at him questioningly. He shook his head, and she did the same. Neither of them had seen any ghostly apparitions in their photos.

As the tour continued, the group heard various tales of tragedy, such as suicides, fatal accidents, and such. They also learned of several ghostly sightings which had been purported throughout the years. The tour continued through the town of Plymouth. Eventually, they were directed along a long brick-and-mortar stairway leading up to Hill Cemetery as the sun began to set. Jolene was certain that if there were any chance of getting the money shot, it would be in this graveyard at night, filled with four-hundred-year-old rotting bodies.

Both she and Terry took many random pictures. Unfortunately, the tour's progress through the graveyard prevented them from having time to examine their photos on the go. They realized they'd have to do so later, perhaps back at the hotel.

As it turned out, the tour ran until ten o'clock, and by the time they returned to their hotel room, they were too tired to look at the pictures. Then, the next day, they were back out doing their typical tourist routines, and reviewing the images simply slipped their minds.

Days later, after the couple returned to their home in Ashton, Pennsylvania, Terry started going through his pictures after loading them onto his computer. His large-screen monitor helped to clarify the images for easier examination.

Unfortunately, all ghost tour pictures seemed to be snapshots of dozens of ancient tombstones. Although interesting to see, the etchings on many were far too weathered after so many years to make out what they said. Combined with the flash photography in total darkness, that did nothing to improve the lack of clarity. Terry hadn't expected to see something strange or unexplainable, and as it turned out, his original assumptions were correct; there was nothing.

Then, suddenly, as he was close to the end of his photos, something caught Terry's attention. It was a shot he had taken of a family plot surrounded by a low, rusted metal fence. The graves were uncared for, and numerous weeds had grown around them. All of the stones were illegible and worn. In the center of the plot, one grave marker was larger and somewhat more visible than the rest. But what caught Terry's attention was how the slightly out-of-focus image on the tombstone appeared to be.

"A skull," Terry whispered. "This image looks just like a death's head staring out and looking right at me. Jolene! Come here and look at this."

His wife came into the study and said, "What's wrong, Babe? You sound like something frightened you."

"It did. Come here and take a look at this, and tell me what you see."

Jolene looked at the image on the screen, and an involuntary gasp caught in her throat. "Oh my God, Terry. Is that? I mean, I see a skull. Is that what you see?"

"Yeah. That's exactly what I see. I've tried zooming in and out, but it never changes. I'm sure it's a skull. What is it doing on a grave marker, or more importantly, on our picture?"

Jolene said, "I don't know. Maybe it was an etching of a face on the tombstone, and over the years, it's become worn away. Combine that with the darkness and the camera's flash, and there you have it, instant skull."

"Yeah. I'm sure you're right, but what if this is a real ghostly apparition? How cool would that be?"

"Extremely. But before you go getting all worked up, Sweetie, why don't we do something to verify what we're seeing and then worry about what it might suggest?"

/ 3 /

Terry hesitated, then said, "I get it. You want me to email the image to the Dead Ringer Ghost Tours folks, right?"

She hesitated, then said, "Yes, I suppose I do. They probably can't do anything more to verify whether you've got an honest-to-goodness ghost there, but they can at least compare it with the actual gravestone during the light of day. If it's only a trick of the light on an old etched tombstone, so be it. But if they examine the tombstone and find only letters or perhaps nothing left on the stone face, they'll have to explain why your picture has a skull face."

"That makes sense to me. Especially since we're five states and eight hours away."

With that, Terry searched for the Dead Ringer website, and within a few minutes, the digital file of the tombstone and an email explanation were on their way to Plymouth, Massachusetts. It was late on a Friday evening, and Terry didn't expect to hear back from the tour guides before Monday. He turned off his computer and headed to the bed where Jolene was already curled up under the covers, almost asleep.

Terry was exhausted and went into the bathroom to get ready for bed. He was grateful the nightly ritual was reflexive and could essentially be done in his sleep. Because at that moment, Terry felt he was more asleep than awake. He stood with his palms pressed against the bathroom vanity as he stared into his reflection in the mirror. He was only thirty-two, but he appeared much older in the glass. Perhaps it was the lighting in the room, or maybe it was simply his fatigue. Either way, the eyes looking at him appeared very old and tired.

As he was about to break eye contact, he thought he saw the image change for a split second. His heart leaped into his throat, and even though the time had been minuscule, Terry was shocked by what he thought he had seen. In place of his reflection, he had seen the skull face from the tombstone picture. He blinked his eyes, and the horrifying image was gone. Then he shook his head to wipe away any thoughts of the disturbing apparition.

Terry realized he must be exhausted more than he had originally thought because he obviously was dreaming while awake and still standing. Nevertheless, the encounter had been so emotionally disturbing that Terry failed to wash his face or brush his teeth without thinking. Instead, he turned away from the mirror, switched off the light, and walked zombie-like out of the bathroom and to bed. Jolene was still fast asleep and didn't even stir when he flopped onto the mattress.

/ 4 /

Terry didn't have the restful sleep he needed and longed for. Instead, his slumber was cursed with nightmare after nightmare, one more horrifying than the last. Unfortunately, he could not awaken from his nocturnal terrors and moved from one surreal, horrifying dreamscape to another.

In one dream, Terry was sitting at his wooden picnic table in his backyard on a hot summer day. Large trees, much larger and fuller than those in his yard, reached high toward the sky, shading him from the sun's burning rays. On the table, sitting on a red and white checkered tablecloth, was a large watermelon. It had been sliced in half across its length in a zig-zag pattern of triangles, resembling shark teeth. The inside of the open watermelon half was filled with bite-sized melon bits, cut into various shapes, including small ball shapes.

He also noticed some bright orange cantaloupe and green honeydew melon carved and balled into similar shapes mixed in the watermelon. The melon sat in a low container of ice that Terry assumed was used to make the melon nice and cold, just like he loved it. Because of the heat of the summer day, Terry's throat was extremely dry, and he felt if he didn't get a piece of the fruit immediately, he'd die of thirst.

He reached his hand into the melon to grab a fistful of the delicious chilled succulent fruit. To his horror, the melon didn't feel icy cold at all. It was quite warm. The consistency of the fruit was all wrong as well. Instead of feeling like cold, crisp, fresh fruit, what his hand grabbed reminded Terry of warm, living human flesh. He turned over his fist and opened his hand, palm up.

In his hand was a revolting horror Terry could scarcely comprehend. There was no fruit of any kind. Sitting in Terry's blood-dripping hand was an assortment of body fragments. Three round eyeballs slowly rolled, floating on a gelatinous bed of crimson gore. No matter how the strange orbs rolled, the pupils never stopped looking at him. Then he saw severed ears, a nose or two, and several severed lips floating in the bloody soup dripping through his fingers and running down his arm like grease from a pizza. Terry screamed in horror and found himself transported to a new location a moment later.

Now, he was standing in a shopping mall in front of a pet store. There was a corral in the entrance to the store made of wooden partitions about two feet tall. A sign hung from the front of the corral reading "Puppies for Sale—Today Only." Terry fancied himself a dog lover, so he approached the enclosure to see what were the store's featured breeds. He noticed a rank stench rising from the pen as he got closer. He thought it was far beyond time for the store employees to clean up the area of dog droppings. However, the odor he was experiencing was far worse than simple animal waste. As he looked down into the corral, what he saw made his blood turn to ice.

There were no puppies; then again, there were, but not what any normal or sane person would want to consider as such. Inside the pen was a charnel house of bloody remnants of what were once several puppies, or perhaps several dozen; it was impossible to tell. Heads, paws, legs, and innards decorated the enclosure floor, and crimson splatter stippled the walls. It looked as if someone with a lawn mower or chainsaw savaged the pack of puppies and hacked them to pieces.

Terry felt the gorge rise in his throat with revulsion. But some alien force he couldn't identify told him what he was looking at wasn't real, nor was it a hallucination. It was something else, something imagined, something dreamlike. A moment later, Terry was catapulted through time and space to yet another twisted version of reality.

He was standing in a dark hallway of a home he didn't recognize, yet one which somehow felt familiar to him. He thought it was strange how he could feel so at home in a place he had never seen before. The hall was dark, save for the moonlight coming in through a window at the end of the hallway. He was holding something in his right hand. Terry lifted his arm to see what it was. The moonlight reflected off the glimmering steel blade of a butcher's knife.

Terry knew who he was, but he also knew he had another name, and that unfamiliar name was Jacob Lightner. Then he heard the steady breathing of someone in the dark adjacent bedroom. It was Jacob's wife, sleeping soundly. He knew what to do next; he would butcher her like a hog.

/ 5 /

Saturday Morning
Terry awoke in a cold sweat, his eyes open as wide as saucers. What a horrible night! What horrifying dreams! As he woke, his muddled mind cleared of the images from those nightmares. Terry got out of bed and stumbled to the bathroom.

After completing his morning bathroom rituals clumsily, Terry headed down the stairs for breakfast. It was Saturday morning, and despite the fact the clock on the microwave oven read 10:00, Terry felt like he had been up all night long. He knew this was a direct result of his frustrating dreams. Although they quickly faded from his memory, Terry realized he must have been experiencing some horrible night-mares; otherwise, he would have felt much more alert and rested.

Before getting his morning bowl of cereal ready, Terry checked his email. This had become another part of his morning ritual, no less important than the rest. To his surprise, Terry saw a reply from Dead Ringer Ghost Tours regarding his inquiry about his picture.

They thanked him for the photo but said it wasn't any sort of ghostly apparition. Their email read: "Dear Mr. Monroe, we have examined the pictures you sent, but unfortunately, we must tell you with great disappointment—no ghosts. There were no supernatural images in this photo. The face on the tombstone is from the Walden

Family Plot. That is a bronze casting of General Charles Walden. It looks spooky, especially at night when its shadows are cast because of flash photography. However, we are sorry to inform you there were no ghostly spirits." They attached a digital photo of the gravestone in daylight, a close-up to clarify what had happened.

Terry was disappointed; the photo had looked like a skull because the original image of General Walden had weathered, and it was likely, as Jolene had suspected, just a trick of the light. Nonetheless, Terry suddenly felt driven to learn more about this character Walden.

While eating his cereal, Terry did a bit of smartphone internet research and learned that General Charles Abraham Walden was born in 1578 and had been one of the Mayflower passengers. He was involved in some early explorations of Cape Cod while the pilgrims sought a permanent settlement location. One of the General's early explorations into the wilderness resulted in the pilgrims' first encounter with Indians. Things didn't go well for the group when they discovered their slow-firing muskets were no match for rapid-fire arrows.

In 1623, Walden brought his family over from England, and during the land division, he was granted two acres. In 1624, his wife, the former Anna Marie Kelsey, gave birth to a son, Charles Abraham Walden Jr., followed in 1626 by a daughter, Sharlot Marie Walden.

Charles Walden and his wife and two children died in 1630. However, the circumstances of their deaths are unknown. It is assumed they may have fallen ill and died from some viral outbreak that hit the settlement that year. He and his family were buried in a family plot on Burial Hill in Plymouth.

Terry did a bit more searching and found several other similar accounts of the General's life, none of which seemed any more noteworthy. The man appeared to be just another settler of the Plymouth Colony, doing what he could to survive. Nothing was written about why he and his family died in the same year.

/ 6 /

Back in Plymouth, the two Dead Ringer Ghost Tours owners were in the middle of a heated discussion.

"I can't believe you lied to that man!" Bob, the tour guide, said, "Doesn't he have the right to know the truth?"

The owner replied, "I didn't lie to him, Bob. There's no truth to tell him. If you mean we should subject him to needless worry based on a ridiculous legend, some coincidence, and old wives' tales, then I still say I'm right, and it's best to keep everything from him. Ignorance, in this case, is definitely blissful."

"But the skull appeared in his picture. That hasn't happened since, well, you know."

"It wasn't a skull. Yes, it looked like one, but it was just the light reflecting the worn image of General Walden's sculpture."

"But what if . . ."

"But what if what? Are you serious, Bob? Those people live far away from us. Even if there was a real ghost, which I can assure you there isn't, do you really think it would follow them all the way back to Pennsylvania?"

"I can only hope not," Bob replied, "I'm serious about this, Nathan. It really concerns me."

"It's just plain ridiculous even to consider the possibility, Bob."

"But what about that couple from Boston? They caught the image of a skull on their picture of the General's tombstone three years ago. Remember what happened to them?"

"Yes, I certainly do. But again, that too was all simply coincidence."

"But the legend says . . ."

"That's a bunch of bull, Bob. I know the legend perfectly well. Everyone in Plymouth does. But that doesn't make it true. It's still all just a series of coincidences. That murdering husband from Boston was obviously a nut-job, and maybe his seeing that supposed skull image in the picture was enough to set him off."

"Yeah, but the way he butchered her and how he killed himself."

"He was just another sick and deranged lunatic, Bob. No one would have given it a second thought if the tabloids hadn't picked up the story and sensationalized it. And as we both know, even though this ghost walk is all a lot of fun, no matter how many stories we tell and how many pictures we display, no one has ever really seen a ghost on any of our tours."

"That may or may not be true depending on your beliefs, but don't you think we should at least make that couple in Pennsylvania aware of what happened? Don't we owe them that?"

"Bob, look at it from my perspective. You're my business partner, so I need you to hear me out. If I were to tell this Pennsylvania couple about the legend, then I'd be putting suggestions into their minds. That would indirectly make us responsible if things suddenly went as bad as they did in Boston. By not telling them, I've removed you, myself, and, more importantly, Dead Ringer from being the potential cause of a tragedy, dare I mention a potential lawsuit. You know all about the power of suggestion."

"And what if it does happen to them, to these nice people? What then?"

"I don't really know. Before I believe anything bad could happen to them, I'd have to accept the premise that this alleged spirit was also responsible for the Lightner tragedy, and I refuse to believe that. But I'll tell you what I'll do for you, Bob; I'll send this couple another email. I don't know; I could ask him to send me some more pictures to check out. That way, when he responds, we'll know everything's all right, and you'll be able to rest easier."

"And what if he doesn't respond? What then?"

"Well, he did leave us his cell phone number. Maybe if we don't hear from him, you can give him a call in a few days and tell him we're doing a phone satisfaction survey, as long as you don't bring up that stupid legend. That might at least make you feel better."

"That might work. It'll be a good excuse to talk to him, listen to what he says, and decide whether he's going bonkers. And what if he has gone wacko?"

"If he has, there'll be little we can do from our end. Maybe if we suspect something's wrong, we can contact the police department and tell them he was acting strange when he was up here, and we wanted to make sure everything was ok, you know, maybe have them stop by and double-check."

"Do we know where he lives?"

"He signed our guest registry with his address. It says he's from a town in Pennsylvania called Ashton."

"Well, then that's fine, I suppose. If that's the way you want to play this. I just want to make sure nothing bad happens to those nice folks."

/ 1 /

"Wow! I'm telling you, I had some really bizarre dreams last night," Terry told Jolene.

"That's a weird coincidence. I had a bunch of strange dreams as well."

Terry was surprised to hear this because Jolene seldom dreamt at all, and on those occasions when she did, she rarely had dreams that were more than an ever-so-slight twist on reality.

"That's way out of character for you, Babe. What sort of dreams did you have?"

Jolene thought for a moment, then said, "I have absolutely no idea what I dreamt about. It's weird because I can't recall a single detail, yet somewhere deep inside, I realize those dreams were bad ones. I don't know if that makes sense, but that's how I feel. What about your dreams?"

"Me? Oh well, first I dreamt . . . hey, what the heck? I can't remember my dreams either, and I usually do. But like you, I somehow know they were horrible. It's just that I have that same feeling I get after having a terrible nightmare, one I can recall. Apparently, it doesn't matter if you remember your dreams or not; the bad sensation remains with you either way."

"Yeah," Jolene agreed, "I suppose you're right. But Terry, it's all so strange."

"Speaking of strange Jo, I checked my email first thing this morning, and believe it or not, I already got a reply from Dead Ringer Ghost Tours."

"It must be good news, or else they wouldn't have replied so fast. Right? So, what did they say?"

"Unfortunately, it was a flop. According to the owners, it was just a trick of the light. The grave belongs to a Plymouth settler who was a general or something. It's his family's plot. That was the reason for the fence around all the graves. The 'skull' resulted from a worn sculpture of the General's image carved on the gravestone. As cool as the picture was, it wasn't any ghost sighting."

"Well, I suppose we sort of knew that already. It's pretty hard to get a ghost picture when there are no such things as ghosts. Still . . ."

"Yeah, I know, it might be cool to make that big payday, even once."

"Oh well," Jolene said, "Maybe next ghost walk."

"You mean to tell me there'll be another walk in our future? I thought maybe this would be our last."

"I don't think so. We'll keep trying and enjoying ghost walks like we always do, and maybe someday, well, who knows?"

Terry was sitting at the kitchen table, and he had just reopened his laptop computer. "Once I saw the email from Plymouth, I completely forgot about checking my other emails. It looks like I have about twenty, which means about sixteen are junk. Hey, what's this? I got another email from Dead Ringer. It's from someone named Nathan Shelbourne. It says he's one of the owners of the ghost walk.

"Maybe they changed their mind. Maybe we got a winner after all."

"No, I don't think so. It says, 'We're sorry your picture wasn't a real ghostly apparition, but we appreciated your sending it our way for examination. Do you perhaps have other pictures for us to check out? You could possibly have something that only one of our experts might identify. Feel free to send them our way. Thanks again from the staff at Dead Ringer Ghost Tours. We hope to hear from you soon."

"Other pictures?" Jolene said, "I didn't think we saw anything strange on any of the other shots. Did you?"

"No, I didn't either. I wonder why they want to see the other pictures."

"Maybe you should email them back and tell them there was nothing special on the other pictures."

"Good idea."

A few moments later, Terry completed his email and sent it on its way. Then, he closed out his email program and shut down his computer. If he had time later, he'd check back to see what reply he received.

In the early afternoon, Terry was out in their garden, building a new retaining wall for a raised flower bed using a variety of stones he had found on the mountain south of their subdivision. Terry liked this kind of work as it was more physical than mental and represented a change from his stressful and mind-numbing office job. He often found the relaxation of hardscaping conducive to stimulating creative ideas. Doing these virtually brainless tasks allowed his mind to relax and open itself to new thoughts.

Suddenly, a name popped into Terry's mind, seemingly out of nowhere: Jacob B. Lightner. He stood up straight with a confused expression as he turned the name over in his mind.

"Lightner? Jacob? Jacob B. Lightner?" He couldn't recall ever meeting anyone with that name, so why had it suddenly appeared in his mind? Perhaps it had been someone from his past, someone he should recall, but he didn't.

Jacob B. Lightner, he thought again. How could he know a name and yet at the same time have no face to associate the name with? It was very odd. Perhaps he had overheard the name somewhere, and it had stuck in his subconscious until it came to the surface today for no reason. He often found his mind tended to work like that.

However, Terry knew deep inside this wasn't true because there was a strange feeling of discomfort down in the pit of his stomach at the recollection of that name, just like the feeling he had that morning. Then he had a partial memory, just a glimpse, a flash. He was standing in a dark hallway outside of a bedroom door, and he could hear the shallow, even breathing of someone sleeping. In the vision, Terry wasn't Terry but was this man, Jacob B. Lightner, and the person asleep in the darkened bedroom was Lightner's wife. A voice was booming in his head, telling him to do terrible things.

"Honey?" Jolene called out as she walked across the backyard toward him. "Do we know anyone named Suzie Lightner?"

/ 8 /

Jolene's voice brought him out of his dream state and back to reality. He hesitated for a moment, then asked, "Did you just say, Lightner?"

"Yes. Suzie Lightner," Jolene replied.

Terry shook his head, clearing the final remnants of fog from his brain, and reluctantly said, "Jolene, I can't explain what's happening, but something really weird is going on."

"What do you mean?"

"Well, you just asked if we know anyone named Suzie Lightner, and by the way, we don't. And I just had the name Jacob B. Lightner pop into my head right before you came out."

"Jacob and Suzie Lightner? You know, we must have heard something about them sometime in the past, or else we wouldn't recognize the names."

"But that's just it, Jolene. I don't recognize the names, and my guess is neither do you. And there's something else. When I first thought of the name, I got a weird negative vibe that made me feel he might somehow be tied to the nightmares I had last night."

"Yeah, me too. When I thought of the name Suzie Lightner, I got a similar weird vibe."

"So now what?"

Jolene said, "I don't know. No, wait. I have an idea. Do you have your phone with you?"

"Of course I do," Terry said, "When don't I have it with me?"

"Very true, Sweetie. Very true. Anyway, mine's in the house. Do me a favor and Google "Jacob and Suzie Lightner.""

Terry reached into one of his many cargo shorts pockets and pulled out his phone. He searched as Jolene had suggested. Suddenly, his eyes grew wide with shock.

"What is it, Terry?" What did you find? You just turned white as a sheet."

"Oh my God. You're not going to believe this, Babe!"

"What, what is it?"

"I found an article that said three years ago, a young couple from the Boston area died in a murder/suicide. It says the killer was Jacob B. Lightner, and the victim was his wife, Suzanne E. Lightner."

"S . . . S . . . Suzie and Jacob?" Jolene stammered.

"The article says the couple had just returned a week earlier from a vacation in . . . holy crap . . . in Plymouth."

"What? Plymouth, Massachusetts?"

"Yeah, that's what it says. They had just returned from a vacation in Plymouth the previous week. It says here most neighbors commented the couple seemed to be a normal, loving pair. However, several neighbors noticed the couple acting differently toward each other."

"Different? How so?"

"One neighbor said he had noticed a far-off look on Jacob's face a few days before the incident. He asked Jacob if everything was all right, and he said Jacob replied in a strange monotone voice that everything would be fine very soon."

"This is all too weird, Terry. They return from Plymouth and start acting strange a week before Terry kills Suzie and then kills himself. We come home and have nightmares we can't remember, and then we think of their names out of nowhere. What the hell is going on?"

"I don't know, Jo. But I have to tell you, there's even more to all this. I remembered part of my nightmare right before you came out when I thought of Jacob's name."

"You did? What did you remember?"

"In my dream, I was standing in a darkened hallway outside of a bedroom. I held a large butcher's knife in my hand, and I wasn't me. I now remember I was this guy, this Jacob Lightner. And the woman sleeping in the bed in the adjacent room was my wife; not you but Jacob's wife. A voice kept telling me she was cheating on me and running around with half the men in town. And I, that is, Jacob, believed what the voice was telling him. It also said he needed to end it, to put an end to her. And he believed the voice again."

"Oh my God, Terry! Are you telling me you saw Jacob kill his wife and then himself in your dream?"

"No. Not really. I mean, I might have, but I don't remember anything but what I just told you about, and that just popped into my mind while I was out here working. I assume I may have seen more, but I can't recall it. More importantly, I have no idea why I should even have such a dream in the first place."

"It's Plymouth Terry. There's something about Plymouth that we have in common with these Lightner people; something we may have done there that they also did."

"The ghost walk!" Terry suddenly shouted. "Do you think they may have taken the same ghost walk tour we took?"

"What?"

"The Dead Ringer Ghost Tour! What if the Lightners went on that ghost walk?"

Jolene argued, "So what if they did? Thousands of people have probably taken that walk in the last three years. It's not like there were a ton of things to do in Plymouth. The tour is open seven days a week, and there were over thirty people in our tour group alone. And if you remember, three separate tour groups were going out at once. That's almost a hundred people a night, seven hundred a week."

"Yeah, I see what you're saying. With so many people taking the tour every year, what could possibly be so special about us that we'd form some sort of . . . I don't know, psychic connection with the dead Lightners? Wait a minute. I suddenly have a crazy idea. Stay with me on this. What if they took the same tour we did? And what if they captured the same strange image we did? And what if capturing that image allowed some sort of spirit or demon to follow them home?"

Jolene looked at her husband with disbelief. She was speechless.

"Hear me out, Jolene. Suppose that same ghost or a similar one followed us home because of one of the pictures we took?"

"Now, wait a minute, Terry. We just discussed how there are no ghosts and how going on a ghost walk was a historical thing. And how we're always hoping for the big payoff which never comes."

"But what if it did come? What if the people at Dead Ringer Tours were lying to us? What if that picture we took actually did stir up a paranormal force? And what if the Lightners had a similar experience? What if photographing that image disturbed a spirit, which somehow latched onto us and followed us home?"

"Stop it, Terry, right now. Don't be ridiculous. As crazy as I know that idea is, you're scaring me with it. Why would the people at Dead Ringer lie to us? What could possibly be gained?"

"I'm not sure. But I intend to find out. Something's going on within that organization. But right now, we don't even know if the Lightners even took the ghost tour, although I strongly suspect they did."

"So, what are we going to do now?"

Terry said, "Research. I'm going to go in the house and find out all I can about the Lightners, Dead Ringer Ghost Tours, and this General Walden character. Then I'm going to call this Nathan Shelbourne at Dead Ringer, and I'm going to find out what's happening to us and why."

"More importantly," Jolene said, "What can we do about it."

/ 9 /

Saturday Afternoon

"Dead Ringer Ghost Tours, Nathan speaking."

"Um, yes, hello. Is this Nathan Shelbourne, owner of Dead Ringer Tours?"

"Why yes, this is he. How may I help you? Are you interested in booking a tour?"

"No, sir. In fact, my wife and I took your tour last week. This is Terry Monroe. My wife Jolene and I were on your tour while visiting Plymouth."

There was silence on the other end of the line. Terry could sense the man tensing up at the obvious recognition of his name. He decided to pretend he didn't notice.

"Just last night, I sent you a picture we thought was a skull image. Do you recall that? You replied to my email and said it wasn't a paranormal sighting."

For several moments, there was even more silence. It was obvious that the man was stalling while he put together whatever lie he was about to tell.

Then Shelbourne said, "Um, yes, Mr. Monroe, I believe I recall the photo." He did his best to sound casual and uninterested, perhaps too much. Terry could tell instantly that the man was holding something back, something very important.

Terry waited for a beat, then said, "Jacob and Suzanne Lightner," hoping to catch the man off guard and succeeding because the phone went dead for a few moments. "They went on one of your tours. Isn't that true, Mr. Shelbourne?"

"Um, um, leave me think about that. Lightner, did you say? Yes, as I recall, they did take our tour several years ago."

"That's odd," Terry said, "a moment ago, you seemed to have trouble remembering the photo I sent you just last night, yet now you had no trouble remembering the Lightner's visit over three years ago. Don't you find that a bit strange?"

"Of course, not Mr. Monroe, not at all. And I'm sure you realize why. If you know about the Lightners, you are aware of their tragic deaths. Poor Mr. Lightner went insane and murdered his wife, then killed himself. The police investigation into the Lightner incident was very thorough. They traced the couple's movements for the previous months. That was how they eventually learned about the couple's visit to Plymouth and took our little tour. Had the detectives not shown up on our doorstep, we never would have known about the tragedy. That being said, you apparently did some research on your own before contacting me."

"Yes. As a matter of fact, I did. The murder/suicide occurred just five days after visiting your ghost walk."

"Yes," Shelbourne agreed, "I recall. That was quite an unfortunate coincidence."

"Coincidence?" Terry asked.

"Yes, coincidence. Nothing more."

Terry asked, "Tell me something, Mr. Shelbourne, did the Lightners take pictures while they were on your ghost tour?"

"I have to assume they did. Everyone does. You know that. We encourage it."

"And did they happen to find anything unusual in their photographs, particularly those taken of General Walden's gravesite?"

"I'm sorry, Mr. Monroe; I couldn't possibly be expected to recall that sort of detail. It was many years ago. We've had thousands of visitors since then."

Terry said, "Fine, so you don't recall. Well, I'm going to go out on a limb here and do a bit of speculating. I'm betting they took photos of Walden's grave, and I'll bet they got a similar image on their photo to the one I got on mine. How am I doing so far?"

"Honestly, Mr. Monroe, as I said, I can't be expected to remember what they did or didn't photograph. It was so long ago."

Terry was quickly losing patience with the man. He went on the offensive, "You have a lot of nerve using words like 'honestly' when it's apparent you're obviously lying through your teeth."

The man was caught off guard and dumbfounded; he stammered, "How d . . . d . . . dare you to accuse me of su . . . su . . . such a thing?"

Terry cut him off, "How dare I? Let me tell you how dare I, Mr. Shelbourne. Until this morning, I had never heard the name Jacob B. Lightner in my life, and neither had my wife. Yet last night, after sending you that photo, my wife and I both had a series of horrible nightmares. I can't recall most of them, but the one I can remember was a replay of the murder of Suzanne Lightner by her husband Jacob and then his suicide. Later, we simultaneously had the couple's names pop into our minds."

"Well, I can't explain that," Shelbourne said, "but I assure you it has nothing to do with me or Dead Ringer Tours."

"Wait, Mr. Shelbourne, there's more. I looked up Jacob Lightner on the internet and was astonished to discover the details of my nightmare matched the news details describing the murder/suicide exactly."

"Oh well then, the answer is simple," Shelbourne said, "you and your wife must have read about or seen something on television about the incident three years ago. Then, you must have simply forgotten about it. Maybe subconsciously, you had even known they had visited Plymouth. Then, your trip to Plymouth triggered the memory in the form of dreams. That sounds like a plausible explanation to me."

"Nice try, Mr. Shelbourne, but I'm not buying it. My wife seldom dreams, and when she does, we don't have simultaneous ideas pop into our heads, which result in us knowing the names of dead people we've never previously heard of."

"Look, I'm sorry you had a bad night, Mr. Monroe, but . . ."

"I also think as soon as you saw the image on our picture, you knew it was a repeat of the situation the Lightners encountered, and it terrified you. I'm guessing you lied to us about the significance of that skull image on the photo so that you could distance yourself from what you're afraid might happen to Jolene and me."

"Nonsense. That's ridiculous, Mr. Monroe. And as I said in my email, there was no skull image."

"Look, Mr. Shelbourne, I understand because of fear of potential legal problems; there's no way you'll admit to knowing anything about what happened. I get that. But I'm just very concerned about what might be going on. And I believe you're just as concerned as we are. Otherwise, you wouldn't have sent me that email requesting to see the other pictures."

"Wait a minute. I was just doing my job to help promote the ghost tour. I was asking for those pictures with the hopes of finding something we could use to get more customers."

"Uh, yeah, right. I think the real reason you contacted me was to make sure I was still alive, that I didn't go crazy and murder my wife as Jacob Lightner did three years ago; that's exactly what I think."

"Mr. Monroe, I assure you I thought nothing of the kind. You're being ridiculous about all of this. And I have a good mind to hang up on you."

"But you haven't hung up on me; I'm certain you won't hang up on me because you're more than a little curious about all this, aren't you? Yes, I believe you are. I think I get it now. You've been running this so-called ghost tour for decades, yet you've never seen any real proof of the existence of ghosts. Here's what I think. I believe when you learned about the Lightner tragedy three years ago, you started to think that maybe, just maybe, you were on your way to finding some sort of proof of a supernatural event. If that happened, your tour business would skyrocket. Then, when the cops brushed the whole thing over as nothing more than a deranged husband who went off the rails, you assumed you were cheated out of a real opportunity."

"Even if what you said was true, Mr. Monroe, what does that have to do with you and your wife?"

"I'm not sure about that yet, but I'll bet the Lightners took a picture of the same tombstone we did. And I'll bet their picture had the same skull image ours had. They probably sent the photo to you, and for whatever reason, you told them the same pack of lies you told us, but then after the murder/suicide, you reexamined the picture they sent you and saw the image of a skull. You realized something supernatural actually had happened, affecting that couple for some reason.

"But then you started thinking about liability, and you figured maybe you didn't want to have your business tied to the event too closely after all. So, for the past three years, you've laid low, watched the pictures coming in from customers, and waited to see if anything similar occurred again. When we sent you a similar image, you panicked, realizing there was a potential to repeat the Lightner incident.

"The first thing you did was what just about anyone in your position would do, and that was to deny, deny, deny. You told us the image was not a skull but was just a trick of the light, which had nothing whatsoever to do with any ghosts, with you, or with your ghost walk, thereby freeing you from any liability. But then, for whatever reason, you started to be concerned and maybe a little curious. So, you emailed us back just to make sure we were ok. Now that we have all the formalities out of the way, I need to know what is going on."

There was a momentary silence on the other end of the line. Terry could hear Shelbourne's troubled breathing for a few seconds, followed by a sigh of frustration or acceptance.

The tour owner said, "OK. You're right about some of your assumptions, Mr. Monroe. The problem is, I don't know for sure what happened during the photographing of the gravesite that might have affected the Lightners, only that there may have been some sort of connection. And now, hearing what you've told me about your dreams, I have to assume a similar connection occurred during your visit. I may run a ghost tour, but I can't pretend to know everything about the supernatural. We provide a fun tourist service, you know, a light, harmless form of entertainment for our customers. I'm no expert on the occult or the supernatural. I'm just a businessman out to earn a few bucks, pay his bills and carry on. I can't pretend to understand your worries, nor can I hope to tell you what to do next."

"I'm afraid I don't know what Jolene and I will do either. This is all new to us. All I know is I don't want us to end up like the Lightners."

Shelburne said, "I have no suggestions other than to wait to see what if anything happens next. If what you fear is true, and I am not suggesting it is true, you have one advantage over the Lightners. From what I've read, all indications suggested they never spoke to anyone about any supernatural experiences. Did he have dreams of the sorts you two are experiencing, or did he hear voices? No one knows."

"I believe he heard a voice," Terry said, "at least I assume so since I heard a voice in my dream."

"You . . . you did? What did the voice say?"

"In my dream, I wasn't myself. I was Jacob Lightner. And the voice inside my head kept repeating, 'Do It' over and over. It was telling Jacob Lightner to kill his wife."

"I must admit that is quite intriguing, Mr. Monroe, but I still think your experience is more the product of a vivid imagination rather than any supernatural occurrence."

"Fine, if that's what you choose to believe, we'll have to agree to disagree, as the saying goes. Look, Mr. Shelbourne, I have to go now and figure out what I will do next. I appreciate your time, although, to be honest, you weren't much help."

"I apologize for that, but I only know what I know. Please call or email anytime. And by all means, call me Nate, please. I want you to know you have a friend up here in Plymouth. I don't know what I can do for you from my end, but if I think of anything, I'll call or email."

"Thanks, Nate. I will. And you can call me Terry."

Terry had no idea why he had been so cordial with the ghost walk owner. It was easy to see the man had been either lying or at least holding something back. This Nathan Shelbourne knew a lot more than he was telling, and the man was covering up something important for whatever reason.

/ 10 /

"So, something did happen in Plymouth to the Lightners, and now the same thing is happening to us," Jolene said with a quivering voice. "What's going on, Terry? What are we going to do?"

"I'm not sure, Babe, but now that we have at least some vague ideas of what might have happened, maybe we can find a way to stop it before it gets any worse."

"How are we supposed to do that? Should we call an exorcist? Do you, by any chance, happen to know an exorcist? What do we do? Go to Exorcisms.com. Or do we just call Ghostbusters? Seriously, what are we supposed to do tonight? We have to sleep. What if this whatever-it-is comes after us in our sleep? Jacob Lightner killed his wife in her sleep. What if this thing takes over one of us and tells us to kill each other?"

"I think we have a bit of time, maybe as long as a week."

"How can you know that, Terry?"

"I'm not sure, but I believe it took a week for it to happen to the Lightners. Also, we have the advantage of being aware of the problem. They didn't know what was happening until it was too late. From what I can determine, only Jacob Lightner was affected. His wife had no idea that her husband had been possessed. The ghost, demon, or whatever it was had a week to influence Jacob. You and I are both aware that something isn't right. We know what to look out for, and we know not to believe any strange thoughts we might have. More importantly, we are communicating and sharing anything that might be out of the ordinary."

"So, what do we do now? Do we just wait to see what happens next?"

"Here's what I think, Jolene. I believe this all ties into that grave up in Plymouth and the man buried under it."

"That general guy?"

"Yes, General Charles Walden. I believe he's the one that's some-how the cause of the ghost problems."

"I thought we didn't believe in ghosts, Terry."

"We don't, or at least we didn't. I have no idea what to believe. I tried to do more in-depth checking into this General Charles Walden character, but unfortunately, I found all the limited information there was available. Still, I can't help but think the more we learn about this man, the better off we'll be."

"I assume from what you are saying, finding that information isn't very likely. What do we do to protect ourselves in the meantime?"

"We go about our lives as close to normal as possible, and we watch out for any weird occurrences. If we see, hear, or dream about anything, we need to let each other know and talk about it. Maybe that will help us stay ahead of whatever this entity might be planning, that is, if there really is an entity."

Jolene said, "I'm starting to believe this ghost thing is real. If this is the payday we've been waiting for while doing all these ghost walks over the years, I'm not exactly thrilled about it. We've said we always wanted to find proof of the existence of ghosts. What if we really have? What are we going to do?"

"I wish I had an answer for you, Babe, but I just don't know."

/ 11 /

Saturday Night
Terry walked through the darkness of the cabin. Only the smallest sliver of moonlight crept through the curtained window. He could smell the musty scent of the damp logs and the earthen floor. He felt the softness beneath his bare feet. Although he could see almost nothing, Terry sensed the cabin consisted of a single room where everything took place, likely divided into sections for eating, sleeping, and other family-related activities.

Terry was aware something unusual was happening to him. He understood he must be dreaming, yet everything felt so real. He also knew he was no longer just Terry but was both himself and someone else. Whoever that other person was, the thought suddenly filled Terry with dread. He could sense something very bad was about to happen. Terry wanted desperately to wake up but couldn't make himself do so.

He looked about the cabin, straining all his senses to gain some feel for his environment. Then he heard the faint sound of breathing. One . . . two . . . no, three people sleeping. One sounded like an adult, and the others seemed much smaller, probably children. Yes, children, but not his children. Terry and Jolene had no children. Whoever the other entity was controlling him, this entity was the father of these two children: a boy and a girl. How did he know that? Surely, it must be one of those dream things you simply knew without understanding how you knew. Or perhaps the knowledge had come from the being whose consciousness he was sharing.

Then Terry realized who this other being was. The thought appeared in his mind with such clarity he knew it had to be true. The other being was General Charles Walden, the man whose grave he had photographed and whose image appeared as a skull in Terry's photo.

In this awful dream, Terry found himself sharing space with the General, sharing a memory. He was in the General's one-room cabin where his wife and children slept. Terry felt something gripped in his right hand and saw he was holding the handle of a knife. That was when he realized he was reliving a night in the General's life. He felt his stomach clench in dreaded anticipation of what was to come. Then, a horrible voice began to fill his head. It spoke to him in English, but Terry sensed this might not be the voice's native language as it didn't seem to use contractions but more formal language.

"You know she is a harlot, Charles. She has been running with all the men in town, and they are all laughing at you behind your back. Many of them are your underlings. What they do with her is not out of affection but their way to get back at you. And the children, what do you think the odds are that either of them is yours? Not very good, I would say. They do not even look anything like you, do they? They are both the results of your trollop wife's fornications. You know what you have to do, Charles. Do it now! Do it now! DO IT NOW!"

After that, Terry heard screaming as he/Charles plunged the knife first into the woman asleep in the General's bed, followed by the soon-silenced cries of the children. Then he felt his hand rising and placing the sharp edge against his own throat, followed by the searing pain as the blade slid across his neck, biting deep into his flesh while a stream of hot blood ran down his chest.

Terry woke up screaming.

/ 12 /

Sunday Morning
"Oh my God, Terry! What's wrong?" Jolene pleaded as she shook Terry's arm, trying to bring him to consciousness.

Terry looked around his bedroom, expecting to still be in the dark cabin, but the room was bright with early morning light. The digital clock on the end table read 8:30 am. Suddenly, reality was slowly coming back into focus. He felt someone tugging his arm and heard his wife's pleading voice. He looked around and saw a frightened Jolene staring at him in terror.

"Wha . . . what happened?" Terry asked, bewildered.

Jolene regained some of her composure and said, "Terry . . . it was so . . . you were . . . oh my God, Terry. You were . . . screaming."

"Screaming? I was . . . I remember now. I was having a nightmare."

"Again? Was the dream about Jacob Lightner again, Terry?"

"Um . . . no. No Babe. This one was different. In this dream, I was that general, General Walden. It was . . ."

"The dead guy from Plymouth? Did you dream about him? What was going on in the dream that freaked you out so badly?"

"I, I want to say . . . but it was so horrible, Jo. I didn't just dream about him. I was the General in my dream. I was walking in the dark in a single-room cabin. I could smell the wood and the dirt floor. It was like I was really there. That part was fascinating, but then everything went horribly wrong. I heard a voice in my head, which was also the General's head. It told me . . . it said my wife was the town slut, and my two children weren't really mine but the product of her whoring around."

"Oh my God! That is horrible."

"But that's not the worst of it. In my dream, I had a knife, killed my wife and children, and woke up as I was slitting my own throat."

"Oh, my Lord, Terry. What in the world is happening to us?"

"I believe what's happening is what we've always waited for. This is the big payday, Jolene. This is the real deal. Somehow and for what reason, I don't know, a ghost or spirit has followed us home from Plymouth as it must have followed the Lightners home. At first, I thought it was the General's ghost. Now, I think it goes much deeper than that. I now know the General's unrecorded secret. Remember how I learned that he and his family all died in the same year?"

"Yes, I recall that. We assumed it might have been from some disease or something."

"I now know that wasn't true. They actually all died the same night; I'm certain of it. I saw him kill his family in my dream and then take his own life. But worse, he could not stop himself from killing them. It was, as I suspect, happened to Jacob Lightner as well. There was a voice inside the General's head, and it was the same voice I heard in Jacob Lightner's head in my dreams."

"Are you saying whatever entity was responsible for Jacob Lightner's murder/suicide may have also been responsible for General Walden's actions as well?"

"Well, yes. I heard that voice clearly in my dream. It spoke to me in English, but it sounded . . . accented."

"You mean like an accent from a foreign country?"

"No, I don't think so. This accent sounded like the accented speech of native Americans like you hear in old western movies."

"American Indians?"

"Yes, just like that. I have to figure out what that voice has to do with the Plymouth and why it was responsible for making the General do what he did. That is, providing I can get some corroboration that the General did, in fact, kill his family and then himself. Nothing I can find online suggests anything of the kind."

"What do the reports say?"

"Just what I told you the other day. They are vague. They say the General and his family all died in the same year. None say anything about them dying on the same day, however. The articles did mention there was lots of sickness hitting the colony that same year, so logic would suggest it was some sort of illness that eventually took the entire family."

"But you don't believe that now, do you?"

"Not one little bit. It all felt hinky to me from the beginning. I felt like Nathan Shelbourne had been keeping something from me. After last night's dream, I'm convinced there was some sort of cover-up, a rewriting of history to hide what Walden actually did. After all, he was a General, an important man in the community. Back then, it would have been easy to control what was officially reported versus what might have actually happened."

"So, you're suggesting some sort of deliberate cover-up?"

"Yes, I think any of his siblings or influential friends might have altered the truth to protect the family name and the General's reputation."

"Maybe that's true, Terry, but where will you get the corroborating story you need? If something like that happened so many years ago, there would be no way to verify it today."

"You're right. There is no record of any tragedy like the one I've been reliving. Unless . . .

"Unless what?"

"There are other possibilities that don't require the written word. Remember, not everyone read back then, so they had to rely on other methods for handing stories down from father to son, mother to daughter, etc. People would use legends, folk tales, and ghost stories to tell their tales.

"Think about it, Jolene. If something horrendous happened so many years ago in Plymouth, there would have been those suspicious of the official reports, and likely that would get the rumor mills churning. If so, wouldn't stories likely be generated from those suspicions? And those stories could have become folk tales and legends, commonly passed down from generation to generation."

"I wonder who would know of such tales if they did exist?"

"Life-long residents of Plymouth, most likely those folks with an interest in the paranormal."

"You mean?"

"Yep. I think it's time I make another call to Nathan Shelbourne at Dead Ringer."

/ 13 /

Sunday Afternoon
"Dead Ringer Ghost Tours, Nathan speaking."

"Nathen . . . Nate, this is Terry, Terry Monroe."

"Terry . . . it's um . . . yes, good to hear from you," Nathan said. Terry noticed something odd in his voice he hadn't heard before. He couldn't put his finger on what it might be, but something was different. He got the distinct impression that Nathan was not happy to hear from him.

"Well, it may not be as good to hear from me as you might think it could be."

Nathan hesitated for a beat, then asked, "Dreams again? Can I assume you are still having them?"

"Yes, I certainly am, but not about Jacob Lightner this time."

"Well, then, who?" Nathan asked with that same odd tone, which led Terry to believe Nathan knew much more than he was letting on.

Terry sighed with frustration, then said, "The General. That General Walden."

"General Walden? Why in the world would you dream of him?"

Terry went on to explain his nightmare, how he believed he was in the General's mind and how a voice took control of the General as it had done to Jacob Lightner and caused the General to murder his family and kill himself.

Then Terry said, "When I researched the General, all I could find was that he, his wife, and his two children all died in the same year."

"Yes, that's what the official documents say as well," Nathan confirmed.

"What I want to know about, Nate, are the unofficial stories. I want to know about rumors and local legends. I figured if anyone knew of such stories, it would be Dead Ringer Ghost Tours."

Nate hesitated for a beat.

Once again, Terry felt the man was holding something back. He assumed it would only be the tip of the proverbial iceberg no matter what Nate told him.

Then Nathan said with resignation, "OK. So, there is something of a local legend, Terry. For all anyone knows, it's likely no more than a steaming pile of nonsense. It's a story we used to make part of our tour whenever the group got close to the General's grave. We had to stop including it in our tour a few years back when a local descendant of the General's brother Walter filed a cease-and-desist order and threatened to file a lawsuit accusing us of defamation of character. They said the story we told as part of our tour could not be proven, and it shed a bad light on the General's reputation. So, rather than looking at our livelihoods and the shirts off our collective backs disappearing, we decided to remove the story from our tour permanently."

"Ok . . . I must assume that had been some story!"

"Not really, Terry. As I said, it was a good tale to add to the tour, but other than that, it wasn't very intriguing. And before you ask, it was not part of the tour when the Lightners were here, so Jacob was not influenced by it. However, based on what you told me about your dream so far, you already know most of it. The story alleges the General murdered his family and then killed himself. What you probably don't know about are the events leading up to that night."

"So, let's hear that story, Nate." Terry wondered why Nathan was trying to downplay the value of the tale. Again, he felt he wouldn't be hearing the whole story, no matter what Nate told him.

"Ok, but it's very likely a complete fantasy based on no factual information."

"I don't care, Nate; let's hear it."

"Well, legend says the General was not a very nice man. In fact, from what little we could gather, he was a tyrannical bully and an egomaniac. Everyone in the colony despised him. However, he was also a very wealthy and powerful man, so locals had little choice but to tolerate him. As the story goes, one day, the General took a group of local men scouting in the nearby woods. There had been some tensions between the settlers and several native tribes.

"If the stories are correct, most of the trouble was caused by the General himself. He insisted on constantly expanding the borders of Plymouth, encroaching on the territories of a small, obscure tribe known as the Wampanaga Indians. Little, if any, information has ever been recorded about the tribe. Anyway, on the scouting mission, it's said the General had been in a particularly foul mood.

"As it happened, his band stumbled upon a cluster of mostly women and children camped in the woods. They were Wampanagas. They had one warrior with them, whose job was to protect them. The General approached the warrior, who offered his hand as a sign of peace, but before the warrior could react, the General shot him right between the eyes. He simply fired and killed the man with no threat, no warning, and without provocation. After that, the scene was chaos. When it was over, every Indian who had not managed to flee was either dead or dying. Old women, small children, the lame, and the sick were all slaughtered."

"Holy cow! That's some story. That General must have been a psychopath or something," Terry said.

"Perhaps he was. It took a certain type of man to rise so high in the ranks. Those were hard times, and only the strongest and hardest men survived. The rest of the legend claims that a month later, the General murdered his wife and two children before slitting his own throat. Of course, this is all just a coincidence, and even the legend itself is based on unfounded theory and conjecture.

"Some even claim the story was fabricated to try to ruin the reputation of one of Plymouth's leading citizens. To this day, no one knows the real truth about what happened that fateful night. All of the surviving print records mention nothing about any murder/suicide. As you've learned, the records are all vague, leaving the reader to come to his own conclusions."

Terry said, "Yes, that may be so, yet I believe I know the truth now. I saw the General murder his family in my dream last night. I was there. I saw everything. I smelled the cabin's wood, the dankness of the dirt floor, and the stink of spilled blood and emptied bowels.

"I had become the General in every way, and I heard a voice in his head telling him to do those horrendous things. Something must have possessed him; something made him do what he did. And that same something made Jacob Lightner do what he did. Are you aware of any other similar deaths, Nate?"

Nathan was silent for a moment, then said, "Why no, only the Lightners."

But Terry didn't completely believe him. There was something about that momentary hesitation. It was only a second or two longer than it should have been, but it might as well have been a full-page ad in the New York Times to Terry. Though it might be true that he wasn't aware of any other deaths, he might have had suspicions but chose to ignore his feelings.

"The fact is, Nate, whatever force, whatever evil spirit arose from that graveyard, it wants me next."

There was another moment of silence, then Nate said, "I'm sorry, Terry, but I just don't know what else to say. The truth is, I don't believe in ghosts. I know that may sound strange, all things considered, but I'm simply not a believer. I wish I could do something to help you, but

I can't. I probably shouldn't have told you about the legend. It might put unhelpful notions in your head. For all we know, these stories are nothing more than a cleverly concocted bit of fiction. If you mention to anyone that I told you about the legend, I'll deny it. There is the potential for legal ramifications, as I mentioned earlier. I have a business to run in this town, and I can't risk doing anything to anger the locals.

Terry could have screamed at the man; he felt he had every right to do so. Instead, Terry decided not to waste any more energy dealing with him. Terry didn't know why Nathan would be less than honest with him, but he supposed the man had his reasons.

Then, as if to insult injury, Nathan asked, "So . . . what are you and your wife planning on doing next?"

Terry decided it was time to end this conversation, and just before he hung up the phone, he said, "I don't know. I just don't know."

/ 14 /

Sunday Night
The room was bright with moonlight as the lone figure shuffled like a robot from the kitchen, past the living room, up the stairs, and down the hall toward the bedroom. The thick-pile carpeting muffled his movements. Although the man was sleepwalking, a silent yet tumultuous argument was playing out inside the mind of the slumbering Terry Monroe.

"You must kill the slut, I tell you. She has been untrue to you. She has lain with every man in town. She does not love you. She is only using you for the money you bring from your job. While you slave your life away, she is bedding man after man at home. They laugh at you behind your back while they rut like savage beasts."

Terry tried to shake his head. In his mind, he argued furiously, "No, you're wrong. It's all lies. My Jolene would never do such a thing. She's my wife, and she loves me more than life. Go away, whoever the Hell you are, and stop tormenting me. I swear by all that's holy, I will never do what you say."

"Oh, you will because I will not leave your mind until you do. I will come to you every night while you sleep until you finally see the truth. You will eventually see how that vile tramp is using you. Sooner or later, you will see things my way. Sooner or later, everyone does, and when you do, you will do what must be done."

Terry said, "No, this isn't real. It's all some horrible nightmare. I have to wake up. I have to get you out of my head."

"Terry? Terry baby, please . . . please wake up."

Terry heard a voice breaking through the barrage of murderous commands repeated by . . . by whom? Who was that? What was that voice trying to get him to do the unthinkable? Then suddenly, the awful, antagonizing voice began fading as the other voice, which made him feel much better, was getting louder.

"Terry? Wake up, Honey. Please wake up; you're scaring me."

It was Jolene's voice, his beautiful wife calling to him. She sounded frightened, perhaps terrified. She needed him. He understood instinctively that he needed to follow her voice to get to the real place, the only place that mattered. He had to get back to Jolene again. If he did, everything would be fine; he knew it would. She could make that horrible other voice go away and stay away. Only she could do that, he was certain. Jolene's love would make everything ok. It always did.

Then, very slowly, Terry began to return to consciousness. When he finally opened his eyes, he was momentarily blinded by the light from the lamp on Jolene's side of their queen-sized bed. As his eyes began to adjust, Terry became aware that Jolene was sitting upright in bed with her covers pulled up to her chin, a look of terror on her face. She was looking at him as if seeing him for the first time. For that briefest of moments, it was as if they were two strangers.

"Babe? What's wrong? Why are you looking at me so strangely?" Terry asked, genuinely confused. He could see Jolene was crying, tears streaming down her cheeks. As bad as that sadness might be, it wasn't nearly as bad as the terror he read in her tear-filled eyes. "Honey, please tell me, what has you so upset?"

Jolene pointed a trembling finger at her husband and stuttered, "I . . . I . . . look in your hand, Terry."

Terry looked down, and his stomach lurched as he saw he held the large carving knife that belonged in the wooden block on the kitchen counter.

"Oh my God, no!" He moaned as he dropped the blade to the floor, fell to his knees, and began to weep uncontrollably, "Jolene, what in the name of God are we going to do?"

/ 15 /

Monday Morning

The phone on the large wooden desk rang, echoing throughout the almost empty office. The man sat alone, staring at the phone, uncertain if he should answer it. He saw the number come up on the caller ID screen, but he knew who it was without even looking. It was time for her to call.

He had no idea why she had to bother him so often. After a few more rings, it stopped. Then it began once again. He knew he had no choice but to answer the damn thing. The crap he had to put up with for financial support from this annoying patron was often unbearable.

"Dead Ringer Ghost Tours, Nathan speaking," he said, pretending as if he had no idea who was calling.

"Why did you not answer my call before?" The voice of the ancient woman asked.

"I'm terribly sorry. I didn't get to the phone on time."

The woman said, "It is more likely that you were sitting, staring at your phone, anticipating my call, yet not wanting to speak with me. Did you honestly think I would simply give up? I suspect you know me better than that. Besides, I am but one of many. When I can no longer call, another will take my place. Tell me, Nathan, have you forgotten what our people, the descendants of the Wampanaga tribe, have done to supplement your pathetic business if you can even call it a business?"

"No, Mother Whispering Tree, I have not, and I am eternally grateful for all you do for my company and me," Nathan said respectfully. He hated feeling like he was groveling at this old hag's feet for a handout, but the truth was, he needed their generous donations to keep his business afloat.

"Then you know the importance of your continued cooperation. We've pumped thousands of dollars into your worthless business over the past thirty years, and we are not sure you appreciate it."

"That is not true, Mother Whispering Tree. What you have done for me over these years has been greatly appreciated."

"So, you say. You have served us well over the years, or perhaps I should say, served him well."

Nathan was genuinely confused by what the old woman was saying. He was not serving her or anyone else, to his knowledge. He took their contributions gratefully and simply ran his ghost walk. He was unaware of what she was talking about. "I'm terribly sorry, Mother Whispering Tree. I don't believe I understand what you are saying."

"You don't? You mean to say all this time, you never once questioned why we would support your business?"

"I suppose I thought perhaps you believed in my business and the service it provided to promote tourism in Plymouth."

"Are you telling me you never wondered if there might be some other reason?"

"Why no, Mother Whispering Tree, I never did," but he was obviously lying to the old woman and himself. The uncertainty in his voice betrayed him. He had wondered about it on many occasions but had feared the answer. And more importantly, whenever he suspected he might be right about the answer, he knew it was one he didn't want to face, couldn't bear to face. So, he pushed the thoughts out of his mind. That was how he survived for the past three decades. It was what allowed him to sleep at night.

With fear in his trembling voice, Nathan said, "I'm quite comfortable with not knowing the reasons for your generosity, Mother Whispering Tree. It is sufficient for me to show my appreciation for your gifts, whatever your motivation. That is more than enough for me."

"So, you don't care to know? The truth is, you never wanted to see the truth. Well, I think it's high time you learned that truth. Did you honestly believe that we would hand you money every month for so long out of the goodness of our hearts?

"We aren't stupid savages, Nathan. We are wealthy businesspeople. We own over a dozen casinos responsible for bringing in millions for our people. Why would we care what happens to just one more failing white businessman? You should already know we have a reason for everything we do. If you didn't realize that, you are every bit the fool many of my people believe you to be.

"Whether you choose to admit it or not, Nathan, you have provided a much-needed service for the money we've given you. You've given the spirit of the great one everything he needed to carry out his revenge."

Nathan's stomach suddenly clenched in pain to realize that he would have to face a reality he didn't believe he could. He continued to plead ignorance. Maybe if he thought hard enough and denied it long enough, he might never have to face the truth.

He asked, "What, what are you saying? You're not making any sense. I've done nothing, and who is this great one you're speaking about? I know of no such person."

The woman said, "The great one is forever. The great one is eternal. The great one is Roaring Bear, the warrior slain by that white devil known as the General. But thanks to you and your ghost walk, he has had his revenge on the white man more times than you could imagine."

"Thanks to me? How, what have I done?"

"You have accepted blood money from the Wampanaga casinos, money that has kept you in business. In exchange, you have serviced people from all around the world while they were in Plymouth. You have walked them through the cemetery and brought them to the feet of Running Bear. He has chosen who must die and has rained death down upon their worthless souls time and time again."

There it was. The truth, spoken aloud, the words Nathan had tried to avoid for most of his life. As long as he had not heard them, he had convinced himself that the various tragic events were simply coincidence; the Lightners and God only knew how many others he wasn't aware of. How many had there been? How many innocents had died because of him? Nathan couldn't speak. The realization of his involvement in these deaths was overwhelming. He was unable to speak.

"Even if you were unaware of helping our people, or perhaps you just chose to turn a blind eye to the truth, you have aided us. You have earned your blood money. The spirit of Roaring Bear must continue to be allowed to seek its vengeance. He must be able to claim victims to avenge the death of his people who were murdered by the devil white General so many years ago."

Nathan was wrought with sorrow. In a weak voice, he pleaded, "But why me? Why did your people choose me, and why my ghost walk?"

"I believe you know that answer, Nathan Melbourne, or have at least figured it out by now. First of all, your business was failing, which provided a solution to your problem. Secondly, the spirit of Roaring Bear haunts the gravesite of that murdering General, the evil one who slaughtered our ancestors. He killed Roaring Bear and then those whom he was charged to protect. This disgraced our people. After the slaughter, an elderly tribal woman cursed the general with her dying breath. She said the spirit of the slain Roaring Bear would haunt the minds of the white man, speaking in their tongues and making them kill their own.

"For many years, the old graveyard remained barren, with few visitors. Then, you started your ghost tour and brought hundreds of thousands of people to the cemetery on the hill. This allowed Roaring Bear to pick and choose all the victims he needed.

"But your so-called business could not support you and your white man's greed, so the Wampanaga people decided to help supplement you financially. Ironically, the money you receive comes from the foolish and greedy white people who throw their wealth away at our casinos. The circle of greed was completed. All you had to do was continue to run your tour and pass by the General's grave. Roaring Bear did the rest.

"He chose his victims, attached himself to them somehow, then followed them home. Even our tribal elders do not understand how Roaring Bear carries out his vengeance. Once he was finished with them, his spirit returned to Plymouth to await his next victims. He repeated this cycle over and over, month after month, year after year.

Nathan said, "If what you say is true, that would mean, for all I know, my ghost walk may have been responsible for more tragedies than I can imagine."

"Most certainly, Nathan. If you only knew!"

"Please, Mother, don't say it. I don't think I can bear to know. Now, for the first time, the Monroes, Terry and his wife, Jolene, have called me personally, seeking my help."

"Help you will never provide," the woman insisted, "Unless . . . what have you told this latest white devil and his whore wife? Have you already assisted him in any way? Because Roaring Bear must have his vengeance. If he does not get it from the one he has chosen, he will choose another. Perhaps he will choose you, Nathan Shelbourne. Maybe he will blame you if his intended victims slip through his grasp."

"I have told them nothing because until now, I had nothing I could tell them. This is the first I have learned of this abomination."

Mother Whispering Tree shouted, "Abomination? The only abomination is the fact that Roaring Bear was not able to kill more of your kind. And remember, the warrior's spirit may have been the blade that killed them, but you and your ghost walk brought him his victims. It is you who have sharpened his blade."

Nathan hesitated, then said, weeping with sad resignation, "Yes. You are right. Sadly, what you say is true. I now see the role I have played in these tragedies, and the realization sickens me to the pit of my soul."

"There is nothing anyone can do for your lost soul, Nathan Shelbourne, but I'm sure when you see the money transferred from the Wampanaga casino to your bank account, your conscience will at least feel much better. You must now make certain you do not accept other calls from these Monroe devils. Roaring Bear must complete his revenge without any interference on your part."

She disconnected the call without any further discussion. As he hung up the phone on his end, Nathan stared at the wall across from his desk. It was decorated with enlarged yellowed photos of alleged ghost sightings from his tour, glowing white orbs, misty shapes, and other such images by the dozens. These were no more than reflections, tricks of the light. They were meant only to increase his profits.

He now knew there was only one real ghost he had to be concerned about, and if he sat by and did nothing, Terry and Jolene Monroe would die. Their deaths would be on him. Somehow, he had to find some way to help them. If he did nothing to help the couple, they would die, likely within the next day or two. But if he did help them, he didn't know what would happen, specifically to him.

/ 16 /

Monday, Early Afternoon

"Bob? It's Nate," Nathan said over his cell phone as he drove faster than he should have, heading south, traveling away from Massachusetts. "Look, I got called away on a family emergency. I'm going to be out of town for a couple of days, and I need you to run the show for me."

"What's wrong, Nate? Where are you heading?" his partner and tour guide asked.

"Um . . . nothing you need to worry about . . . just family stuff. You know I come from a large family. Look, I promise I'll fill you in when I get back."

"Ah . . . sure . . . no problem, Nate. I'll cover for you. Take care of your business, and I'll hold down the fort 'till you get back."

"Thanks, Bob. I knew I could count on you. I should be back in a day or so."

"Anything else you need me to take care of, Nate?"

"Um . . . well, yes. If that Indian woman who calls herself Mother Whisper Tree calls looking for me, don't mention I went out of town. Just tell her I called, said I wasn't feeling great, and asked you to cover for me."

"I think we're supposed to call them Native Americans now, Nate."

"What?"

"You said Indian. That's not really politically correct, Nate."

"Whatever! I don't give a flying . . . never mind. Can you handle that for me, Bob?"

"Well, sure. The only thing is, I've spoken with her before; she's a very strong-willed old lady. She's a force to be reckoned with, and to be honest, she's pretty creepy. I'm not sure how I feel about trying to lie to her. I think she'd know."

"I'm not asking you to lie, Bob. Tell her the truth. Say I called and asked you to mind the fort for a few days. That's true, isn't it?"

"Well, Yes, I suppose it is."

"And do I sound okay to you, Bob, you know, normal?"

"No, you don't sound all that normal to me at all."

"Great. Then you tell her I didn't sound very well, not like myself, and I asked you to cover for me. That's The truth, isn't it, Bob?"

"Yeah, I guess it is."

"Good, then you can tell her that exactly, and then you won't be lying."

"What if she wants to know where you went."

This was one of those times when Nathan questioned his decision to partner with Bob Allsgate. The man was a hell of a tour guide and knew more about the history of Plymouth than just about anyone, especially the darker side of Plymouth's history. Nathan realized that, as always, he had to be patient with the man. He asked, "Bob, do you have any idea whatsoever where I am going? Do you?"

"No, Nate. I suppose I don't."

"So, if Mother Whispering Tree or, for that matter, anyone at all asks you where I went, what can you tell them?"

"Well, I guess I could tell them I have absolutely no idea where you went."

"And that also would be the truth. Am I right, Bob?"

"Yep. That most certainly would be correct."

"Ok. So, you know what to say. Right?"

"Right, Nate."

"Very well. Look, I gotta go, Bob. I'll call to check on things when I can, and I'll see you in a few days."

"Ok, Nate. Don't worry. Everything will be under control. You know what I always like to say."

Nathan thought, *Don't say it. Please don't say it, Bob. I'm really not in the mood.*

"You're in good hands with Allsgate."

Damn, he said it anyway, Nathan thought. But always the diplomatic businessman, Nathan just said what he said every time Bob used that tired, lame joke, "Good one, Bob. But I gotta go now. I'll call when I can, and I'll see you when I get back."

Bob replied, "No sweat, Nate, I'll see ya when I see ya."

Nathan disconnected the call and returned to concentrating on his driving while trying to figure out what he could do to help the Monroes. It was ten minutes past three, and he still had another seven-hour drive ahead of him. He should arrive in Ashton, Pennsylvania, sometime after 11, maybe midnight, if traffic were against him. He was going to have to come clean with Terry and Jolene Monroe. He had to tell them all he knew. He didn't know if it would help, but he had to try at least.

/ 17 /

Monday Night

"YOU HAVE TO DO IT! SHE DESERVES IT!" The voice screamed inside Terry Monroe's head.

"No . . . stop saying that . . . you don't know my wife. She loves me. She would never do anything to hurt me, and I could never hurt her."

"But you can and you will. I command you to do what must be done."

Terry was standing in his kitchen, leaning against their granite countertop, stretching his arm out to grab a long butcher's knife from the block of knives next to the toaster. He was trying to stop himself from taking the knife, but the voice inside his head was too powerful.

"Go ahead. Take the knife. Go back and slaughter that sleeping sow. She deserves to die. You both need to die," The voice chanted repeatedly.

"I . . . I don't want to . . . please don't make me . . . I love my wife."

Terry felt the handle of the knife in his hand. He was still standing in the darkness of their kitchen. He couldn't recall removing the blade from the block, yet he held it tightly in his grasp. Maybe the voice was right. What if Jolene was being unfaithful to him? He would be hurt, broken-hearted, and probably furious if it were true. But even if he did believe she had been unfaithful, he still couldn't hurt her, could he?

"You can," the voice interrupted his thoughts, "you must butcher the pig. It is the only way. You must slay her where she sleeps."

"But I can't. I can't hurt my Jolene."

"No? Well, I can," the voice proclaimed.

Terry suddenly lost the ability to think, to reason. He felt a presence coming to the front of his mind, forcing his control back to his subconscious.

"That's better. You must relax and let Roaring Bear do what must be done."

Suddenly, Terry was blinded by a bright light. His hand opened reflexively, and the knife clattered to the tile floor.

"Wha . . . what's happening . . . where am I . . ." Terry stammered.

"Terry. It's me, Baby. It's Jolene. Can you hear me, Terry?"

"Yeah, Babe . . . I hear you. What am I doing in the kitchen? Was I sleepwalking again?"

"More than that, Honey. You had a knife again. Do you remember anything about your dream?"

"Yes, I do. I know who the spirit is that caused the Lightner's death and who wants to cause ours."

"You do? How?"

"He said his name in my dream. He said his name was Roaring Bear. He took over my mind when I fought back and resisted his control. Had you not come in here and turned on the bright light, I might never have been able to wrestle control back from him."

"Then, thank goodness the doorbell rang. That's what woke me up."

"The doorbell?" Terry asked, looking at the kitchen wall clock, "It's 1:34. Why would our doorbell be ringing at this time of the night?"

"That's why I came to find you. I have no intention of opening any door in the middle of the night without you," she said.

Then Terry heard the doorbell chime again. "Well, whoever it is, we owe him some thanks since I suppose he is the reason I'm awake and we're both still alive."

"What a terrible thought!"

"Maybe so, Babe. But the facts are the facts. Let's go see who needs to speak to us so urgently."

The couple left the kitchen and walked to the front door.

"Do you have your cell phone?" Terry asked. Jolene nodded that she did, and Terry said, "Be ready to dial 911 if the person at the door is a lunatic or something."

"Lunatic? Maybe we shouldn't answer it, Terry."

"I think it will be ok, Babe. Just have that phone ready in case I'm wrong."

Before Jolene could respond, Terry opened the front door and found himself face-to-face with someone he had never seen before. It was a short, overweight, balding man in his mid to late fifties. The man looked exhausted as if he had been traveling for a long time.

/ 18 /

"Can I help you?" Terry asked.

"Are you Terry Monroe?" The man asked in an obvious New England accent, making 'are you' sound like 'ah yoo.'"

"Yes, I am. And I recognize your voice. You're Nathan Shelbourne, Nate, right?"

"Yes, that's me."

Terry turned to his wife and said, "Honey, this is Nathan, the guy who owns Dead Ringer Ghost Tours." Then, turning back to his guest, Terry said, "What the heck are you doing here, Nate? You're a very long way from home."

"Yes, that's for sure. I left Plymouth this afternoon and put my partner, Bob, in charge. You remember Bob, your tour guide?"

"I remember Bob."

Nathan said, "Well, besides being a tour guide, Bob is my business partner. He doesn't know I'm here. I told him I had to go out of town for a bit."

"So, tell me, why are you here? The last time we spoke, I had the impression that you had washed your hands of our problems."

"You were right about that assumption."

"I also had a feeling you might be lying to me. Was I right about that as well?"

Nathan took a deep breath and said, "Not so much lying as being uninformed. I had been holding back some information as well. I'm very ashamed of that, as my motives were strictly self-serving. However, this morning, I learned the truth and found out about many other bad things I had unknowingly been involved in over the years. Things I have done, or I suppose I should say things I have not done."

"I'm sorry, Nate. I'm having some difficulty following you here. Maybe I'm still half asleep, or maybe you need some sleep," Terry said.

"Sleep is the last thing either of us needs right now. Look, Terry and Jolene, this is very hard for me to tell you. In fact, it's hard for me to come to terms with it myself. But I've had a lot of alone time behind the wheel on the way down here, and I think I'm here to do the right thing. If you will, I must come clean to confess my sins."

"I'm no priest, Nate. I can't offer you absolution for whatever you've done or think you've done."

"I get that, Terry, but I need you to do this. I think it might be the first step in finding a way for me to help you both. When you hear what I have to tell you, likely, you might not be very happy with me. God knows I'm not happy with myself."

Terry said, "Then don't stand there in the doorway; come inside, sit down, and you can tell me all about it."

Nathan, Terry, and Jolene sat on chairs in their living room, drinking the black coffee that Jolene had prepared. Nathan said, "I'm not sure where exactly to begin."

"Just cut to the chase, Nate. The last two nights, I woke up with a butcher's knife in my hand and no idea how it got there. Tonight, I lost my ability to control my actions. If Jolene hadn't turned on the kitchen light and woke me, God only knows what would have happened. What aren't you telling me, Nate? And who the Hell is this Roaring Bear?"

"Roaring Bear? How do you know that name?" Nathan asked.

"Tonight, in my dream, the creature that took control of me said he was called Roaring Bear. What does that mean, Nate?"

Nathan took a deep, cleansing breath, let out a sigh, and told Terry and Jolene his entire story, recapping the legend and then informing them of Mother Whispering Tree's call that morning. He didn't leave out or try to gloss over a single detail, including the money he received every month for the previous three decades.

"As I said, Terry, when you heard the truth, you'd know what a poor excuse for a man I am. I have no idea how many people have died because of me. And to be honest, I don't want to know. I don't think I could live with that knowledge. I turned a blind eye; I looked away from the truth, all for money."

"Isn't that always the case?" Terry asked.

"Yes, I suppose it is," Nathan said, "But that's no excuse for my actions."

The three people sat silently in the Monroe's living room for a few minutes. Terry sat on one side of the sofa in his sleep pants and athletic tee shirt while Jolene sat beside him, wrapped in her robe. As Nathan sat across from them on a plush armchair with his coat resting on his lap, he could feel the tension, thick as soup, in the air around him.

Finally, Terry broke the uncomfortable silence, "OK, Nate. I get that confessing probably takes a weight off your chest and likely makes you feel better. But I have to tell you, putting that monkey on our back doesn't help us one bit. What about all those who have died because of your greed? What about us? If the only reason you came here was to confess, then you might as well leave because it isn't going to do us any good."

"I suppose you're right about that," Nathan said, "Confession was not my intention."

"I feel like I should turn you over to the police, but what the Hell could I tell them? Officer, I want this man arrested and charged with aiding and abetting a series of murders. What murders did you say? Well, it's like this. The spirit of a long-dead Indian warrior who follows people home from Plymouth then takes over people's minds and makes them kill their loved ones and eventually themselves.

"You see, officer, Nathan Shelbourne helps facilitate the ghost's murderous plans for profit by encouraging people to take pictures on his ghost tour. If the ghost appears as a skull in their pictures, they are marked for death. Yes, officer, I know what that sounds like. Crazy? Me? Why no officer? I'm as sane as the next guy. Nate, how long do you think it would take them to lock me up? Not very long, I would think."

"I realize what you're saying is true, Terry. But believe me, I'm not a horrible human being, and perhaps I deserve every insult you hurl my way and more. Hell, I probably don't even deserve to live. I may not have known what was going on, but as Mother Whispering Tree told me, they didn't give me money out of the goodness of their hearts. Ok, I was ignorant, perhaps because I chose to be ignorant.

"However, now that I have faced the facts and accepted my sins, I have to find a way to live with myself. There is nothing I can do to either change the past or make up for my part in these tragedies, but perhaps I can help you and Jolene."

"And how, may I ask, do you propose to do that?" Terry asked.

Jolene said, "Yes, it's not that we don't want or appreciate the help, but I don't see how you can do anything."

"I have a theory; it might work, it might not, but it's worth trying," Nathan said.

"Tell me about your plan, Nate. Because right now, I have nothing," Terry said.

/ 19 /

"It's like this. This Roaring Bear's spirit was a native of the Plymouth area. That is still his home base. Yet somehow, he has followed you to Pennsylvania. Likewise, he has followed others. Some might not even have been in this country. Yet, in every case, when he is finished with his business, so to speak, he returns to Plymouth. Some of the many questions I've been asking myself are how he gets to his victims' residences and back to Plymouth. For example, does he follow someone to France or England and return to Plymouth? If he does, then how?"

Terry said, "I've been wondering the same thing. At first, I thought perhaps he attached himself to the photo we took or maybe to our phone's camera, but I don't think that's right."

"Nor do I. I think, for whatever reason, the spirit attaches itself directly to its victim, in this case, you, Terry. Once it does, I believe it leaves a trail of sorts leading back home to Plymouth. Think of them as cosmic breadcrumbs or perhaps a portal of some sort. Whatever the case, once its business is finished . . ."

"You mean once we're dead," Terry interjected.

"Um, yes, well, there is that. Once that happens, the entity follows that trail back to Plymouth until it's time to choose another victim. I have no idea how it determines when to do that either."

Jolene said, "If that's the case and the ghost is inside Terry, why did I have dreams the first night, and why did I think of the name Suzie Lightner?"

"I don't know. Perhaps it was some kind of spiritual bleed-over from you being connected maritally to Terry. Or maybe some part of the victim's spirit stays with Roaring Bear. For all I know, maybe Roaring Bear collects the souls of all his victims and makes them part of him."

"That might explain why I first dreamt of the Lightners and then the General. Maybe it was never really them in my dreams, but Roaring Bear used their spirits to put thoughts in my head. But why?"

Nathan said, "I don't know. Perhaps the reason was to plant ideas in your head so it would be easier to take control when he came forward."

"If what you are theorizing is true, then this entity is inside me now. Why doesn't it just take over and kill us all now?"

"I thought about this as well. I believe it cannot control you while you are awake, Terry. When you are alert, you will never let anything control you. But when you sleep, you dream, and when we dream, we tend to accept our dreams as reality at face value. We accept things that would make absolutely no sense in the waking world as truth in our dreams. Think about it: how often have you had ridiculous dreams you could still recall when you awoke and wondered how they could have seemed so real while you were sleeping?"

"Many times," Terry said, "dreams often seem real while you have them, then in the light of day, you realize how impossible they were."

"If I'm right, I think that's the situation we have now. As I said, I have given this a lot of thought during my long drive to get here. I believe Roaring Bear is helpless to influence you while you are awake but can only do so while you sleep."

"Wonderful," Terry said with more than a hint of sarcasm, "So all I have to do is try to stay awake forever, and I'll never have to worry about anything . . . other than eventually falling asleep and killing Jolene and then myself. Sounds easy enough."

"Yeah, I get it. You're frustrated, confused, and scared. No one can blame you. If my theory is correct, it does nothing to make your plight any easier, but it's information, knowledge we didn't previously have, and that's at least something."

As his temper steadily grew, Terry said, "OK. So, let's assume you're correct. Let's assume this spirit, this Roaring Bear, sits dormant inside me, waiting to fall asleep. What can we do about it? How can we get rid of it? You're supposed to be the expert on ghosts, Mr. Ghostwalk. You're the one who sold his soul for a few shekels and is probably indirectly responsible for more deaths than the Manson family and Jim Jones combined. What the Hell are you going to do for me?"

Nathan was quiet for a few minutes, then said, "I think I might have an idea. It's risky, but I don't see as we have any other choice."

/ 20 /

Nathan sat silently and then looked first at Jolene and then at Terry. Finally, he said, "Look, I realize neither of you trusts me, and you have no reason to now, especially when I tell you what I have in mind. But you will have to trust me if this plan has the slightest chance of working."

Terry looked over at his wife, and she gave him an imperceptible nod so slight only her husband, who knew her so well, could have noticed.

He turned back to Nathan and said, "Alright, Nate, I suppose you're right. We really have no choice but to trust you. We have no way of getting ourselves out of this mess without some sort of help, and right now, like it or not, you're the only game in town. Just so you know, even if this works, it won't do anything to make me forgive or forget what you've done."

"I understand, Terry. Now, here's what I have in mind. Jolene, every time Terry was sleepwalking, it was your voice that brought him back to reality, am I right?"

"Um, yes, it was. I called his name until he responded last night and this evening."

"I assumed so. Your voice is apparently one of the few things that can break the spirit's grip on your husband. So, until we figure something else out, we have to ensure you are awake while Terry sleeps. This way, you can watch him. If he starts to sleepwalk, you can immediately call him and wake him up."

Terry said, "But how long do we have to do this sleeping in shifts? A week? A month? A year?"

"At this time, I honestly don't know. Nathan replied, "Perhaps a short while, perhaps even longer. This vengeful spirit is accustomed to getting the results it wants."

"So that's your plan; we sleep in shifts until Roaring Bear gets bored and moves on?"

"Well . . . ok, so I don't really have a plan yet. This is just a precaution to buy us time until I actually do come up with a plan. Besides, I sincerely doubt he will just get frustrated and leave."

Jolene asked, "What happens if I fall asleep when I'm supposed to be watching Terry?"

"Unfortunately, we all know what will happen," Nathan said.

"Oh my God, Terry. What can we do?"

Terry hesitated, then said, "Look, Babe, I'm not tired now. Why don't you go back to bed and sleep for a while? I'll stay here with Nathan and see what we can come up with."

"Yes, Jolene, I agree with Terry. You should sleep while you can."

"But what about work? We both have jobs."

Terry said, "You're right. But to be honest, I was pretty worthless at my job today. Between exhaustion from poor sleep and simply dealing with this crap, I plan to call in sick for a few days until we get this all figured out."

"I don't see that we have a choice," Jolene agreed, "but my boss won't be happy about it since we were just on vacation last week."

"All things considered, getting fired is the least of our worries, Babe."

Nathan said, "If you don't mind, Terry, I'm not in a very good planning frame of mind. I need to rest my brain. If it is ok with you both, I may stretch out on that sofa for a bit. That ride from Massachusetts took a lot out of me."

"Well then, it looks like I'm going to be on my own for a bit," Terry said.

"Whatever you do, just don't fall asleep, Terry," Nathan cautioned.

Jolene agreed, "Yes, Sweetie. Please don't fall asleep."

"Not to worry. I'm too hyped up on adrenaline to fall asleep. Besides, I have a lot to think about."

/ 21 /

Nathan was asleep on the sofa, and Jolene slept in her bed. They had been for more than two hours. Terry was wearing tracks in their carpeting, walking back and forth from room to room around the house. He was trying to recall as much as possible about the dreams he had been having, every nuance, anything that might provide a clue into how he might beat this horrible spirit. He was not, however, having much luck. Then Terry thought perhaps if he sat in his favorite chair, he could come up with the answers he desperately needed. He didn't feel tired, so he figured it wouldn't hurt to rest his legs for a bit.

Terry wondered if what Nathan had said was possibly true. Maybe there was some psychic link not only between the ghost and himself but between the ghost and Plymouth. If he could only find a way to locate and break that link, Terry knew he and Jolene could get back to living their normal lives again. But what could he do? How could he defeat this entity?

After a few seconds of quiet contemplation, Terry stood up, yawned, and stretched. It had felt good to sit and rest his legs, even for a short while. He took a deep breath and suddenly noticed a strange coppery scent in the air, accompanied by other less pleasant aromas. He smelled sweat, urine, and the reek of released bowels.

Terry looked down at his hands and saw they were covered in blood, as were his clothes. Glancing over at the sofa, Terry saw Nathan appearing to be sleeping comfortably. But then he realized the man was dead. His shirt was wet and saturated with crimson gore. On the floor near the sofa was a knife, its blade caked with blood and bits of flesh.

"What? Nathan! Oh, my Lord! Jolene!" A voice screamed inside his brain as Terry turned and raced toward his bedroom. As he burst into the room, he was stopped by a sight that chilled him to his core and seemed to crush his heart as it thudded in his chest.

The bed no longer looked like a bed. It looked more like the floor of a slaughterhouse. The formerly crisp, floral-printed sheets were now a deep crimson, saturated with Jolene's blood. Terry stood staring, mouth agape, as the full horror came into focus.

Jolene, his beautiful wife, lay dead among the sodden sheets. Her nightgown had been ripped off, and the place where her upper body had been now looked like a hundred pounds of bloody ground beef. Her mouth hung open in a silent scream as her lifeless eyes bugged out of her head in terror.

Terry wondered if he might be hallucinating, having a horrible waking nightmare. He was sure he hadn't fallen asleep; he didn't believe he had. That was when he heard the voice.

"You did sleep, white man. And I came to you. Look at the great work you did, Terry. You butchered them like the swine they were."

Terry fell to his knees sobbing, "No, please, no. It can't be. I couldn't have done this."

The voice said, "But you did. And now you know what you must do. You must finish it."

As Terry keeled sobbing by the side of the bed where his wife's body lay, he saw a bloody butcher's knife from his kitchen knife block on the carpet. He grabbed the handle, lifted the blade to his neck, and felt the burn as it slid across his throat, leaving a gaping slit in its wake.

/ 22 /

"Welcome to the Dead Ringer ghost walk," the tour guide, Bob, said. "Please feel free to take as many pictures as you want. At Dead Ringer, we encourage it. Some of the best shots we've ever gotten have been from people just like you. Remember, if you capture any strange images, please email copies to us, and we'll be happy to verify them for you."

Then Bob said, "I know some of you probably don't believe in ghosts, spirits, or anything supernatural. Hopefully, by the end of this tour, you might completely change your mind. Or, at the very least, maybe you will consider the possibility of the existence of otherworldly beings."

The walkers turned and started up a long brick-and-mortar stairway leading up to Hill Cemetery as the sun began to set. An elderly Native-American woman watched the procession from a nearby park bench. She smiled a knowing smile.

HEADS, YOU LOSE

"Ok. What in the Hell is that thing?" Bruno inquired of his equally perplexed partner in crime.

"I have no idea, but I don't like what I'm seeing," Chaz replied.

The two thieves were staring at a blue-and-white crate labeled "Exempt Human Specimen." They had broken into a refrigerated freight truck parked in a local storage lot a few hours earlier, and using a hand cart they found inside the truck; they moved all the boxes to their truck. The thieves had gotten away cleanly, with no one seeing them.

Once inside their warehouse hideaway, the pair examined their loot and found an abundant supply of drugs and supplies. However, one of the remaining boxes was causing them consternation.

Bruno said, "I gotta ask, what the Hell did we just steal, and what does 'Exempt Human Specimen' mean?"

Chaz thought for a moment, then said, "Um . . . I don't really know. The truck was supposed to be transporting drugs, hypos, and other medical junk I figured we could sell on the street. But I have no idea what 'Exempt Human Specimen' even means."

Bruno stared at the label, perplexed, as if trying to parse the meaning of the sentence one word at a time. He, of course, knew what "Human" was because, on a good day, he was almost qualified to be considered one. And had a pretty good handle on what "Specimen" meant because he had left plenty of those with women all around the city. But his ninth-grade education didn't provide him with the ammunition to decipher the word "Exempt," even with two years spent in each of the seventh, eighth, and ninth grades. He stared at the strange word with complete befuddlement on his face.

Chaz was apparently having an equal amount of trouble with the phrase. "So wadda ya think, Bruno?"

"Well, I ain't really thinking so good at the moment. I can't seem to figure this thing out."

"Do you think it's from the blow we did last night or the weed we smoked this morning?" Chaz asked.

"Not sure. Maybe both. Or it might not have nothin' to do with any of that. It might just be 'cause I have no idea what the Hell 'Exempt' means."

"Well, as you know, I ain't exactly no 'Rouges Scollar' or nothin' like that neither, but I think 'Exempt' might have something to do with not bein' part of something else."

"What the Hell is that supposed to mean, Chaz?"

"OK. Leave me think about it for a minute. If I remember correctly. Back when I had a job . . ."

"You had a job?"

"Yeah. Once, a long time ago. You know, way back when I was stupid, back before I got smart and started hangin' with you. Anyway, I had this job working for a company that described its workers as 'Exempt' and 'Non-Exempt.'"

"Ok . . . and . . ."

Chaz said, "Well, here is where it gets a bit confusing for me. One of the two types of workers got paid for overtime and were, you know, hourly workers, and the others were salaried and didn't get paid no overtime."

Bruno asked, "What kinda horse's ass would work without getting paid overtime?"

"I don't know, Bruno. That was a question I was askin' myself the whole time I was working there. The problem is I don't know which type of worker was considered exempt and which was non-exempt."

"Ok, so far, you've been as useless as nipples on a bull in this here discussion, Chaz. So, how's about we get back to the problem at hand?

We now know that 'exempt' don't mean radioactive or explosive or infected, right?"

"Yeah, Bruno, that sounds about right to me."

"So, what do you think it means?"

Chaz thought for a long moment, then said, "I think it might mean there is a human body in there. You know, like one of them stiffs that get sent to medical schools so wanna-be docs can cut them up and crap."

"Ok, well, let's assume you're right. What the Hell are we gonna do with it?"

"Hum . . . well, beats me. I got nothin'"'

Bruno suggested, "Let's open up that stupid box and see what we have in there."

The pair got out their pry bars and hammers and began removing the top of the mysterious blue and white crate. When they removed the lid and the sides, the pair discovered a large metal cooler fastened with a digital locking device.

Chaz asked, "Now what?"

Bruno replied, "I don't know. I guess we break off the lock."

"It's digital."

"I don't care if it's nuclear," Bruno said, "Let's smash it, get inside and see what we have in there. Maybe we can sell it to a lab or something if it's a body."

"That makes no sense, Bruno. First of all, the cooler is too small to have a whole body in it. Second, if it's supposed to be going to a lab in the first place, and we show up with whatever is in there, the lab will know we stole it. I ain't no wiz at math, but that doesn't add up for me."

Bruno said, "Yeah, you're probably right. Well, let's break the lock and get out whatever is in there. If it's worthless to us, we can always get rid of it."

Chaz chuckled, "Yeah. It won't be the first time we had to get rid of a body. Haha."

"Right you are, Chaz, my man. Let's do this thing."

The two pried and smashed at the unit containing the digital locking device until it shattered and fell off the side of the cooler. The lid popped open, and a cloud of steam rose from the opening. When the mist cleared, the two robbers crept slowly toward the open cooler, looking like they were being asked to defuse a bomb that was mere seconds from detonating. Chaz looked inside and saw what looked like five clear bags full of some sort of liquid surrounded by pieces of ice.

"Ok," Bruno said, "pull out one of those bags and let's see what we got."

Chaz reached in and grabbed the top of one of the bags. His hand felt like he had just stuck it in a freezer. He pulled it away and shouted, "Man, that's cold! What if they packed these things in that crap I saw on a movie once where the dude put his hand in the stuff then banged it on a table, and his hand shattered into like a million fleshy pieces?"

Bruno laughed, "No, man. I'm sure it ain't that stuff. That was like liquid something or other, hydrogen, nitrogen, oxygen, or some crap."

"Do we have work gloves or something I can use?"

Bruno reached into a toolbox and found a pair of thick canvas gloves, tossing them to Chaz.

"What if these ain't good enough? I don't want my hand breaking into pieces, man,"

"Give me the damned gloves," Bruno said in frustration. He reached in, grabbed one of the bags by the top, and pulled it out of the box.

"Holy crap. Is that what I think it is?" Chaz shouted.

"Well, if you think it's some dead dude's head, then yeah, it's what you think it is."

Chaz started to panic, "A fricken' head? What the Hell are we gonna do with a head?"

"Make that five heads," Bruno said as he removed the remainder of the bagged heads one at a time, placing each one on a nearby work table.

"Ok. So, excuse me all to Hell! What are we gonna do with five heads?"

"Hum . . . I don't really know. I've never had to deal with something like this before. It's what they call uncharted waters."

"Who calls it uncharted waters?"

Bruno said, "I don't know. I think I heard it on TV or something."

"Well, I can't swim for squat, and I have no interest in drowning in them waters. Look, Bruno. I got things to do. I gotta go unload some of these pills with Butch and Vinnie. I ain't got no time to deal with no dead heads right now."

"But they're kinda cool, Chaz. Don't you think so?"

"No, I don't really think so. Besides, all's I see are five water-filled bags with heads in 'em. Ain't nothin' awe-inspirin' about that. Gettin' money from Butch and Vinnie, now that's some kinda special. Tell ya what, Bruno. You hang out with your 'Exempt Human Specimens' for a while, then when I get back, if you're finished playin' with them, let me know, and I'll make sure they join Rocko and Sledge in the bottom of the river. Sound good?"

But Bruno didn't reply; he was too engaged in the work of opening the bags to get a better look at their contents. As each bag was removed, a foul chemical-smelling fluid spilled onto the wooden workbench and then down onto the concrete warehouse floor.

In frustration, Chaz said, " Fine, fine, don't worry about me. I don't care. Just go ahead and play with your new toys. I'll be back in a few hours." Chaz left the warehouse with his bag of goodies, hopped into his beat-up VW Bug, and took off to an even seedier part of town to find Butch and Vinnie.

Bruno was staring at the five heads, captivated by them. He believed two heads were female, while the other three were male. At least, he thought that was the case, although it was difficult to be certain. All of their heads were shaved, as were their faces. Most of them appeared quite old and wrinkled, although some of those wrinkles might have been from the liquid in which they were stored. Bruno didn't know.

The head closest to the front appeared to be significantly younger than the others, perhaps a man in his early to mid-thirties. All the heads sat silently atop their beds of crumpled bags and rapidly depleting liquid.

"This is so strange, and yet, man, it's so cool," Bruno said as he gawked at the heads, not wondering what he would eventually have to do with them but just staring as if in rapture at their bizarre appearance. Then, the younger head at the front opened its eyes.

Bruno jumped back and let out a scream that would have made any thirteen-year-old girl sit up and take notice. He was too stunned to speak; his mouth hung open, and his eyes bugged out of his head as his mind struggled to make sense of what had happened.

Just when he thought his heart was about to explode in his chest, Bruno realized what had caused the eyes to open. He breathed a nervous sigh of relief and said to the empty warehouse. "Oh, crap. That was so weird, but I get it now. These stupid heads were frozen, and now they're thawing out. That's what must have caused the eyelids to pop open. Yeah, that's all it was. Jeezus, that was creepy!"

The head seemed to stare at Bruno through sightless, gray-filmed orbs. Although it freaked him out to the extreme, Bruno couldn't help but still be curious. He walked up to the workbench and bent over to get a better look at the grizzly remnant. He could smell the chemical fluid that surrounded the thing. He didn't believe it was formaldehyde because he was familiar with that smell. It was something different, which he didn't recognize. He also sensed the presence of another underlying aroma he knew to be the stench of decomposition. Bruno had disposed of enough corpses in his life never to forget that pall.

"I wonder who you were before you died and what your life was like," he said to the head. Were you a doctor, a teacher, or a low-life criminal like me?" Then he chuckled at his foolishness. If Chas could see him talking to a decapitated head, he'd probably think Bruno was a few cards short of a full deck. Bruno decided he'd have Chaz get rid of the ugly things when he returned. Bruno turned to walk away but only made it a few feet when he found his legs were no longer working. Then he heard a voice in his head. "Turn around, Bruno, my friend. I would like to speak to you . . . face-to-face." Then he heard a maniacal laugh that seemed to reverberate inside his skull.

Bruno felt his body being forced to turn around as if some puppet master controlled his movements. He was unable to resist or stop the action. Moments later, he found himself bent over with his face inches from the face of the severed head. Its dead eyes seemed to stare right at him.

However, now the head wore a hideous grin, revealing a mouth full of brown and yellowed teeth. The stench coming from inside that mouth was one of the foulest things Bruno had ever smelled. Then its lips moved, and although no voice passed from its mouth, Bruno could hear the words in his head as clearly as if it had.

"I want to thank you, Bruno, for rescuing my friends and me from these accursed bags. You have no idea how awful it was for us inside."

"Um . . . you're welcome, I guess." It was the only thing that Bruno's thoughts could produce. He was still incapable of speaking. He couldn't believe how ridiculous this was. How could he be carrying on a conversation with a severed head? As if that were not strange enough, he was doing so with what . . . mind-reading?

"Yes, Bruno. You can think of it as mind reading. It's called telepathy. I speak to you through that maggot-infested vestigial organ you call a brain," the voice in his head said, "Although the Lord only knows how you've managed to survive so long with that worthless mound of unused gray jelly between your ears is beyond me."

Despite his fear, Bruno found himself becoming angry. He thought, *I might not be the sharpest bulb in the shed, but I think you may have just insulted me.*

"Nice one, Einstein. Believe me, Bruno, no insult I could hurl at you could compare to the affront on humanity that occurred when your junkie mother brought you onto this orb."

Bruno thought, *There you go. I think you just did it again. I don't know how you come off, so all-fired high and mighty, like your turds don't stink. Hell, you ain't even a person. All's you are is a ridiculous head.*

"Perhaps, Bruno. But I am a ridiculous head that has taken control of your body and soul and can do whatever I want with you."

Bruno's last rational thought was, *Oops, my bad.*

* * *

Bruno awoke to hear Chaz calling his name, "Bruno! Bruno! Where the Hell are you?"

"I'm right here, Chaz. Where else would I be?" He could see Chaz walking across the warehouse toward him. Chaz seemed to be walking through a mist or fog.

"Whatever," Chaz said aloud, "I don't know where he got to, but I see he left a mess for me to clean up as usual. Jeezus, look at those disgusting heads."

Chaz grabbed two large plastic trash bags and reached for the first head in the front. "Ugh! These things stink! And why the Hell are its eyes open?" Chaz picked up the first head by the ear to put it into the bag.

Bruno tried to call out but could not as he felt himself lifted in the air and dropped into darkness.

ACROSS THE GREAT EXPANSE

/ 1 /

"Nick, buddy. Look. I think we need to have a heart-to-heart, dude," Chuck said.

Two men in their mid-thirties sat across the table from each other, nursing their favorite alcoholic beverages. The pair were situated in their number one watering hole, a local corner combination pub and restaurant. It was called Joe's Beef and Beer. Joe had been dead for decades, and the place was presently owned by a Lebanese investor and run by a local man named Joe Rosen. So, one might argue the pub still was living up to its name.

Although some people with a more discerning pallet might disagree with the restaurant portion of the "pub and restaurant" description, Chuck and Nick liked it just fine, thank you very much. Some locals called it Joe's Barf and Belch, but anyone with the sense of humor sophomoric enough to come up with such a juvenile name probably should be ignored, in Nick's opinion.

The pair had just ordered their choices of pub fare entrees and appetizers and were waiting for said cuisine to arrive. Chuck liked the name pub fare rather than the less appetizing term bar food. He felt it gave the place a slightly classier feel. This is to say, assuming one could ignore the loud music, pool table, dartboard, rowdy patrons, and bank of ten big-screen televisions tuned to five different sporting events.

Chuck Edison had known his best friend Nick Morton since kindergarten. There was almost nothing the pair couldn't discuss, no subject off-limits, yet Chuck knew what he was about to bring up had the potential to strain their lifelong friendship. Nonetheless, Chuck felt this was the time to broach this sticky subject with Nick yet again. He hoped he was right.

Nick said, "Sure thing, Chuckster. Go ahead and ask away."

"Well, Ellen and I were discussing your situation . . ."

"And what situation might it be that you and your lovely wife of ten years were discussing?" Nick asked, knowing fully well what subject Chuck was about to discuss, but he figured he'd let his friend sweat it out for a time. There was no way Nick would make it easy for the man. Besides, he knew it wasn't entirely Chuck's idea to approach him. It was likely Ellen's, and Chuck was going along with it because he had no choice.

Nick tolerated Ellen, but he wasn't afraid to admit the woman got on his nerves, more often than not. She could sometimes be a buttinsky to the tenth degree. Most times, Nick could simply ignore Ellen's interferences. Unfortunately, this was not going to be one of those times. Nick decided he'd let things play out for no reason other than to make it easier on his friend.

Chuck said, "I know what you're thinking, Nick. Hell, I always know what you're thinking. But for your information, this wasn't Ellen's idea. It was one hundred percent mine. I'm concerned about you, Dude. You're alone. You got nobody but me, and most of my time is dedicated to Ellen and the kids."

"I know that, Chuck. I got no problem with that. It's the way things are supposed to be. You're a man with a family; you have responsibilities. I get it."

"But you're my best friend, Nick. You're like my brother, Dude. I'm not just blowing smoke up your ass, either. You know how happy me, Ellen, and the kids are. That's what I want for you."

"I know you do, Chuck. But like I told you before, it's complicated."

"Complicated my ass, Nick. It's simple. You simply go out into the world and find a woman. Then you marry her and start making babies."

"Unfortunately, it's not that easy for me."

"Look, Nick. If you're trying to tell me you're . . . you know, gay . . . well, I got no problem with that."

"What?"

"You know. If that's the way your gate swings, it don't mean Jack Squat to me. Sure . . . I might have to get used to it, but I'm sure I will . . . eventually. I mean, it's not like you ever tried to grab my junk or anything."

"Can you listen to yourself for a minute, Chuck? Do you seriously hear what you're saying?"

"Of course I do, Nick. Do you? Look, brother. I'm telling you I'm ok if you don't go for chicks. I may not be able to relate, being the stud I am, but I'm cool with you doing whatever those people do. I just prefer not to hear any of the horny details, if you know what I mean."

"Chuck . . . Chuck . . . just shut your pie hole for one second, and listen to me. Ok?"

"Um . . . sure, Pal. Go ahead," Chuck said, chastened.

"I'm not gay, Chuck. I . . . AM . . . NOT . . . GAY . . . I like women, ok? If I were gay, I'd admit it and be open about it. I have no problem with people being gay. Got it?"

"Yeah, yeah. I get it. But even if you're still in my camp, you're alone, Dude. You don't date. You're thirty-five. People wonder . . . you know?"

"Yeah, Chuck, I know. People always wonder about stupid things. But it really isn't any of their business, now, is it?"

"No, I suppose it isn't. But what about me? We've been buds since the Stone Age and will be for life. Womb to tomb, right?"

"Damn straight. Womb to tomb," Nick agreed.

"So, level with me, Nick. What's up? Why the solo act?"

"You already know the answer, Chuck. We've had conversations like this before. I'm still looking for the right one."

"Yeah, I get that. I remember the whole routine about knowing who will be the one as soon as your eyes meet. Yeah, that would be all well and good if this was a book or a movie, but that ain't how reality works. In the real world, you meet someone you like or are attracted to, you date them for a while, get to know them, take them for a few test rides, nudge, nudge, wink, wink, then marry them, procreate and settle down."

"That might work for you, Chuck, But I need more than that. I can't settle for good enough. I need more. I need bells and whistles, sparks, and fireworks. I want the whole shebang, no pun intended."

"But listen, Nick. At your age, that chance is somewhere less than nonexistent. Most of the available babes out there have more mileage on them than a road-worn Harley. They carry more baggage with them than Mrs. Howell on Gilligan's Island. You know what I'm saying; times are tough out there; it's a jungle. You can't afford to be so picky, Nicky. You gotta learn to settle a bit."

"Look, Chuck. I know you mean well, but you don't understand. It's hard to explain, but I know what I'm looking for, and I'll know when I find it."

"Ok, ok. If you insist, I'll try to butt out . . . again. But just so you know, I'm here for you, Bro, and always will be."

"I know. Thanks, Dude, much appreciated."

The rest of the time at dinner went without incident, although it took a few minutes to recover from that discussion and get on with a less controversial conversation.

/ 2 /

Being alone was not the same as being lonely. At least, that was how Nick Morton saw things. Sure, he lived alone in a three-bedroom townhouse far larger than he required. But when he bought it a decade earlier, it was not just a place to hang his hat; it had been an investment in his future.

Nick sat on a faux wicker chair, looking out over the lush, manicured lawns, painstakingly cared for as part of the hefty fee he paid to the Fairway Estates Homeowners Association every month. Another expense feature was maintaining the on-site golf course, care of the tennis courts, and the community clubhouse and swimming pool. However, these amenities meant nothing to Nick since he never used them.

But he did enjoy relaxing on his postage-stamp deck and looking out over the grounds. His unit was located at the rear of the complex, so he had more privacy than many residents. He also had an excellent view of the forest that surrounded the property. It was not uncommon for Nick to sit for hours watching squirrels scamper about the grounds or the occasional deer peek out from the trees.

The house had given Nick many tranquil moments during his time here, yet he still felt this was not enough. He was getting close to thirty-five years old and had yet to find the right woman to share his life with. It's not that he hadn't dated because he had tried to do so as much as his busy schedule would permit. It was simply that none of the women had met his stringent requirements.

Like his best friend, Chuck, many of Nick's friends called him a hopeless romantic, unwilling to accept reality while waiting for a fantasy that would ever be fulfilled. They often told him things like, "You set your expectations too high," "There's no such thing as a soul mate," "The perfect woman doesn't exist," or, his least favorite, "You have to consider what you have for bait when you're trying to land a prize catch."

However, knew what he wanted and would settle for nothing less. Nick had never shared the reason for this particular desire with anyone, largely out of embarrassment and mostly because he didn't want people to think he was weirder than they already did. If he told them his deepest, most personal reason for being so selective, someone might try to have him locked up in a loonie bin.

Nick believed . . . no, Nick was certain that he had lived before, perhaps many times. He had fragments of memories that usually came to him in dreams but occasionally while awake. He was always someone else in these recollections, yet the memories were as vivid as if they were his own. This was initially as hard for Nick to believe as he was sure it would be for others. After all, the idea of reincarnation was not something that made him feel comfortable.

He realized that perhaps reincarnation wasn't the right word for his feelings. It wasn't like he remembered being someone else, a specific person. It was more that he had bits and pieces of many other people's memories over many lifetimes.

Nick couldn't claim to have been a train conductor in the 1800s, but he did have the occasional blip of a memory of being on a steam train in that period. Likewise, he might not believe that he was ever a slave in ancient Egypt, yet he had vivid glimpses of the pyramids under construction. Some might argue that his memories were of nothing more than the recreated scenes from movies he had seen as a kid.

Typically, Nick might agree with them if it wasn't for that other memory, the one he had repeatedly appeared to him. In those dreams, Nick was with the love of his life, his soul mate during those possible memories, a woman more perfect for him than he could ever have imagined. He didn't know her name, and her appearance was not cohesive. She might have been blonde or brunette or maybe even a redhead. She might have been short, tall, medium, heavy, thin, he couldn't say.

However, the thing he did know was this love connection he seemed to have with this nonexistent woman, or perhaps many women over the many years, surpassed typical human sexual attraction. No matter what form the woman took, Nick loved her, and she loved him. As far as Nick was concerned, their love was legendary and immortal. Their souls were joined so completely that not even death could completely sever that tie.

That didn't stop the universe from trying. In every memory, every scenario Nick could recall, either his lover was taken from him or he was taken from her. War, famine, disease, pestilence, and life's tragic comedies conspired to keep them apart. But no matter what obstacles life put in their way, these two lost souls always managed to find each other again somewhere along history's timeline, regardless of what tragedies befell them.

Nick sensed in his heart that his love was somewhere in this world, perhaps nearby. He couldn't recall any of her names in the past and had no idea what her name would be now. He believed that when they met and locked eyes, something incredible would pass between these two supposed strangers, and the soul link would reconnect. He would be reunited with the love of this and many other lives.

This was why he could never share his beliefs with anyone. They would, at best, think him a bit odd and, at worst, a raving lunatic. Yet he believed. He felt it with every fiber of his being. Recently, his conviction was further solidified when he went to the local high school presentation of the Elton John / Tim Rice musical Aida.

It was a play about two lovers, Aida and Radames, who tragically were lost to each other in ancient times. In the end, in modern times, two strangers meet in a museum. The man and the woman looked into each other's eyes and were instantly drawn to each other. They were the reincarnations of Aida and Radames, finding each other after so many centuries. Nick was not usually someone to show emotions, but tears streamed down his face after that final scene. Then he knew he was right. His lover was out there somewhere, waiting for the right moment when their eyes would meet, and they, too, would know.

Nick was so certain he would be soon reunited with his lost soulmate that he had decided to put his current house up for sale and look for something bigger, nicer, and worthy of the love of his life. As things worked out, his investment had paid off a year after the latest pandemic in a series of economic upheavals and raw material shortages. His home had more than doubled in value. That, combined with the money he had managed to squirrel away over the past ten years, provided Nick with a large enough down payment, so he would likely have a lower mortgage on his next home than he did on his current residence. That was, of course, assuming he could find a home.

After several weeks of attending open houses, he still had not found a place. Often, the homes he looked at didn't meet his requirements. Another problem was when he did find a house he liked, it usually sold before he had a chance to even put in a bid. Because of the reduction in new home construction caused by the lack of available building supplies caused by the pandemic, people were going to ridiculous extremes to buy existing houses.

It was not uncommon for a house listed for $300,000 to sell in a few days for $360,000. The extra $60,000 was often offered in cash. Sometimes, buyers would also agree to pay all the closing costs for themselves and the seller and then skip any home inspection.

Nick found himself frustrated time after time. When he was about to give up what he considered an exercise in futility, his realtor called with a possible home that had not even hit the market. Something told him this was a good sign and that something was right.

/ 3 /

"What do you think, Terry? Is it really something I should check out, or will it be just another wild goose chase?" Nick asked his realtor as he pulled out onto the expressway. His cell phone was in hands-free mode. It always amazed Nick how clear someone could sound over his car sound system as they spoke via Wi-Fi.

"I'm telling you, Nick. This place has you all over it. Believe me, it checks all your boxes, and the price is also right," she replied.

Nick and Terry had a unique sort of relationship. They had previously dated a few times and had 'done the deed,' the 'horizontal mambo' a few times as well. But somewhere between the first and last boinks, Terry decided she wasn't really into men and was going to pitch for the other team. Despite the fact she had assured Nick that the rethinking of her sexual preferences had nothing to do with him or his performance, the blow to his ego took a while for him to overcome.

Nick asked, "So what's the deal? Why hasn't anyone snagged this place up yet?"

"I told you; it hasn't hit the multi-list yet. I'm the listing agent for the place, and I wanted to give you a shot before we toss the place to the thundering hoards," she explained for what seemed like the twentieth time.

"I get that, but is that legal or even ethical?"

"Nick, Nick, my man. You know I'm not the sort to bog myself down with annoying encumbrances like ethics. And as far as its legality goes, I'm a firm believer in 'don't ask, don't tell,' and I'm pretty sure you are as well."

"Um . . . ok. So, according to my GPS, I'm about a block or two from the address you sent me. Are you there yet?"

"You bet. I'm standing right out front, ready, willing, and able. I'm sure you'll love this place, Nick. See you shortly."

"Ok, Terry . . . Ready or not, here I come."

Nick turned right into a cul-de-sac named Harington Court and studied the address numbers on the houses and mailboxes, looking for

107. When he passed under the canopy of a massive oak tree, he saw an amazing multi-level brick, stone, metal, wood, and glass building. Its style was hard to describe, part modern, part traditional, leaning towards industrial. Nick looked around at the other homes in the cul-de-sac and noticed they were more traditional-style homes. There were a few colonial-style homes, some farmhouses, a few split levels, and a sprawling rancher or two. But none had the curb appeal of this house at 107.

Nick was sure he had never been in this neighborhood before and had certainly never set eyes on this house. It wasn't the sort of place you could easily forget. But despite having never previously seen the house, Nick felt there was something about the place that screamed "home!" He couldn't believe how incredible he felt. This place, this amazing house on this gorgeous street, was exactly what he wanted.

He realized how ridiculous such an idea was. After all, he hadn't even seen the inside of the house yet. Maybe it was a dump. Perhaps the rooms were small and choppy. Perhaps there were issues with the electrical service or plumbing. No matter how comfortable he felt with the exterior, if there were infrastructure problems, that could prove to be a deal-breaker, depending upon their severity. Yet, in his heart, Nick knew he was lying to himself. This house would be his, and there was nothing to stop him.

"I'm ready to put in an offer," Nick told his realtor.

"Don't you think maybe you might want to look inside first?" Terry asked.

"If you insist. But I can tell already the place is perfect."

"Well, do you think maybe you might want to know the listing price?" She asked with a chuckle.

"Oh . . . yeah . . . I suppose that matters," Nick said absentmindedly.

"Well, it's below your budgeted amount by at least twenty thousand."

"What? You've got to be kidding me. Now, I have to see the inside. Something must really be screwed up in there."

"Rest assured, Nick, my man. You are going to love the inside every bit as much as the outside."

/ 4 /

Terry was right. Nick did love the inside of the house. He couldn't believe he could have fallen in love with the place so quickly. He put in an offer on the house at ten thousand below the asking price, and the owner accepted without question or negotiation. The man they dealt with was the estate's executor for the former owner. The owner had been an elderly woman who had died in her sleep several weeks earlier. The executor was the deceased woman's much younger brother. When his offer was accepted so quickly, Nick assumed that the executor might be out of touch with the current housing market. Nick discussed it with his realtor. He felt guilty about his offer being so low, especially since the estate would have easily gotten at least fifty grand over their asking price had this home made it to market. He was beginning to feel like he was stealing from the estate.

Terry explained that the executor's brother was already a wealthy businessman who was very much aware of the current real estate market. He was a very busy man and just wanted the place sold as soon as possible. Terry said the brother was completely satisfied with Nick's offer, and there was no reason for Nick to feel guilty. Terry said she suspected that because the man's sister had died in the home, he might have been concerned the sale would drag on unnecessarily. People can feel strange about such things.

Despite his odd opinion regarding the theoretical mystery woman who would someday stumble into him and become the love of his life, Nick was not typically superstitious. When it came to people dying in a bed in a house he wanted to buy, Nick had no problem dealing with that. Death was a natural part of the life cycle, as far as Nick was concerned. It made no difference to him whether the woman had passed away in her bed or a guest room in a retirement home a hundred miles away.

Nick stood outside the house on the front porch with the key to his new home in his hand. The closing and settlement for the property were conducted flawlessly. As he inserted his key into the lock, Nick hesitated for a second in an attempt to relax, although it seemed like a futile idea. This house, this incredible home, was his now, and that was quite a bit for him to wrap his head around.

He opened the door and walked into the grand foyer, looking at the empty expanse of the place. He was certain once the home was furnished, it would seem much less hollow. He had decided to wait two weeks, until after he closed on the sale of his current home, to move his possessions into this new home.

Nick used the available time and the money he saved on the sale price to do some remodeling. The following day, he had painters scheduled to come in and start repainting all the rooms with brighter, more natural shades. Three days later, tile and flooring contractors would upgrade all the tile, carpet, and hardwood areas. The electricity and plumbing had recently been upgraded, and the bathrooms and kitchen had been remodeled and modernized. There was nothing Nick needed to do to the house, and the things he had chosen to have done were essentially cosmetic.

Walking through the place, Nick couldn't get over the amazing feeling of absolute comfort he experienced with the house. The home was simultaneously new to him yet familiar at the same time. It all seemed so incredibly overwhelming to him.

Nick stepped into the first-floor powder room and took a look around. Everything was immaculate, with new flooring, wall tile, and a new sink and toilet. He looked at the mirror hanging on the wall and realized it wasn't new and seemed quite old. He hadn't noticed that before. The mirror hung in an ornately carved mahogany frame, depicting various trees, leaves, and forest animals. Although Nick felt the piece was extremely gaudy, bordering on tacky, he certainly could appreciate the intricate carvings' time, effort, and craftsmanship. It just wasn't his proverbial cup of tea.

He decided that anything derived from that level of workmanship would have to be worth a good deal of money from the right antique dealer. Since it didn't fit his plans for the house, he'd get rid of it as soon as possible. Yet, he had this strange feeling, this unidentifiable sensation there was something familiar about the piece, something Nick believed he should remember but couldn't.

Nick turned to leave the powder room and thought he saw something from the corner of his eye. It was a slight movement reflected in the mirror. He turned back and quickly scoured the room, looking for any source for a reflection. He found none. Nor did he find any reflections in the mirror save for his own. Nick shook his head and walked out of the room. He turned to look back at the antique mirror a few times, unsure why he had done so.

He left through the front door and locked the place up for the night. Nick had already planned to return each night to check the painters' progress and verify they had properly locked the property when they left. Another addition Nick planned for the house was a wireless security system. That installation was scheduled for later the following week, just before moving day.

As he drove away, Nick had a strange feeling in the pit of his stomach. Call it post-purchase cognitive dissonance, if you prefer. He was starting to wonder if buying the house was a good idea. The place seemed so perfect, perhaps too perfect. He had been impulsive, perhaps too much so. And what was that thing that happened with the bathroom mirror? Was that just the result of him freaking out from being alone in the big, empty, echoing home? He suspected that was probably what had happened.

Yet something deep inside him, in the pit of his gut, made Nick feel uneasy. Maybe this feeling was normal when making the biggest single purchase of one's life. He didn't recall feeling that way when he bought his current townhouse. Maybe because that home was always meant to be a temporary residence. But now, the feeling was almost overwhelming.

"Get hold of yourself, Nick," he said aloud. "this house is amazing and will fit you like a glove. There's nothing to think about but planning for the move in two weeks."

Nick decided to take his own advice.

/ 5 /

Moving day had gone surprisingly well, with all of Nick's possessions arriving on time and intact. The movers had put Nick's larger furnishings in place, and after they left, he had set to work emptying boxes and putting everything in its place. Being the sort of person Nick's friend,

Chuck, referred to as ultra-anal, Nick had labeled every box denoting their contents and which room in the house they should go to. The movers had placed all the boxes in the appropriate rooms. Later that evening, Chuck and Ellen brought over pizza and beer, which gave Nick a chance to take a much-needed break.

Chuck and Ellen were both amazed by how nice the house was and how much it seemed perfect for Nick.

"This place is awesome, Nick," Chuck said as they took a tour. "Terry did a great job finding this place for you. Too bad she switched teams; I always thought you two might make a good couple."

"I agree," Ellen said. Then she asked, "You and Terry always had so much in common. So, Nick. I suppose the important question is, how do you like the house so far?"

"I love it," He replied, "I felt right at home from the minute I saw it. It's like I always lived here."

"All this place needs now is a woman's touch," she added.

Chuck interrupted, "El, I told you not to beat that dead horse tonight."

"What?" She asked innocently, "You were the one who brought up Terry. Besides, I wasn't beating . . ."

"It's ok," Nick said, trying to smooth things over.

"Thanks, Bro. But I promised you I'd give it a rest, and I asked my beloved to do so as well." He gave his wife the stink eye. She gave it right back at him, only with more stink.

Nick said, "Not a big deal, Chuck. Look, Ellen, I think we need to address the elephant in the room. I'm not opposed to dating or even marriage, for that matter. But as I've told Chuck many times, I don't want to waste my time and energy dating many different women when I know instantly that they're not who I'm looking for."

"Know instantly, Nick? How can you even imagine instantly knowing whether someone's "the one"?" Ellen asked, forming annoying air quotes with her fingers. God, how Nick hated it when she did that. Ellen had more annoying peculiarities than Nick could list, but if he did make a list, her propensity to overuse air quotes would top it. She was the queen of air quotes as far as Nick was concerned.

Chuck interrupted again, trying to keep a bad situation from worsening, "Ellen, Babe. How's about we let this go for now?"

She glared at Chuck and whispered through gritted teeth, "I'll let this go when I'm good and ready to let it go, and don't you ever embarrass me like that again. Do I make myself perfectly clear, Darling?"

Chuck had pushed his luck too far. Ellen could be a real force to reckon with when she was determined, and she had just turned that force on him. He felt his rectum slam shut and his testicles creep up inside him like a turtle tucking into its shell. If such a thing could make a sound, the noise would have been as deafening as a major explosion. Chuck knew from painful experiences that if Ellen weren't happy, then nobody would be satisfied. Since he had no desire to be in the dog house, he backed down and let Ellen continue. He hoped Nick would understand.

Nick said as diplomatically as he was able, "Look, Ellen. You need to understand something, and although I've tried to explain this to you many times, I'll try once more because you're the wife of my best friend in the world. But this is the last time I'll be nice about this."

"Save your breath, Nick. My problem with you isn't tied to your lame excuse about waiting for 'Miss Perfect.'" she said, making those infernal air quotes again. "My problem is that you are hiding behind that aforementioned 'lame excuse' to keep people from knowing the real reason for your 'avoiding commitment.'" She emphasized "lame excuse" and "avoiding excuses" with still more inappropriately placed air quotes.

Chuck could see his wife had gone too far and had pushed his friend further than she had any right to. Things were about to get ugly.

Nick's face reddened with anger and frustration. He said through gritted teeth, "You're wrong, Ellen. And what's worse, you're clueless. You don't know me. All you know is what you think you see. Maybe if you were capable of finishing a sentence without using those damnable air quotes, you could muster the intelligence to actually pay attention to what someone says. But no. You're like most brainless women. You're too busy thinking about what you'll say next to listen to what's being said. Like many of your, quote "sista girls," you're shallow and empty; nothing more than a life support system for a vagina."

Chuck stood speechless with his mouth agape. He had never seen Nick get this angry before. Nor had he seen Ellen pushed so far. Nick even had the nerve to use his own set of air quotes when he said "sista girls" to mock Ellen further. Chuck knew this was not going to end well.

Ellen gasped as her eyes bulged from her skull in anger. No one had ever dared to speak to her like that, not even her husband. As she regained control, she said with newfound confidence, "Well, there it is, isn't it? The real reason you're alone, Nick. You're not waiting for the woman of your dreams because that woman doesn't exist. She never did, and she most certainly never could. Your problem is, Nick, that you hate and disrespect all women. You've created a perfect fictional woman in your twisted mind, one you will never meet. This way, you can lie confidently to everyone, including yourself. You'll never meet this woman, Nick. You'll never marry, never have children, and you'll die a lonely old man with no friends and no family to care for you."

Chuck started to say something, and Nick raised his palm in a stop gesture and said, "No, Chuck. Don't bother. I think it would be best if you both just left now."

"But, Nick, buddy."

"Just go," Nick said, opening the front door and never making eye contact with his former friends as they walked past him.

/ 6 /

Nick sat alone on his sofa, looking around his living room. This should have been a night of celebration shared with his closest friend, but all that had come crashing down around him. He suspected the days of being Chuck's best friend might be over. It would be tough to come back from this terrible encounter. Nick always knew that the growing tension between him and Ellen would come to an unpleasant show-down sooner or later. It was like she was jealous of Chuck and Nick's friendship. Well, he supposed she got what she wanted tonight.

He had always heard the expression about blood being thicker than water, but apparently, marriage vows were thicker than a lifetime of friendship. Nick understood that concept deep down inside, but it didn't make the current situation any easier. The best he might hope for was to patch things up with Chuck, but the days of including Ellen in his life were over.

How could she have said such awful things to him? She acted like everything Nick had believed in was a lie. She said he was even lying to himself, but that was ridiculous. Wasn't it? Of course, it was. He didn't hate women, although he did find many of them annoying and didn't enjoy engaging them in conversation. Nick always believed when he met the right woman, the one he would instantly connect with, he would enjoy having hours of discussion with her. And why not? She would be his perfect partner.

However, what if Ellen was right? He hated speculating about that because if she were right, he had been essentially sabotaging every relationship, deliberately torpedoing every opportunity. And for what? For some nonexistent fantasy girl he would never meet. Nick took a deep gulp of his fourth or fifth vodka on the rocks and decided it was time to go to bed. Suddenly, he was hit with the urge to empty his bladder.

"What goes in must come out," Nick mumbled to no one in particular as he staggered into the downstairs powder room. He hadn't been in that room since his strange encounter with the old mirror two weeks earlier. Nick had gotten the contractors to haul it away and had asked them to buy a new mirror and install it. He told them to find something modern-looking in a frame that was perhaps shiny silver or chrome. They certainly had come through for him but at the cost of several hundred dollars. Still, Nick felt it was worth it.

He did a closer inspection of his stylish new mirror. The mirror portion was large and oval but was rotated counterclockwise at a slight angle, maybe twenty or thirty degrees. The mirror rested in a highly polished silver rectangular frame and was sleek and contemporary. The metal was textured in the area with no mirrored surface, making the glass and the highly polished chrome frame stand out.

The three-by-five frame had hints of retro art-deco but with an ultra-modern flare. Then, as Nick looked closer at the oval glass, he noticed something that made his anger rise. He suddenly realized although initially different in appearance, this new mirror was actually the same mirror that had been there previously. He had been swindled. The contractors must have taken the original oval mirror out of its antique frame, rotated it at an angle, and then placed it in this glitzy and glamorous new frame. Now that Nick thought about it, they must have had this fancy frame left over from another remodeling job.

"They probably put this mirror together for next to nothing and charged me a couple hundred bucks. I'll call that crook first thing tomorrow morning and read him the riot act," Nick said, trying desperately not to slur his words but not doing a very good job. "First thing tomorrow," came out, "Firsch ting tamarra."

Then something strange and frightening happened, catching Nick off guard. As he looked at the mirror, its surface began to change and ripple like a pond's surface after a pebble was tossed inside. Nick wasn't sure if this was actually occurring or if it was an alcohol-induced hallucination. Whatever the cause, Nick was astounded to see a beautiful woman's face appearing beneath the rippling mirror surface.

As the rippling stopped, the face became as clear as if she were standing right in front of him. He probably should have been terrified by the visage, but he wasn't. Even more unbelievable was when his eyes met those of the woman in the mirror; Nick's heart skipped a beat. He couldn't believe what was happening. It was like he had fallen instantly in love with the incredible vision. But how could that be? Unless the woman in the mirror was his long-lost soulmate, the woman of his dreams. That must be the case.

He didn't know how he knew this, but he did. Even though the smiling vision before him was probably the most beautiful woman he had ever seen, that wasn't what mattered. There was a different connection of sorts, a psychic linking between the woman and himself. It was just as he had always imagined it would be. Their eyes met, and in an instant, he knew this was the one he had waited for his entire life.

"It's you," Nick whispered. "You're the one."

She looked back with an expression of absolute adoration, and as her lips slowly moved, Nick heard a soft and melodious voice, "Yes, I am for you as you are for me."

It caught him off guard, as he hadn't heard her words in his ears, but they seemed to pop miraculously into his mind. "I have been looking for you for centuries, my love, all over the world and across time. I have crossed the great expanse of space and time, hoping to find you again. And now I have."

/ 7 /

"I can't believe you've found me. It's so strange. Although your beautiful face is a mystery to me, somehow, I still recognize you," Nick said in astonishment. "I have waited for you my entire life. I hoped we would reunite with all my heart but never believed it would happen."

The woman said, "Yes, Nick, I heard your thoughts and heard you calling for me in your dreams."

"I did dream of you but didn't know what name to call. How is it you know my name?"

"I only know what I heard your friends call you. I sensed your presence and heard them call you Nick."

Nick felt embarrassed knowing she may have overheard him losing his temper with Ellen. Then again, he was defending his right to love who he wanted, and now he was glad he did. If this woman had heard him, she would know his level of devotion. Yet Nick couldn't wrap his head around how she had managed to find him.

"But how did you find me?" Nick asked.

She said, "It was this house. I was attracted to this house just as you were. I believed if it drew me, I knew you too would find this place in whatever form you occupied, and we would be reunited again."

Nick stared into the eyes of the vision and asked, "I know we've been together many times in the past and have had many different names. What is your name now? What should I call you?"

"I have no name in this place. There is no need for names in this vast landscape of nothingness. I will not require one until we are together again, but if you like, you can call me Lorena."

"Lorena, yes, that's a beautiful name, fitting a beautiful woman. Tell me about this world on the other side of my mirror. What is that place?"

She replied, "It's a waiting area where lost souls, such as ours, must wait. The mirror is just a type of window from your world into mine."

Nick asked, "You said you and others must wait. Wait for what?"

"I don't exactly know. Perhaps to be reborn. I'm not sure. All I do know is, in my case, I was waiting for you."

"But you're over there, wherever there is, and I'm here. Oh, Lorena, I want us to be together again more than anything in life, but I don't know how to get you over here with me. What can I do?"

"That's what I feel is most tragic. I can't come into your place of existence without occupying a body. And, of course, I can't occupy a living body unless it is a human soul about to be conceived. The universe dictates this. But entering a body at the time of conception will do us no good either since once I enter the new body and am born, I will remember nothing. I might be reborn in your country or on the other side of the world. Eventually, like yourself, I will begin to have feelings. I'll believe you're out there looking for me. But by the time I'm thirty, you will be in your mid-sixties. Since we have made contact now and you have seen me, you will likely waste your entire life looking for me, knowing I'm out in the world somewhere and that you might never find me."

Nick said, "But isn't that what I'm doing now? I've been unwilling to settle down and marry someone here because I've always believed I'd find you. But not like this. This way is wrong. You're so close I can almost touch you. Yet you may as well be a million miles away." Nick reached up and placed his hand flat against the shimmering mirror surface. Lorena did the same, but when their fingers overlapped, Nick felt nothing but the cold surface of the glass. He was heartsick.

Nick said, "This is so unfair. I want to be with you. I need to be with you. My life has been so empty, knowing you were somewhere but not having you with me. Now that I've seen you and know you really exist, how can I go back to living without you? My life will be nothing if I can't have you. Surely, Lorena, there must be some way for us to be together."

The woman in the mirror hesitated momentarily, then said, "There is, Nick. But I suspect you won't like it very much."

/ 8 /

"What do you mean? Of course, I'll do anything, whatever it takes for us to be together, my love."

"You must take time to consider this, as once you do what must be done, there is no turning back."

"It doesn't matter. We must be together."

Lorena said, "Before you decide, you must know all the facts. The final decision must be yours alone."

"Fine, fine. Please explain to me what it is I need to know. I understand you can't come to me, but I must come to you. How can I come to you?"

"You asked me earlier what this place was where I exist. Sadly, Nick, this place where I am is a world of the dead. Everyone on this side of the great expanse is dead. We are souls waiting for, well, for something. Some of us will be slated to be reborn. It might happen any minute, or it could take centuries for it to happen. None of us knows for sure. Time, as we know it, does not exist here. Some may move on to another plane of existence. Some will remain. We are all but lost souls floating in this in-between place."

"But you're here now and appear to already have a beautiful body."

"Appear is the keyword. In truth, I have no shape and no form. What you see before you is what your mind requires you to see. Your mind can't begin to comprehend the actual image your eyes are sending your brain, so it automatically goes into survival mode and produces an image it knows it can accept. Trying to process my appearance in this world would shatter your mind and leave you a drooling vegetable. What you see is how your mind has decided to see me. Does that make sense to you?"

"I suppose it does," Nick said, not very convincingly. "So please, tell me, Lorena, what must I do to come to you?"

"I think you should have already figured that out," she said.

"You mean?"

"Yes, Nick. To live in this world, you must die in yours."

Nick was caught off guard, "Die in my world. But how will that get us together?"

"When your soul leaves your body, it will travel here, and we will be together for eternity."

"But how can that be? If I remember correctly, we've been together many times before and always lost each other," Nick said.

The woman replied, "That's because we have always been together as living, breathing creatures. We've never been together as pure souls before. I'm not sure, but I believe if we come together in this place, nothing will ever be able to separate us. We will finally be together for eternity. That's what I want more than anything else, and I'm sure that's what you want, too, isn't it?"

"Of course . . . I do."

She noticed Nick's obvious hesitation and asked, "What's wrong, Nick? I sense your uncertainty."

"It's just that I'm quite healthy and in no danger of dying any time soon. That means I would have to . . ."

"Yes, my love. You would have to take your own life."

"But . . . but that would be committing suicide. If what I've always believed is true, suicide is a mortal sin. That would mean my soul wouldn't come to you; it would go straight to Hell."

Lorena hesitated for a moment, then said, "That's not true, Nick. You have been misled. Someone has lied to you. I promise you that you will be sent directly to me when your life ends on your side. As frightening as it may seem, it's our only solution."

"I . . . well, I really have to take some time to think about this. I've always dreamed of us being together, and I want to be with you more than I can say. But suicide goes against every human survival instinct. I'm not even sure I could do it."

"You will have to decide on your own, Nick. I will be waiting for you for as long as I can."

"Are you saying you might be unable to wait for long?"

"I'm sorry, Nick. I just don't know how long I will be permitted to stay. I hope you can decide soon. I long to hold you in my arms again."

/ 9 /

Nick visited Lorena in his powder room mirror multiple times daily for the next several weeks. Each visit, he seemed to fall more in love with her. Finally, he decided he had no choice but to do whatever he must to be with his love. Nick told Lorena he had decided to take his own life and come to her, but he had to take care of some important final business first.

Nick visited a local attorney and drew up a will, leaving his home and all his possessions to his friend Chuck. Although he was still angry with Ellen and regretted her benefiting from his death, Nick realized Chuck was the only friend he had in the world, and as such, he wanted Chuck to have his possessions. Nick had no living relatives to leave anything to or anyone else, so his decision was an easy one.

His life insurance policy would cover the balance of his mortgage if it didn't have a suicide clause. Nick couldn't recall if it did or not, but he didn't have time to deal with that. Besides, Chuck could always sell the house for much more than Nick paid, which would wipe out the remainder of the mortgage and still provide his friend with a nice financial windfall.

After stopping at a local funeral parlor, where Nick made arrangements for the disposition of his earthly remains, he headed for home. He stopped at a local ice cream shop and got an extra-large, thick vanilla milkshake. Nick also picked up a large meat-lovers pizza at his favorite Italian restaurant. If he were checking out tonight as planned, caloric content would be the last thing on his mind.

Nick returned home and sat on a stool in front of the bathroom mirror for a final time, waiting for his beloved Lorena to appear. After a few minutes, the surface of the glass began to ripple, and his beautiful Lorena faced him.

"I'm going to be with you this very night, my love," Nick said, holding out his palm and showing her a mass of pills he held there.

"Pills?" Lorena said, sounding slightly disappointed, "That's usually a woman's way to end things. Are you sure that will do the job?"

"Yes, my Darling, I'm sure. There is enough power here in my hand to kill an elephant. Believe me, I have no chance of surviving this."

"I'm so glad to hear you say you'll be coming to me. It will be incredible, my Darling. You will hold me in your arms once more."

"Yes, Lorina. I will be with you soon, and nothing can change that."

"Come to me, my love. Come to me now."

Nick swallowed the mountain of pills he held cupped in his hand and washed them down with a glass of straight whiskey.

/ 10 /

Nick opened his eyes and found himself in a strange, dark place with no landscape or substance. A light seemed to be coming in off to his right through a window, and he cautiously approached it. As he got closer, he realized the window was not really what he had first thought but was actually the mirror in his downstairs powder room.

Nick walked over to the mirror and looked through it. What he saw terrified him. He saw his own dead body lying on the bathroom tile floor. His head looked damaged, as if it had been cracked open; a puddle of blood spread slowly across the tile floor, filling in the grouted spaces between the tile. The stool he had been sitting on was lying on its side. Apparently, when the drugs had done their job, he must have passed out, toppled off the chair, and crashed to the floor, striking his skull against the granite tile.

To Nick, this strange place seemed like a vast world of nothingness. He began to panic. Had he done the right thing? Where was his beloved Lorena?

He felt something gently touch his shoulder and turned to find Lorena standing behind him with her arms outstretched.

"Come to me, my love," she said as Nick fell into her waiting arms.

"Oh Lorena, my darling. I can hardly believe we are finally together."

She replied, "But we are and will always be for all eternity."

Nick suddenly felt strange, like something was wrong. He had believed holding Lorena in his arms would be the most incredible feeling he had ever experienced. He had been sure of it and had dreamt of it his whole life. But that was not what he felt as he wrapped her in his arms. Instead, Nick felt nothing, as if holding this woman was no different than trying to grab mist.

"What's the matter, my love?" Lorena asked.

Nick said, "I . . . don't know. Something feels wrong."

"Wrong? Wrong, how?"

"I . . . I don't quite know how to explain it. Everything feels different than I expected."

"Oh, that? That's nothing. It's just your soul getting acclimated to this place. Please allow me to explain," Lorena said as she stood back and smiled in a way that troubled Nick. "You were expecting fireworks and all kinds of things like you've always dreamed you would experience. Am I right?"

"Yes. That's right, Lorena. I'm sorry if I seem a little disappointed; it's just that when I was on the other side, our feelings seemed so strong. But now, well, it's like I feel nothing. How can that be?"

"It's because those senses you used as a living being are gone now that you're dead. But don't fret, my love. Soon, you'll develop new senses similar to what you had in life. When that occurs, everything will work out, and you'll be fine. You can already see and hear, can't you?"

"Yes, but when Lorena? How soon?" Then Nick realized he could answer his question as he noticed a strange sulfur stench in the air. Next, he could feel the temperature in the room start to rise.

/ 11 /

"What's happening, Lorena? What's that horrible smell?"

"Smell? What are you talking about . . . what smell?"

"That disgusting stench. It smells like three-day-old roadkill."

Lorena stepped back a few paces from Nick and stared at him. Her face changed slightly, and the loving beauty he had originally seen was gone, replaced by a stern, almost angry countenance.

"I don't know what you're talking about, Nick. There is no horrible smell in here. It must be your imagination."

"Lorena, I'm dead. How much imagination can I still possibly have? None of this makes sense. I'm sorry, Lorena. I'm having trouble getting my head screwed on straight and struggling to understand."

"Well then, Nick. Let me set things straight for you," Lorena said, her voice suddenly taking on a sharp, angry tone.

"Please do," Nick said, sounding a bit haughty himself.

"I had hoped to keep this from you for a while, but then again, I suppose there's no point. The fact is, Nick. You're an idiot and a fool."

"Lorena, what are you saying?"

"I'm saying you've spent your adult life waiting for some magical woman to appear who never existed."

"But you did exist; you do exist. You're right here in front of me."

"Do I really exist, Nick?"

"Of course you do."

"Here's the truth, Nick. I'm not the lost love of your life. My name's not even Lorena. Your tiny human mind couldn't even begin to pronounce my real name. You see, dear Nick, I'm not even close to who you wish I was. I'm a demon, and this place is Hell. That looking glass in your house is a window that allows us on this side to see and hear things happening in your world. The glass itself is ancient. The mirrored backing is also very old but has been replaced many times over the centuries, always to our specifications. It makes our work easier.

"Foolish Nick, my job here in Hell is to use any means and deceit necessary to find and capture souls for Hell. I've lured thousands of unsuspecting souls over the centuries. So don't feel so bad about being deceived. This ain't my first rodeo, as humans are fond of saying.

"The former owner of your house picked up the original mirror at a yard sale a few months before she died. Her husband apparently had crossed over a year earlier, but he's not with us. Old Homer went up to that other place we in the soul-stealing business prefer not to discuss. She was quite depressed and lonely over her husband's passing.

"It didn't take much to convince her that I was her beloved husband and was waiting for her to join me on this side. A little creative deception goes a long way. She eventually committed suicide in a way not so different from your own. She took pills, went to bed, and eventually woke up on this side. As you pointed out, Nick, suicide is a mortal sin and guarantees a one-way ticket to the center city of Hell. Go to Hell, go directly to Hell, do not pass go, do not collect two hundred dollars. She had a first-class on the suicide express, traveling nonstop from your home to our side. And for your information, she is presently being tortured and tormented in ways you couldn't imagine."

"But . . . but none of this is possible. I looked into your eyes and felt the love we shared so many times throughout history. Something like that cannot be faked."

"Of course it can, Nick. This is Hell. We are great deceivers who can make humans believe anything we want them to."

Her appearance suddenly changed, and the lovely face returned, filling Nick's heart with joy. Then, just as quickly, the face disappeared, being replaced by that of a hideous snarling demon with a pig-like snot-dripping snout and a wide mouth full of tusks and razor-sharp teeth. When the Lorena beast opened her huge maw and laughed, a revolting stench hit Nick, and he felt light-headed.

Long ram-like horns protruded from both sides of her forehead, leading back to a greasy mane of long, black, matted hair. Her dress and lovely figure were also gone. Standing before Nick was a monstrously obese creature with huge, sagging, pendulous breasts swinging from side to side. They hung down so low that Nick couldn't have seen between her legs if he had wanted to, which he certainly did not. The monster's skin was covered with hair and glistened with sweat.

When he looked again, the beast was gone, and beautiful Lorena had returned. She came closer to Nick, placed her arms around his neck, and kissed him passionately on the lips. He was horrified at first, having seen what he had just seen, but now she was back to her beautiful form. Perhaps he was wrong about what he thought he had just seen. Eventually, he gave in to his manly urges, closed his eyes, took her in his arms, and slid his tongue into her waiting mouth. Then he smelled that foul stench again.

Opening his eyes once more, Nick saw his lovely Lorena was gone again, replaced by the demonic and hideous pig-snouted creature. He tried to pull away but couldn't. The revolting monster smiled at him with that mouth full of piranha teeth and said in a deep, guttural voice, barely recognizable as human dialect, "Don't worry, Nick, my love. I swear no one here will harm you as long as you are mine. And as I promised, you will be mine for eternity."

Nick heard an ear-piercing scream like a wounded animal and realized the sound was coming from his mouth.